I0706123

SCORCHED EARTH

SCORCHED EARTH

JUSTICE BEGINS™ BOOK SIX

MICHAEL ANDERLE

This book is a work of fiction. All of the characters, organizations, and events portrayed in this novel are either products of the author's imagination or are used fictitiously. Sometimes both.

Copyright © 2022 by Michael Anderle
Cover Art by Jake @ J Caleb Design
http://jcalebdesign.com / jcalebdesign@gmail.com
Cover copyright © LMBPN Publishing
A Michael Anderle Production

LMBPN Publishing supports the right to free expression and the value of copyright. The purpose of copyright is to encourage writers and artists to produce the creative works that enrich our culture.

The distribution of this book without permission is a theft of the author's intellectual property. If you would like permission to use material from the book (other than for review purposes), please contact support@lmbpn.com. Thank you for your support of the author's rights.

LMBPN Publishing
PMB 196, 2540 South Maryland Pkwy
Las Vegas, NV 89109

Version 1.00, February 2022
ebook ISBN: 979-8-88541-172-1
Print ISBN: 979-8-88541-173-8

THE SCORCHED EARTH TEAM

Thanks to the JIT Readers

Dorothy Lloyd
Rachel Beckford
Zacc Pelter
Diane L. Smith
Wendy L Bonell
Dave Hicks
Deb Mader
Jeff Goode

If I've missed anyone, please let me know!

Editor
The Skyhunter Editing Team

DEDICATION

To Family, Friends and
Those Who Love
to Read.
May We All Enjoy Grace
to Live the Life We Are
Called.

— Michael

Dante Costa, M.D., fourth among the Executioners, stood by the truck and checked his pistol while he waited for Eleanor. He carried a Colt 1911 in .45 ACP, much like Ty Katakura preferred. It was in sound working order and loaded with a round chambered and the safety on. He slid it into the holster at the back of his waistband, where his light jacket would cover it.

"Too bad there's no way to conceal my shotgun," he muttered. Still, a handgun was far better than nothing.

The truck was parked next to a house near the cove that demarcated the edge of Atlantica Metro's docks and harbor district. The day was on the cooler side, overcast and damp. It wasn't *raining*, exactly, but the humidity sometimes turned into more of a mist that occasionally became a drizzle.

The house's side door opened and Eleanor came out, moving at her usual brisk, striding clip like the self-assured business-woman she was. By now Dante knew her well enough to detect something "off" in how she moved, an underlying nervousness.

He didn't blame her. He felt it too. Their plan was audacious and came with nothing remotely like a guarantee of success.

However, the element of disguise would be a key factor in

how well things went. It looked as though his partner had that part well under wraps.

Eleanor had put her hair up in a tight bun. In the past, Dante had always seen her with her hair down in some fashion, so it made her look noticeably different. She'd also applied her makeup more thickly and used different colors, ironically drawing more attention to her face while making it far less familiar. The magic that women could work on themselves with cosmetics never ceased to amaze him.

She also wore snappy-casual athletic clothes, nothing like the business suits or formal dresses she usually wore. Her boots were stylish but practical and would allow her to run fast if necessary.

Dante smiled at her. "You look good. From more than five yards, I could probably mistake you for someone else in public."

She tried to return the gesture with mixed success. "Thank you. As for yourself... it's difficult to say. You do appear different."

"Of course." He adjusted his fake glasses and ran a hand through his black hair, to which he'd added a couple of stripes of spray-on gray. "Older, more distinguished and erudite, but just as devastatingly handsome as always, I'm sure."

She walked past him to the passenger's side of the truck's cab. "Something like that. Come, let us leave as soon as possible unless you have anything else to do. You have the paperwork?"

Dante opened the door and held her hand as she stepped up and settled into the seat. "I have it." He patted his jacket, feeling the manila folder within. "I'm all set. Let's go."

As Eleanor pulled the door shut, he went around and climbed into the driver's seat.

The vehicle was a modest-sized military-style one, armored with plenty of storage but not so large that it affected its acceleration speed or maneuverability greatly. It was a standard-issue Autocutioner, one of the trucks issued to their order.

Most people would never recognize it as such. Gage Gurung, the third Executioner, had disguised it with a new tan paint job, some frame elements foreign to the original style, a chrome grille, and some other minor details that Dante hadn't paid much attention to.

It was as necessary these days to cloak their rides in deception as it was to disguise themselves. The Executioners, once the dispensers of justice on the island of Atlantica, had become outlaws.

Dante pulled the truck away from Daria's house, which lay in a neighborhood populated mostly by dockworkers. There was a small maze of residential streets to get through before they encountered the main road that abutted the harbor facilities and led into the city proper. The relative anonymity of the place was one reason that the Executives hadn't yet found them.

Eleanor adjusted her bun. "We're going into an upscale part of town, you realize. It's the stratum of society where I was most active before I became an outlaw like you. There might be people around there who would recognize me."

"Don't worry," Dante reassured her, trying to sound blithely confident. "The disguise looks great. You're basically unrecognizable. In a good way, I mean. Lots of rich people are superficial enough that if you change your hairstyle and dress down a bit, they wouldn't even notice you. Right?"

He had his doubts but chose not to express them. The bulk of the persuasion would fall upon Eleanor, not himself, so he wanted her to feel as cocky about it as he hoped he sounded.

Eleanor sighed. "Perhaps that is true. If I turn suddenly toward a wall, or if I take your arm and guide you someplace else, do not question me. Play along. It's probably because I've seen someone I know who could identify me."

"Got it." He made himself grin. "No problem at all. I mean, I might have the same problem, but probably not. I didn't generally associate much with the society types. Then again someone from Atlantica General Hospital might have moved up in the world.

Or some of the gun runners and brothel keepers I used to know could've made enough money to end up there."

His grin faded. "Damn. Why did I think of that?"

Eleanor closed her eyes and leaned back in her chair. "Let's try not to worry. We've done everything we can. Now we must trust our plan and trust to luck."

Dante nodded and drove on.

Lunch hour for most businesses was drawing to an end right as they had departed, so traffic wasn't as bad as it could've been. Nonetheless, the streets buzzed with cars, trucks, and motorcycles. The business people, construction workers, taxis, and random citizens who could afford to drive zipped to and from their errands, jobs, or recreational pursuits.

Around and above them, the city with its mostly new and ultra-modern skyscrapers glimmered. Skeletal frames and pools of concrete lay in the few remaining gaps in downtown's dense real estate. More buildings would fill the skyline soon enough.

There were rumors of security checkpoints at a handful of major intersections. Dante saw none so far. Still, they had to be ready for anything. The Executive Security forces were simply waiting for them to drop into their laps sometime.

There was something else.

Dante broke the brief silence since the subject refused to leave his mind. "Have you heard any more about the Hellbreakers? I haven't seen the bastards since we left them behind at that facility a month ago."

"No. There have been vague stories. There are so many violent people on this island that it's impossible to determine if a particular crime or skirmish or act of destruction is their work or someone else's. We can no longer conduct investigations of such things ourselves, can we?"

Dante didn't reply. It was unnecessary. They both knew she was right.

At a busy intersection where skyscrapers blotted out most of the heavens, they stopped at a traffic light between a Citroen and an Aston-Martin. On the cross-street was a nondescript black van, like those used by Exec Security.

Dante tensed but didn't react. They would have to trust the effectiveness of their disguises.

On the passenger's side, a kid ambled by, hawking newspapers. Eleanor opened the window and flagged him down, slipped him a few coins, and took one of the papers.

"If there is word of the Hellbreakers, or *us*, this would be the place to hear it," she pointed out to Dante. "Since by now the Executives largely control the press, we can gain some insight into where their minds are and what their next plans might be."

"Well, I'm glad you're taking the plunge, so I don't have to."

The light changed, and they drove ahead, the black van doing nothing to indicate it had any interest in them. So far. Security was far more prominent in the city than it had been a month or two ago. Of that much, Dante was sure.

Eleanor groaned as she read the main details of a story about the "increasing threat" posed by the rogue organization known as the Executioners. Once widely respected if feared, the article alleged that they had now been "infiltrated by an extremist element" and were not to be trusted. Worse, the reporter tried to imply that several random acts of violence outside the city were potentially the Executioners' work.

In fact, the six of them had spent almost all their time within the city ever since the destruction of the centrifugal super-generator at the water treatment plant. Any clashes taking place out on the frontier were likely the responsibility of either disgruntled citizens trying to repel the Executives' heavy-handed servants or criminal elements preying on the citizenry.

Dante gritted his teeth. It was all about what he would have expected, but there was still something profoundly infuriating about being slandered. Having "respectable" sources lie about and insult him and his friends, and knowing that at least some average people would believe it. The gossip he'd heard lately suggested the public opinion was slowly becoming more and more hostile toward the Executioners.

Eleanor tossed the paper aside. "If they must publish libel against us, we must be doing something right, yes? Anyway. Let us focus on what we must do today."

"Sure." Dante looked at her. "Good job keeping in shape, by the way. If you walked into my old office, I'd believe that you were a pro athlete. Seriously."

She gave a subdued smile while looking out the windshield. "Thank you."

Soon after, they arrived at the clinic. There were no obvious markings. As with many facilities that catered primarily to wealthy, elite clients, they preferred to keep a low profile to avoid undue attention from the general populace. Still, Dante had seen enough medical facilities in his day that it looked like a surgical clinic to him. It wasn't much different from any other sleek, modern building that contained more glass than concrete. What gave it away was something more obscure, something he couldn't put into words. He wasn't much of an architecture buff.

At the gate, a booth guard stopped them and asked if they had an appointment. After giving the man their fake information, he checked something on a clipboard, nodded, and waved them in.

Dante sighed in relief as he pulled in, choosing a spot with a fairly straight path back to the gate and backing into it. He opted not to voice aloud his concern that if someone *did* discover them, it would be all too easy for them to be trapped within. Being found out at the gate would have meant that at least they could have fled back into the metropolis.

He shifted into park and killed the engine. "Let's do this. And let's do it right."

"There is no other way *to* do it," Eleanor observed.

They climbed down, locked up the truck, and strode to the entrance, pushing through a pair of reinforced glass doors and ending up in a clean, bright, ultra-modern lobby. Dante quickly noted the locations of the security cameras and positioned himself so his face would be mostly out of sight, trying not to be too obvious about it.

He glanced around. Two other people were waiting there, a man and a woman, both dressed in expensive but tasteful clothes that reflected the tastes of the day. Dante and Eleanor had selected outfits that were a notch or two down the swankiness scale but still likely to be within the establishment's acceptable parameters.

This had to be the place. He could feel it.

A contact of Daria's, a former smuggler turned high-end drug dealer, had been the one to drop the clinic in their lap. Based on his admittedly somewhat erratic and poorly described report, though, certain details began to fall into place. It was hard not to assume that *something* was going on here beyond what they advertised openly.

Namely, people sometimes came out with parts of their bodies bandaged up that had nothing to do with the procedures they had originally, nominally requested. There seemed to be more warm bodies in the surgical wards and operating theaters than actual *customers*.

Thus the Executioners had concluded that it was a possible front for the Coven of Miracles. Here, they reasoned, the shadow cabal might be performing its bizarre experiments and implanting its incredibly advanced technology into the bodies of clients whom they knew, whom they trusted, and who could afford to pay the undoubtedly steep fees.

An attractive receptionist with pointed glasses greeted them from behind a spotless white desk. "Hello. How may I be of service? Do you have an appointment?"

Eleanor smiled. "Yes, indeed. My name is Maria Salazar-Ramirez, and this is Dr. Anton Toscani." She had thickened her natural Mexican accent, and Dante felt, altered it in subtle ways to suggest she came from somewhere farther south. "We are here to speak to Dr. Pembrose about a, ah, knee procedure?"

They had agreed in advance that she would "forget" the word she was looking for.

Dante stepped up next to her. "A knee arthroscopy," he clarified, adjusting his fake glasses and taking the folder full of paperwork and fabricated X-rays from his jacket. "She had a recent injury, you understand, and wishes to return to athletics with all haste." He spoke in a more posh fashion than he was used to, with an affected Mid-Atlantic accent.

The receptionist nodded. "Ah, yes, we have been expecting you. I will need you to fill out these forms. Let me know when you finish, and I'll take you to see the doctor."

They went through the charade of writing nonsense on the forms, ensuring that it was consistent with their false IDs in case someone thought to check. Atlanticans conducted much of their business on a discreet basis—it would've been considered "under the table" in a country with actual laws. Under normal circumstances, Dante doubted they'd have had anything to worry about.

Still, with the Executives growing more paranoid and heavyhanded, and the ever more overbearing presence of Exec Security...

He and Eleanor handed back their paperwork. The receptionist glanced over it, seemed satisfied, and gathered a few other things. "Right this way, please."

The pair followed her. She unlocked a door and led them down a short white hallway to an elevator. They rode it to the second floor, much like the first, where the woman took them around a corner before depositing them in a fairly standard, albeit comfortable and extensively furnished, office. The more esoteric parts of the facility must have laid deeper within the building.

"Wait here," the receptionist instructed them. "We were going to have you speak to someone else first, but I believe that Dr.

Lionel Pembrose, our head surgeon, is available today, so he might visit you himself to handle your case personally." She smiled and excused herself.

Dante adjusted his tie. "Good to know we don't have to go through the rigmarole of getting our blood pressure taken first. Of course, *you* will have that pleasure after you come back for your arthroscopy. Am I right?" He elbowed Eleanor in the side and grinned.

"When we come back, yes." She sighed. Dante seemed to be enjoying the farcical pretense of their visit a little too much. "First, let us hear what this Pembrose has to say."

It took about six or seven minutes before they heard footsteps approaching again. They'd spent their time glancing around the room, looking for anything that might qualify as a clue. Unfortunately, there was a camera in one of the upper corners, so they didn't dare poke around in the desk's drawers. The readily visible stuff was banal and standard, nothing to imply guilt or point them toward any useful revelations.

The door opened, and a man strode in. He was sixtyish and on the shorter side of average, with broad shoulders and meaty hands, though his fingers were thin and steady, as a surgeon's should be. He had a large round nose, a bushy unibrow, and carried himself with an air of aloof dignity.

Dante disliked him at once. The vibe he gave off was typical of upper-crust doctors who considered themselves above such plebeian concerns as basic medical practice for the average person. Still, they had a mission to accomplish. He kept his feelings to himself.

"Hello," the man began in a deep drawl. "I'm Dr. Pembrose. I understand you're here for an arthroscopy? Normally one of the other doctors would handle such a thing, but I'm afraid they're all engaged elsewhere. I, on the other hand, have just returned from an errand."

Dante and Eleanor both stood and shook the man's hand,

introducing themselves politely and confirming all he'd said. Before he could brush them off with technical details followed by scheduling arrangements, Eleanor proceeded with the plan.

"Dr. Pembrose," she started, using a higher-pitched and somehow more girlish voice than her usual, along with her artificially altered accent. "I am so glad you could see us. You might be my only chance. You see, sir, I'm an Olympic hopeful. Unless I regain the *full* use of my knee, my career might be over forever."

The surgeon had wandered behind his desk as though he meant to pull out the massive leather-backed chair and sit, but for whatever reason he hovered in place, standing with his hands in the pocket of his clean white coat.

"Mmm, yes, I see. Well, arthroscopy is still a young procedure, not much past the experimental phase, but it has proven effective in diagnosing injuries of that nature. We should be able to determine whether or not you have a chance at recovery after it's complete. I understand you have X-rays?"

Dante beamed and produced the folder again. "Yes, yes. I'm Ms. Salazar-Ramirez's physician. I treated her after the initial accident. Sadly, the type of care she'll probably need is a bit above my pay grade. Ha, ha." He handed the folder over.

Eleanor added, "Please, recommend *whatever* you think might help."

Pembrose accepted it, finally seating himself, flipping open the front, then looking through the X-ray photographs. "Mmm. I see. The damage appears fairly extensive, but again, we'll know more after the procedure. These are from three weeks ago? She seems able to stand without too much difficulty. Allow my receptionist to schedule a date for you, then." He stood, looking slightly bored and irritated that they were wasting his time on something so basic.

"Doctor!" Eleanor interjected. "Please. Knowing your reputation, we had hoped you could tell us more." She gestured at the folder with a slim hand. "Based on what you can see there, do you think that I can perform again? I cannot take the uncertainty any longer. Please, give me *some* sort of prognosis."

Pembrose frowned. "Mmm, yes," he drawled once again, folding his thick hands in front of himself. "We cannot of course say what the problem might be, exactly, until we have performed the procedure. Then, it is difficult to say what outcomes may be possible. Many patients with knee injuries can attain full functionality for normal activities. For a professional athlete, however, it becomes far more complicated."

Now, Dante thought. *The time was now.* He looked at Eleanor, keeping his expression neutral but ensuring that she caught his intense gaze.

Her eyes flicked briefly toward his, then toward Pembrose, before turning to the floor. She drew a deep breath and let her chest and back heave before letting it out in a long, slow sigh.

Then she looked up at the surgeon with a fast, snapping head motion. "I see," she said. She turned her head partway to the left and looked at him sidelong. "Is there anything else you can do that will guarantee I am back to normal? I have heard that, ah, you do other things here as well. Interesting and experimental things, yes? Surely you must know of another procedure that will give me hope. We can pay for it, of course."

The man blinked and bristled, his body jittering briefly as though someone had unexpectedly insulted him or accused him of wrongdoing. "I don't know what you're talking about, miss. I've explained to you what we can and cannot do. That is all."

Dante raised his index finger. "Now, see here," he began in his faux Mid-Atlantic accent. "We've had reliable reports that this place is on the cutting edge of experimental surgery. Part of the reason we came here was because of the rumors that you could potentially do things that go beyond what most people can find anywhere else. Not only is my client in desperate need, but I am quite curious for professional reasons of my own, I must say."

Again, Pembrose bristled, but this time his posture was more aggressive, and his unibrow angled down in the middle as his jaw muscles tightened. "How dare you. Come into my clinic talking about wild rumors and gossip, suggesting that we perform unethical procedures? I never. I am a well-respected surgeon, and all I have done in my career is well within the bounds of—"

Eleanor burst into tears, her face falling into her hands as her loud, high-pitched sobs interrupted the doctor and made him fall silent. She hunched her shoulders and appeared to shrivel, instantly becoming the picture of pitiful vulnerability.

Dante was about as surprised as Dr. Pembrose seemed to be. Eleanor didn't have the same background in violence and human ugliness that Dante and the other Executioners did, yet she was still a fairly tough-minded woman. He'd never seen her like this.

The surgeon's standoffish demeanor softened, but he still squirmed with awkward discomfort, probably embarrassed on her behalf.

"*Doctor*," Eleanor sobbed. "Oh, please. You do not understand." She looked up at him with big, tearful eyes. "I come from a poor and tiny village in Guatemala. It was so difficult for me to begin to compete in athletics. When I showed that I had talent, our government noticed. They are not good people. They rule my country with an iron fist, and no one may oppose them. My career is not my own. They...they expect certain things of me."

Dante racked his brain, trying to remember more of the details of Eleanor's background. He knew she was from the vicinity of Guadalajara in Mexico, not Guatemala. Otherwise, he found it frustratingly difficult to recall the rest.

Pembrose relaxed a little. He frowned in concern, but he might've feigned it. "I am, ah, sorry to hear that, ma'am. We can—"

"I am no more than their instrument," Eleanor went on, "an instrument for making the country look good to foreigners. They wish to use me to compete in the Olympics and bring investment to our nation. They do not care about me as a person, only what I can do to help their reputation. If I cannot perform as an athlete..."

She looked down at her hands, which shook in front of her.

"I will have nothing. Our leaders will cast me aside, and there will be no choice for me but to live the rest of my life doing backbreaking labor in the rural lands or become a prostitute in the city. I *must* come back from Atlantica not only as good as new, but *better* than I was. Or my life is over. I might as well die."

Flustered and beginning to warm up to the seriousness of her predicament, Pembrose hemmed and hawed, trying to think of something to say. Dante stayed out of it, allowing his partner to work her magic.

She reached toward the surgeon. "You are my only hope, Doctor. I am so terribly afraid. But I have heard that you can work miracles."

Pembrose blinked. His unappealing face was a mishmash of emotions and uncertainties. His more casual body language suggested that Eleanor's performance was winning him over, though.

"Hmm, mm. Yes." He stroked his chin. "Given your, ah, predicament, there might be something we can do for you today. Please follow me."

Eleanor's face lit up. She stopped crying, and her excitement was palpable, charging the air like an electric current. "Oh, thank you!"

Dante smiled. "Indeed. Thanks."

They stood and followed the squat surgeon out of his office and into another room down the hall, something closer to a standard examination room in any doctor's office, not unlike Dante's back in New York.

Pembrose gestured vaguely. "Wait here. I will return in a few minutes." He wandered out, closing the door behind him.

Eleanor took a seat on the examination couch and Dante in

one of the chairs beside it. The elation that sprouted between them was wholly genuine. It wasn't a part of their act.

Dante turned to his partner. "Well, that was an impressive performance. Convincing, even. Do you have any training as an actress? Or was any part of that real? As in, if we're honest here, I'm wondering if half of that was you telling him the truth."

She flapped a hand at him. "It doesn't matter. What's important is that we have come to the next stage. Whatever this man has to say next should be far more interesting."

"Well, yeah," Dante muttered, "but that's not what I'm curious about right now, is it? You know my background. Why don't I know more about yours? I have to wonder. Did you end up here because some repressive regime back in Mexico kicked you out? I mean, you know that I got mixed up with La Cosa Nostra. Atlantica was my chance for a fresh start. From them, and some bad habits I had picked up." He grimaced.

A shudder went through his body. With no laws to speak of, a person could purchase *anything* on the streets of Atlantica Metro if one knew where to look and whom to ask. An addict like himself could easily drown in every awful, poisonous, mind-altering substance known to man, plus a few brand-new cocktails of which humankind was better off remaining ignorant.

He'd resisted the temptation for more than a year. Every single aspect of his life was better for it.

Eleanor looked at him pointedly, her dark eyes beguiling. "I thought I told you about my origins, Dante. No, very little of that act had anything to do with real life. My family was wealthy and respected. I simply came here to make my fortune rather than go to work for them. It would've been boring to remain in Jalisco."

Dante shrugged. "Well, I almost bought it, anyway. I think our boy Pembrose did too."

Eleanor pursed her lips as something suddenly occurred to her. "Do you think that the part about 'working miracles' was too, um, what is the expression...too 'on the nose?'"

"No, I mean, yeah. Yes, that's the expression, but no, no it wasn't. It was just right. Seems like it worked, right?"

She rolled her shoulders. "I suppose it did. It sounds like he's coming back." She raised a finger to her lips.

It belatedly occurred to Dante that there was a slim chance of surveillance bugs in the room. He doubted it. There was no security cam, either. If by some chance they'd been overheard, serious problems could result.

It sounded like Pembrose had other people with him. At least one or two.

When the door opened, though, the head surgeon himself was the only one who stepped through. He was pushing a small cart atop which was a truly bizarre device, unlike anything Dante had seen. It appeared to be a clamp of sorts, made of bright silvery metal. It resembled a giant spider.

Two wires ran out of it, each of them connecting to a pair of golf-ball-sized Atlanticore crystals mounted in metal stands that rested upon the cart. The man picked up the spider clamp and moved toward Eleanor. His face was blank of any particular expression.

"Doctor," she began, "what is that thing?"

He flashed a brief smile. "A device that will help you. Dr. Toscani, put it onto her knee, with the central underbelly directly over the injured part of the joint, then secure the limbs tightly around her."

The pair exchanged a half-alarmed glance, then Dante stood and stared full into the smaller man's face. "Dr. Pembrose, I'm afraid I cannot, in good conscience, do that to my patient without knowing more about what this thing is and what, precisely, it does. I must consider my patient's welfare in all things, as well as the importance of my Hippocratic Oath."

Since Dante *was* an actual doctor, he was telling the truth. Only the posh accent was fake.

Pembrose gave him a barely disguised sneer, then looked at

Eleanor with exasperation. "If you want your miracle, ma'am, you need to put this on your leg. Now."

Everything felt wrong. Dante wondered if Eleanor had been as successful with her persuasive routine as they'd believed. It was possible that even if they had convinced Pembrose, he might've spoken to someone else behind the scenes who'd expressed an entirely different opinion and instructed Pembrose to do as ordered.

Someone who might take unkindly to people throwing around that word, "miracles."

Dante cleared his throat. "Dr. Pembrose. We realize that your time is valuable and that we cannot expect you to brief us on the minutiae of every device and procedure you have access to. But I refuse to subject my patient, without even a modicum of explanation, to potentially dangerous and experimental—"

Pembrose barked, "Guards! Restrain this man."

Two men burst into the room from the hallway outside, both clad in the distinctive black armored uniforms of Executive Security. Pistols and shock batons hung at their waists, and they made straight for Dante while Pembrose advanced on Eleanor with the mechanical spider-thing.

Dante exhaled. "Oh, shit."

CHAPTER TWO

There was no time for Dante to draw his concealed pistol, and even if he had managed to finagle it out of his pants, he didn't want to fire it in such a small room, anyway. Squeezing the trigger while wrestling with two men, there was too much risk of hitting Eleanor.

One of the security thugs shouted, "Give it up, pal!" in his face, then both of them were on him, grabbing his arms and lifting him to slam his back against the wall and pin him in place. Dante was no expert in hand-to-hand combat. He lacked the military training and extensive wartime experience that Ty and Gage had.

Still, he'd been in his share of street fights. When he and Gage had first worked together, Dante had, improbably, managed to defeat the giant Soviet agent known as Koschei. He could handle himself better than the average person.

And he felt confident that he could have slipped one of his feet behind the right guard's knee, leaned into him, and thrown him to the ground. But that would only invite the other guy to draw his baton or pistol and take Dante out of the fight altogether. Perhaps permanently. He needed a way of dealing with both men at once.

A yard and a half away, Pembrose lurched toward Eleanor, brandishing the weird arachnoid device. "Stop being a fool," he drawled. "This will get you nice and taken care of, young lady. Just extend your leg and let it happen..."

Eleanor was no expert in combat or martial arts either. She *was* in exceedingly good physical condition, and the other Executioners had been gradually teaching her more and more about fighting over the last few weeks. Pembrose underestimated her.

"No." She kicked the surgeon in the chest.

He grunted and staggered back, the spidery clamp nearly falling from his grasp. One of the security guards turned away to see if his boss needed help, loosening his grasp on Dante's left arm.

It was enough of an opening for Dante to act. He stuck his foot out and tripped the man on the right, heaving against him and bowling him over at the same instant he pulled his left arm free from the distracted guard. By the time the man turned back to him and reached for his baton, Dante had already gripped the hilt.

Dante pulled it free and clicked the button on the side. It crackled with power as the now-panicking goon fumbled for his pistol. Dante shoved the glowing tip up under the man's chin. He made a terrible hollow squawking sound and stumbled back, sparks rising from his armor and gripping his throat. It hadn't fatally injured the guard, but an electrical spasm around the larynx would keep him out of the fight for a hot minute or two. Maybe more like a hot hour.

Dr. Pembrose recovered from the kick a little too quickly. Despite his advancing age and squat physique, he'd adjusted to the reality of the situation and looked like a cornered animal. His meaty fist lashed out and caught Dante on the jaw as the younger doctor prepared to neutralize the second guard.

Dante cursed and stumbled into the man he'd tripped. He dropped the baton, which rolled off behind the examination couch. Then their thrashing limbs intertwined as both sought to get atop the other, the two bodies slamming one another against the walls and floor as they rolled back and forth.

Eleanor hopped down from the couch, seized a glass jar filled with wooden tongue depressors, and hurled it at Pembrose. The man saw her in time to raise his free arm to protect his face, but he failed to move out of the way. The jar slammed into his elbow, spun over his forearm, and *thunked* against his forehead before falling and shattering on the floor.

Pembrose exclaimed, "Goddamn you! It's only a—" He stopped, unsure what to say next, and advanced again toward the woman. "Hold still."

Footsteps pounded the floor outside, and another security guard swung into the room. "Do you need help? Jesus!" Taking in the scene at a glance, he pulled aside the man Dante had shocked in the throat and plunged into the fray.

Eleanor flung open a cabinet door. It wasn't much, but she had nothing else to throw within reach, and it delayed Pembrose and the new guard for a split second. Enough time for her to vault over the couch and practically land on top of Dante.

Instead, she twisted and brought her foot down hard on the head of the guard struggling with her partner. He yelped as his skull collided with the base of the couch, then slumped unconscious. Dante pulled back from him while Eleanor found her balance.

Before either of them could do anything, Pembrose and the fresh guard were upon them. The man Dante had throat-shocked was climbing back to his feet, gasping and coughing, but he'd probably be back in the fight in another twenty or thirty seconds.

Eleanor snapped, "Dante, shoot the bastards!"

He reached for his pistol. The new guard did the same, and both handguns came out simultaneously.

Pembrose sneered, "No, no, no. Don't be foolish. This will be far easier for everyone if you simply cooperate. We're not trying to hurt you. You wanted help, didn't you?"

"Cut the bullshit," Dante grunted.

Pembrose responded by lunging at Eleanor with the spider clamp. To everyone's surprise, she snatched it away from him. The third guard interposed himself, reaching for Eleanor's arm as Pembrose froze in horror. She jerked away from him and shoved the clamp toward his chest.

He stumbled back. "No—*no!*" His eyes bulged in abject fear, a reaction not lost on the two Executioners. They'd been right to mistrust the clamp.

Dante raised his pistol again, getting the drop on the security goon with the sore throat. "Ah-ah," he chided. "You stay right where you are."

Eleanor pressed forward with the bizarre device. The terrified guard threw himself aside, falling over the couch as Eleanor shot out her arm. The spider-thing passed through the air the man had vacated. Instead, its underbelly connected with Dr. Pembrose's neck and chin. The metal legs reflexively wrapped themselves around his head and shoulders.

"Oh my God," he gasped. "Get it off! Get off me!" It began to glow and hum. So did the two crystals it was hooked to, even though the cart lay half-tipped against the counter and one of the stones had fallen to the floor.

The guard whose head Eleanor had stomped on came to again and wrapped his arms around Dante's legs, trying to pull him off-balance. As the Executioner's gun wavered off-target, the man with the sore throat moved in.

Then everyone stopped as a sound like splintering glass accompanied by a flash of blue light filled the room.

Dr. Pembrose had frozen in place, wailing in anguish. Light from the arachnoid device flowed over his body. His eyes looked as though they'd turned to ice. Since his mouth hung open in a now mostly silent scream, they saw the inside of his throat turning from red flesh to blue crystal. The veins in his neck and forehead were following suit.

One of the guards exclaimed, "Jesus Christ almighty!" It was the man on the floor, the one gripping Dante's legs.

The tall physician came down on the man's head with the butt of his 1911, slamming it into his temple and sending him back into unconsciousness. He kicked the man's arms away. Ahead of him, the guy who'd taken the baton to the Adam's apple was paralyzed in horror as he watched Pembrose's transformation.

"Sorry, pal." Dante shot him in the head. The man fell without a sound, the gunshot ringing painfully in their ears.

The last of the guards—the man who'd stumbled over the couch in his haste to escape the clamp-thing—rose to his feet, panicking. Eleanor braced herself against the sofa with her hands and swung her legs into his lower back, knocking him into the cabinets. While he was briefly stunned, she pounced on him, grabbed his hair and collar, and slammed his head twice more into the wooden surface. He slumped over, drooling and twitching.

With the immediate threat of the security thugs neutralized, Dante and Eleanor turned their attention toward the increasingly loud crackling and humming sounds, like an electrical charge spreading through ice, that filled the chamber from where Dr. Pembrose stood.

He was still there but no longer human. The crystallization process, the bizarre transformation from flesh and bone to Atlanticore, had proceeded to the point that his entire upper body was now a solid mass of shining blue stone.

His head, shoulders, and upper arms were rigid and statue-like. Creeping veins of Atlanticore spread through his lower neck, chest, and forearms. Faint, twitching spasms still ran through his lower body, and his legs held firm. He continued to stand, even though there was every reason to believe that the crystal engulfing his entire head had killed him by now.

Dante snapped his fingers as something came to him. "Shit. He's going to become unstable and fall over. You remember what happens to destabilized Atlanticore?"

"I do," Eleanor huffed, her head swiveling and gaze darting around to see if anyone else was going to burst into the room to detain or kill them. She snatched a pistol from one of the fallen guards, a Browning nine-millimeter like the one Daria carried. "It would make a good distraction, though. We must get deeper into this clinic."

Dante's face brightened in a crazy, stupid grin. "Let's kick him out the window! He was a prick, anyway. All the damage will be on the first floor and in the parking lot. Meanwhile, we bolt in the opposite direction. We should do it together, though. All that crystal has to be heavy."

Eleanor shot him a squinty, skeptical look, then shook her head and agreed. "Fine. On three, yes? One, two..."

"Three," Dante finished.

They both surged forward, legs lashing out, their feet planting themselves hard in Pembrose's still mostly human chest and stomach. The impact drove him back, the dense blue crystal tipping him over backward as his legs gave out. His head crashed through the glass, and his whole body tumbled out into the open air.

Dante turned and grabbed Eleanor's arm. "Run!"

They sprinted, not waiting around to observe the effects of their handiwork. A faint rustling of the breeze was audible through the window as the half-transmogrified body toppled toward the pavement. Otherwise, they heard only their pounding footsteps. They plunged out of the examination room into the hallway, slammed the door behind them, and raced toward the parts of the clinic that were better hidden from outsiders.

When the explosion came, it rattled the whole building.

Though it was loud enough to set his ears to ringing, Dante heard debris crashing against the door behind them. He was glad they'd thought to close it.

Eleanor stumbled as the building shook. She was glad she was wearing good practical boots instead of high heels. She managed to keep her balance, but Dante caught her arm anyway. She took it, braced her upper body, and used him to launch herself back into a jog down the hall.

Both instinctively made for a double door up ahead on the right. Between Eleanor's long experience in corporate offices and Dante's equally long experience in hospitals, they identified it as the type of door that could only open upon something important.

Dante flung himself at it and yanked on the right handle, probably expecting it to be locked, but it opened easily, disclosing a conference room. "Nope," he grumbled. "Holy shit." He blinked and stared toward the right side of the chamber.

Eleanor came up behind him and poked her head into the room. Part of the wall had collapsed, and through the hole, she saw that the Atlanticore explosion—the results of Dr. Pembrose's defenestration—had blown away most of the doctor's office as well as a large chunk of the front of the building. It also put a shallow crater in the adjacent parking lot. Rubble and glass from the building itself, probably the first floor, lay strewn around it as well.

Dante turned to leave. "We need to keep moving. Looks like we got our distraction, but someone probably noticed where Pembrose fell from."

Eleanor shook her head. "I hope we didn't hurt any innocent people with that." The blast appeared to have missed the lobby, at least, but she couldn't tell what else it might have damaged.

"Well, at least we can confirm that we were right to suspect this place," Dante added as they jogged toward another double door at the end of the hallway. "Pretty sure most high-end clinics don't call in armed guards while they try to turn people into

Atlanticore statues, even if they *do* see through bullshit Olympics stories and fake accents."

Eleanor tried not to roll her eyes as she ran behind him. "This is true, yes." Dante's propensity for sarcastic jokes was sometimes a relief, but he seemed unable to stop himself even when they'd narrowly escaped death mere minutes before.

They crashed through the doors into the clinic's rear wing, which looked nothing at all like the front. The entire atmosphere changed at once. The combination of whites and warm browns in the "commercial" part of the building gave way to cold, eerie blues and metallic tones. Something about the place reminded Eleanor less of a hospital than it did a government morgue.

She also saw a small red light flashing above the doorframe they'd passed through. This must be a restricted area, and they'd likely tripped a silent alarm. With a gigantic hole blown in the front corner of the building and at least two men dead, she didn't think an extra security alert for trespassing would make much difference.

An orderly appeared, pushing a body on a gurney, covered with a sheet. He froze when he saw the two of them, especially since Eleanor's confiscated pistol, while tucked away for the moment, created unmistakable lines through her clothes.

Dante grabbed the man's sleeve. "Where do they make those clamp things that look like mechanical spiders? Hooked up to blue crystals? Don't pretend like you don't know what I'm talking about. We just saw one of the goddamn things ourselves."

The orderly was a young, red-haired guy who seemed baffled and frightened by the intrusion. His fear appeared to contain a definite element of...guilt, though. Or so it seemed to Eleanor.

He stammered, "I, ah, I don't know what all they make back there, but—"

"Where?" Dante demanded.

Behind them, it sounded like boots were pounding the stairs. More security personnel must have been rushing up to investigate the source of the blast. Eleanor realized that Dr. Pembrose's detonation might have rendered the elevators inoperable.

The orderly pointed a shaking hand down the hallway to the right. "Back corner. Through the blue door. That's where they do all the experimental stuff. Okay?"

Dante let him go. "Don't fucking tell anyone you saw us." There was no way to enforce the threat, but the thought counted.

The pair sprinted down the hall in the direction the redhead had indicated, leaving the young man behind with his thoughts. As her heart pounded and the various noises of the facility crowded in around her consciousness, Eleanor wondered who'd been on the gurney. What lay beneath the sheet.

Down the hallway, another short corridor branched off to the side, and they barely glimpsed a blue door at the end. Dante, out in front, veered that way and grabbed Eleanor's shoulder to guide her in the same direction.

Between breaths, she scolded him, "I can run by myself, you know."

"Sorry," he shot back. "Force of habit." Then he forced himself to a halt, his heels scraping the floor half a meter from the blue surface before them. The door wasn't the swinging variety. It had a lever, along with a stop to hold it open in case someone needed to push a gurney or cart through.

Eleanor braced herself for a useless *click*, guessing that the orderly had probably locked it, but it wasn't. It opened outward as Dante depressed the handle and pulled it clear of the threshold. She ran through first, and he swung in behind her, allowing the door to fall shut behind them.

They both stopped. The area where, according to the orderly, the "experimental stuff" was done wasn't what they'd expected. It did confirm Eleanor's earlier impression. They stood in a morgue.

The air was chilly, and their breath formed clouds in front of them. Bodies, at least a dozen covered by transparent plastic sheets, lay on white slabs.

"Jesus," Dante breathed. "It looks like all of these people died in the middle of operations. I know a surgical fuck-up when I see one. But I can't tell...if..."

He moved closer to the corpse nearest to him, peering at it and trying to guess what had happened to the victim in the limited time he had available. With the clinic's security detail doubtless closing in, there was no way he could do anything remotely close to a sufficient autopsy. His best first-impression guess as a doctor was the only thing possible.

Eleanor rubbed her shoulders as she glanced around. "These people look...wrong, for this place. They look like poor people or very unhealthy. Hobos and the sick."

"Yeah." The tall physician moved on to another one. "People who had health conditions to begin with, I'd say. I'm wondering if the bastards were experimenting on them under the pretense of trying to cure them. That way, if they died, they could say, 'Oops, the procedure failed to save them,' or something."

Eleanor felt something within her turn to jagged ice, and it had nothing to do with the frigid air. It was the abrupt and unwanted realization that *she*, in her role as a servant and go-between for the Executives, had helped *this* to happen.

Dante moved toward the far end of the chamber. "Come on. Let's see what else these sons of bitches have been up to."

"I'm not sure I want to." Eleanor's voice was small and soft, a direct contradiction of the rage that slowly swelled up from her gut.

A swinging door separated the refrigerated morgue from what lay beyond. Dante pushed it open and held it for Eleanor, then together, they rushed down the hall. At a T-intersection, the corridor branched off toward a storage room to the left, and something else lay behind a screen to the right. Human voices were talking in that direction.

Dante hesitated, looking at the storage room and probably wanting to ransack it for clues or samples of Coven devices. Eleanor, however, had already veered right. The Browning pistol was out in her hand.

Noticing her, Dante scowled and ran behind her, hoping she wasn't about to give them away and ruin their chances.

Past the screen was an operating theater. Various people—doctors, nurses, and perhaps members of the Executives' Junior Board or their representatives—stood in a semicircle around the open depression where a surgeon and three nurses or technologists were about to operate. On the table amid them was a little girl, maybe ten years old at most.

Eleanor gasped, raising a hand to her mouth. She couldn't help it. Children were rare on Atlantica. A few families brought their adolescents with them to help work and save money, and occasionally so did wealthy people who came to tour the city or sample the island's strange and rowdy delights. Some of the more permanent residents in the city or the distant villages had begun to have babies. In general, most understood that Atlantica was a place too sordid and dangerous for anyone but adults.

It was one of the things that had made Eleanor's job bearable all these years. The knowledge that, no matter what else happened, children—little boys or little girls, like the one she'd once been—wouldn't be harmed.

"*No!*" she exclaimed, pushing forward in a mad rush and brandishing the handgun.

Everyone turned to look at her, and two of the observers, a man and a woman, reached out to restrain her. "Hey! You can't be here! What the hell—"

Eleanor shot the man in the leg. He fell, moaning in pain. The woman tried to tackle her, and Eleanor fired again, putting a round through her shoulder and sending her scuttling to the far wall mewling in agony and clutching the bloody wound.

Dante came up behind Eleanor as everyone fell silent, frozen in shock and trepidation.

Ms. Cervantes gestured at the girl on the operating table. "Stop this at once! Get all of those fucking tubes off of her. What do you people think you are *doing?*"

When the surgeon hesitated, Eleanor raised her gun, aiming it at his face.

"Wait!" Dante interjected, stepping in behind her and putting his hand on her arm. He called to the medical crew, "What's that she's hooked up to, and why? I'm a doctor, by the way."

The surgeon continued to balk, but one of the masked nurses said, in a Slavic accent, "She is on ventilator. There is damage to her lungs from serious infection. If we take her off machine, she will die."

Dante pressed gently down on Eleanor's arm. It infuriated her that he was trying to control her behavior, but she'd heard the nurse as well as he had. She lowered the pistol. "What are you doing in this place? What happened to all of those people in the morgue?"

"What's the deal with those spider things?" Dante added, drawing his 1911 to emphasize that he meant business too, but keeping it aimed at the floor for now. "We want some answers or a lot more of you than those two are going to end up with extra ventilation of your own." He gestured at the two wounded observers.

At last, the surgeon down in the theater started talking. In a Received Pronunciation British accent, he explained, "We work for a group affiliated with the Executives, performing advanced medical research here."

Dante nodded. "A group, meaning the Coven of Miracles, right? Don't play dumb with me, pal."

The surgeon's shoulders slumped in defeat. "Yes. That is what they call themselves, although we aren't privy to the specifics of their, ah, agenda. We do what they pay us to do."

Eleanor stared at him with loathing. "Advanced medical

research, you say. Tell us more, please." Her quiet, frigid tone didn't disguise the underlying menace in her voice.

The surgeon and the nurses, with input from one or two of the observers, told the rest of the story. Dante and Eleanor commanded them to hurry up when they started rambling too much. It was only a matter of time before security forces showed up, and they needed as much information as possible before making their escape.

Through the efforts of its members and hirelings sworn to secrecy, the Coven had been experimenting with technology on a smaller and more "personal" level. That was in addition to the industrial scale the Executioners had seen at the coastal facility a month ago. Various "candidates" had been found, both on the island and off, for use in the procedures.

Typically, the operations dealt with implanted technology. Devices powered by Atlanticore, of increasing sophistication, but with great potential for dangerous side effects or the body to reject the foreign materials, much like with organ transplants or certain types of prosthetics.

"Right," Dante said. "As I figured, you can always say that the cancer is what killed them if the experiments go wrong. Right? What are you planning to implant in that little girl?"

The surgeon swallowed a massive gulp of saliva. "Nothing. We're trying to bring her back to stable condition so we can test a bracelet that produces a kind of, er, protective field."

Dante and Eleanor looked at one another. Gage had recovered a similar bracelet from Jori Singh after the Hellbreakers had seemingly killed him.

Eleanor pointed out, "That wouldn't help her with a lung infection, though. It makes no sense."

"Well, no, but our assignment was to see how its effects would interact with her compromised body systems," one of the other nurses riposted. "A longitudinal study, you see."

Dante frowned. "We see. In other words, she's probably dead

no matter what, so you're going to do nothing except use her as a guinea pig while she has a few months left. What do you say, Eleanor? Should we shoot these pricks and unplug the girl to spare her all of that nonsense? Or should we—"

The observers, nurses, and surgeon all tensed up at Dante's threat, and it looked for an instant like a couple of them were about to try pouncing on the intruders in a desperate bid to save their own lives. Before they could act or Eleanor could comment, tramping footsteps suddenly came up behind them.

"Freeze!" a man's voice bellowed. "Drop the guns!"

Eleanor cursed under her breath. The security goons must have narrowed down where they were, reasoned that they weren't going anywhere right away, and approached slowly and quietly enough to spring an ambush.

She was about to drop her pistol when the woman she'd shot in the shoulder earlier, who'd been pressing herself against the sidewall the whole time, sprang to her feet and ran toward the screen, around which the men had clustered. "They shot me!" she squealed. "They threatened to kill us! Shoot them! They deserve it."

One of the guards ranted, "Get the fuck out of the way, you stupid bitch!"

The woman passed in front of Eleanor, blocking her from the guards' sight for a second. Eleanor stepped back and swung the pistol up, firing over the woman's shoulder at the nearest goon.

The man cried out. Eleanor couldn't tell if she'd hit him or not, but what happened next was obvious enough. Eleanor and Dante dove to the sides of the central depression while the guards opened fire.

The shrill-voiced woman with the wounded shoulder screamed as over a dozen bullets ripped through her torso, spinning her around in a bloody mess and leaving her collapsed against the railing over the theater proper. Everyone else screamed, too.

Dante rolled up from the floor with his 1911 ready and squeezed off three shots at the guards. One of them took a round in the arm and dropped his submachine gun. It was hard to tell about the others, and there wasn't time to stick around and find out. Dante rolled again, this time around the periphery of the theater, and blind-fired twice behind him to keep the security thugs pinned down while he looked for Eleanor.

Eleanor, keeping low to the floor, had scrambled around the theater from the opposite direction. As soon as she had a clear line of fire, she blasted a few more rounds from her pistol. The guards shot back in short bursts, but the muzzle flares in the dim space giving away their positions combined with the general confusion meant they weren't hitting much yet.

She saw a corridor ahead, which, mercifully, looked like it bent around to the left. "This way!"

She and Dante reached it at the same time, bolting into it as the guards regained enough presence of mind to open fire on full auto, spraying haphazardly to bring down their targets through sheer volume of fire. The one good thing, Dante noted, was that they all seemed to have submachine guns or machine pistols rather than rifles—presumably to reduce the chances of firing through too many walls in such a sensitive location.

Then again, he and Eleanor only had handguns themselves. Plus, all the guards were armored, so torso hits were out of the picture.

"We need to get back to the truck," he barked. "If there's a way out in this direction."

Eleanor gritted her teeth as they dashed along, keeping their heads down while plaster chipped and debris sprayed all around them. Dante had a gift for stating the obvious during desperate situations.

As they plunged ahead, trusting more to luck than anything else, another thing occurred to her. The girl. They'd left her behind, to whatever fate the Coven had in store.

CHAPTER THREE

Dante kicked open the door, well aware that someone, seemingly an orderly, was standing in front of it. The door slammed into the person from behind and knocked them over. Which was good—it meant they were out of the way when Dante and Eleanor bolted through.

"Excuse me!" Dante shouted. "Coming through." They burst into what looked like a lounge or something, with tables and comfy chairs set up for important people to discuss things over coffee, cigars, cognac, or whatever. Only three or four individuals languished there, though. They seemed bizarrely oblivious to the earlier explosion and the gunfire from a minute ago or less.

Eleanor asked him, "Is that necessary? Everyone with any sense should already be out of our way."

Someone, a guard, sprang up at her from behind a chair, aiming a compact submachine gun and snarling in animalistic rage. She knocked the gun aside as it spat out three or four rounds, which sprayed into a leather chair behind her.

Dante pivoted, aimed, and pumped a round of .45 ACP into the guard's neck. Blood sprayed, and the man collapsed to his knees, squawking. Eleanor snatched the gun from his hands and left him there to die. They both sprinted toward the door at the far end of the lounge.

Past it, another door displayed "EMERGENCY EXIT."

"Finally," Dante sighed. "Now, where the hell *are* we in relation to where we parked?"

Eleanor had a fairly good sense of direction when it came to buildings. "I believe we're on the north side, and I think we parked on the west. So, turn left."

Dante ejected his pistol's magazine and slapped in another. They had a rifle in the truck, but many things could go wrong between now and then. He only hoped that Exec Security hadn't seized or disabled their ride.

They sprang out through the emergency exit, probably setting off yet another alarm, and emerged into an empty alleyway, running to the left as Eleanor had suggested. When they rounded the corner, they saw the parking lot before them. The disguised Autocutioner was right where they'd left it.

So far, so good.

Another security thug stood guard next to the truck's cab, though. He had a rifle and probably drew the outdoor duty assignment for that very reason. They all caught sight of each other at the same time.

Eleanor already had her borrowed submachine gun at chest level. She blasted it haphazardly at the man, peppering him with a couple of dozen rounds of nine-millimeter and emptying the magazine before tossing the gun aside. The guard moaned and slumped over. Whether he was dead or whether his armor had protected him and he'd merely been battered unconscious by the barrage of lead wasn't their problem.

The Autocutioner's armor had certainly protected *it*. There was nary a dent in the hull, but a handful of stray rounds had chipped off some of the paint job, exposing the dark military green beneath.

Dante tossed Eleanor the keys while he stopped to retrieve

the fallen guard's rifle. He kicked the man in the ribs for good measure when he twitched. Apparently, he wasn't dead, after all.

Eleanor opened the door, slid into the driver's seat, and fired up the engine at once. It looked like dark silhouettes were massing in the lobby, probably yet more of the Coven's hired minions getting ready to storm their position.

Dante ran around to the passenger's side and jumped in. "We have an extra rifle, even. You drive. I'll shoot."

"I'm already driving." Eleanor pulled out of the space, grateful that they'd backed in. "Why aren't you shooting?"

Dante checked the gun to ensure the guard had chambered a round and the safety was off. "No need to be impatient. I'm sure more of our friends will be along any moment."

As they barreled toward the gates, the radio crackled, and Tyler Katakura's voice came through. "This is Number One. Report. We heard a blast. Over."

Irritated, Dante snatched up the microphone. "Just a second. We're busy." He let it hang while Ty cursed up a storm, his voice fading to static as the truck picked up speed.

The gate was closed, of course, but Eleanor was pushing the gas pedal toward the floor and looping around to give them an extra second or two to gain momentum. The truck rattled as it picked up speed.

A guard appeared before the gate, aiming a rifle. Dante was about to shoot him but decided there was no need. The man lacked instinct for self-preservation. Trying to line up a perfect shot on the truck's cabin, he failed to get out of the way in time.

The Autocutioner knocked down the gate after crunching it in the middle. The bent metal sent the guard sprawling into the street, and Eleanor adjusted her course a little so the front left wheel perfectly lined up with his body. They felt an ever-so-slight bump, and they were out on the road with maddened drivers swerving to avoid them.

Dante exhaled. "Okay." He picked up the microphone. "Hi,

Number One, this is Number Four. We had to blow up part of the building and shoot some people. Lots of interesting stuff to discuss, but let's talk about that later. So far, no pursuit, but that could change any minute. You guys are in the vicinity, aren't you? We're heading, uh, south. Over."

"Turn west," Ty instructed them. "We'll intercept you. Out for now." The radio fell quiet.

Eleanor took the next right turn. The cool-warm tingling sensation of relief spread through her, but beneath it remained a cold, nauseating horror.

The girl. She couldn't stop thinking about her.

The street to the west was a major thoroughfare through the southwestern part of town, and all six lanes had cars speeding down them. Traffic wasn't bad enough to be congested, exactly, but there were enough other drivers that Eleanor had to pay attention to what she was doing.

Because she was paying attention, she noticed instantly when a black van pulled out from a side street about twenty meters ahead of them. "We have company," she told Dante.

He glanced into the rearview mirrors. "There's another one coming up from behind us. And—wait. Holy shit, is this for real?"

"What?" Eleanor didn't dare look around too much since she had to watch the van out in front.

Dante opened the window and leaned out, looking behind them. He pulled himself back in. "Yup. There's a black helicopter closing in on us. No idea if it's *theirs* or not, but knowing our luck, it probably is."

Eleanor bit her lip. "Our luck has been very good, considering how much danger we always seem to be in."

Then came the distant sound of crackling gunfire, and what sounded like a hail of stones landed on the roof.

Dante brought up his new rifle. "It's one of theirs. Good thing they only seem to have a gun and not a rocket launcher or something."

The vans were closing in. The one out in front of them was deliberately driving slower than the rest of the traffic, allowing itself to slip back toward them. Meanwhile, the one that had come up behind was accelerating and passing other cars wherever it could.

Eleanor said, "What if they have a firebomb? They could drop it on us from above if they get overhead."

There was another volley of fire, which ricocheted off the truck's armor but drove home the fact that they weren't about to get away so easily. Some of the other cars on the street pulled over and let them pass or turned off at the first opportunity. They were smart. They recognized a disaster about to happen and wanted nothing to do with it.

That freed up space on the road. Eleanor passed to the left of the car ahead of them and came up fast on the black van out in front. It was barely ten yards ahead.

Dante aimed his rifle out the window. A second after he took a bead on the van, a human silhouette with a gun appeared in the rear left window of the security vehicle. "Nope." He fired a short burst.

Glass shattered, metal cracked, and the silhouette vanished from sight. The van swerved, and Dante struggled against the wind as he blasted again at the van's tires. At least one popped, and the black vehicle veered aside to crash into an embankment. The Autocutioner rocketed past.

Dante pulled his head and arms back into the cab. "They'll have to do better than that. Heh, heh." He checked the rifle's magazine. It was still about half-full. Nonetheless, he reached for the spare rifle they'd hidden there earlier and propped it next to his seat in case they needed more firepower.

As Eleanor passed again to the right, seeking to keep well ahead of the rear van and stay out of their line of fire, something else came down at them from above. It sounded like a thunderclap and blew a crater the size of a chair seat in the asphalt.

Eleanor cursed in Spanish. "What was that? An explosive?"

Dante had gone pale. "No. Fifty cal. The helicopter sniper brought a *serious* rifle in addition to a normal one. That damn thing might be able to penetrate our armor. Drive, woman, drive!"

Eleanor slammed the gas pedal down, tearing ahead and swerving uncomfortably as the road curved northward. Seeing what they were doing, the black van behind them picked up speed, no longer bothering with the pretense of anything except a high-speed chase. Eleanor wove between lanes whenever she could.

Dante snatched up the microphone and flipped the switch. "This is Four. We got a helicopter on our ass with what I'm pretty sure is a fifty-cal BMG, okay? We'd like to get off this damn street and go someplace they can't tail us. Oh, there's a van also. We just passed..." he rattled off the names of a couple of side streets and local businesses.

Ty responded, "I know where you are. Do not turn off the road. I'll be there in half a minute. Number Five is waiting. Out."

Dante slammed the microphone back in place. "For fuck's sake. If we can get into a nice little canyon of a street between some skyscrapers, that chopper won't be able to—"

It fired again. Eleanor jerked the steering wheel left, cutting off a pickup that honked madly at them and nearly capsizing the Autocutioner. She narrowly avoided the heavy round, which once again created an impressive pothole. The black van was gaining.

From a side street to the left, another Autocutioner—also disguised, but Eleanor and Dante recognized it—shot out into the street, cutting across three lanes of opposing traffic and heading straight for the black van. It tried to swerve aside, but with the driver's obsessive focus on pursuing his original target, it was too slow.

The heavier, armored truck crunched the side of the van and

sent it flying across the rest of the street, rolling once in midair before smashing into a lamppost and the side of an auto repair shop.

"Hah!" Dante laughed. "Good work, Ty. I get the impression those vans were only marking us for the chopper to follow, though."

As Ty's vehicle fishtailed from the impact and tried to straighten, Eleanor swerved as well, also dropping back a car's length or two. Her timing was fortunate since the fifty-caliber sent another slug her way. It struck the base of a tree planted in the dividing embankment in the highway's center and cut it down, the trunk creaking to fall across the road. Cars behind them screeched to a halt.

Eleanor said, "Whatever other plan Tyler might have had, he needs to do it now. I cannot dodge this thing forever."

As though reading their minds, Ty's voice came through the speakers again. "Hold," he ordered them. "Hold..."

Ahead of them was an underpass. Right as the nose of their Autocutioner slipped into the shadows beneath the elevated crossroad, another rifle shot rang out, though this one was fainter and less booming than that from the fifty-cal BMG.

"What the hell?" Dante leaned out the window again as the overpass fell away behind them.

The helicopter spun in midair and lurched crazily at an angle, gradually descending. A man holding a massive gun fell from the open side door and splattered against the front grille of an oncoming semi-truck. Before the chopper crashed into an empty lot and burst into flames, Dante glimpsed a blood-spattered hole in its windshield.

"Ohh," he mused as he withdrew from the window again. "Amahle must have a nice perch somewhere nearby."

Ty's voice barked, "Take the next right. See that building with the blue sign out front? Swing by the west side and pick up

Number Five. Then head back to HQ Number Two. Then we go for a green escape. Over."

"Roger," Dante said. "Out until further notice." He hung up the microphone and stuck his head out the window, scoping out the structure ahead for the best place to pull up.

In the basic code that the Executioners had developed some time ago, they referred to their members in the order they'd joined. Thus, Ty was Number One, whereas Number Five was Amahle. Eleanor had planned to pick up the sniper no matter what, but she hadn't been sure which building Amahle was in, so Ty's directions were still helpful.

HQ Number Two meant Daria's house. Eleanor had her doubts about how good an idea that was. Someone *had* to go there to ensure that Jori Singh was still secure, but if ever there was a time when the Execs might try to drop the hammer on the little house by the cove, *now* might well be it.

As for "green escape," she might well have guessed the meaning even if she didn't already know it for sure from experience. They would flee north into the jungle. Far away from friends and resources, but also far from the center of the Coven's power. There, the obscure wilderness trails would offer them concealment from their enemies' efforts to track them down.

Eleanor piloted the truck to the right, skirting the shoulder and looking for Amahle. They neared a wing of the building that was only two stories tall, far shorter than the rest, and Dante pointed at the section's roof.

"There she is. Get closer." He waved at Amahle, who was jogging toward the edge.

Eleanor was briefly alarmed that their companion was going to take a flying leap onto the truck while it was in motion, but once Amahle glimpsed them, she slowed to a stop a meter or so back from the brink. Eleanor drove onto the shoulder, the wheels grinding partially against the base of the fence around the property, and stopped the vehicle.

Dante shouted, "We have a minute if you want to climb out and—uhh, nope, she's gonna jump." He slid back fully into the truck and looked at Eleanor. "She's jumping. Hope she knows what she's doing."

"I heard." Eleanor grimaced. "I hope the same."

Amahle disappeared as she retreated toward the center of the side wing's roof. Then she took a running start toward the edge of the building before leaping off, her slim dark form clearing the two full meters of air between structure and vehicle. When she *thudded* onto the truck's top, though, it sounded as though she'd struck it too far toward the opposite side. Eleanor feared she might roll off into the street.

Amahle caught herself at the last second and stabilized. Then she swung down in front of the driver's side window.

"Good afternoon," Eleanor greeted her, opening the door. "Thank you for your excellent shooting, once again."

Amahle nodded and crawled in, maneuvering with ease through the tight space toward the opening behind the truck's front seats, though the rifle she had slung over her shoulder nearly got snagged on Eleanor's armrest.

Once she was safely inside, Eleanor took her foot off the brake and rolled back out onto the road. No one else was chasing them yet. Traffic was getting heavier as they approached rush hour, and cars honked mindlessly—even those in different lanes that didn't appear to be competing for the same space. Rudeness while driving was simply a normal habit in Atlantica Metro.

Eleanor accelerated, driving faster than she usually would to get them far from the area of the recent fighting and destruction, but then veered off into a mass of side streets to the east before bearing south.

Amahle noticed the general trend of where they seemed to be going. "I thought we were heading for the jungle? Didn't Ty order a green escape?"

"Yep," Dante replied. "He wants us back at Daria's place first, probably to collect the old man. The wilderness it is after we do that. We made enough of a mess today that it's probably the only safe and sane option. Well, as 'safe' as anything can be on Atlantica. Let's not even talk about 'sane.'"

The Autocutioner rumbled down a narrow road in a district of warehouses and lumberyards. Although still within the city limits, a substantial amount of the coastal plain's original vegetation here hadn't yet been clear-cut. Local industry made use of it, on a moderate basis, to provide timber and wood supplies to the rest of the town.

Amahle glanced at a thicket between buildings, staring into the deep green shadows of the trees, vines, and ferns.

"Our time is running out," she observed in a soft voice, her face distant and contemplative. She unslung her rifle and loaded it to capacity with cartridges from her bandolier, the motions of her hands at once absentminded and self-assured.

Eleanor glanced back at her before returning her attention to the road. "What do you mean? Have you heard anything new? We haven't been in contact for several days."

Amahle shook her head. "I don't mean anything like that. There has been little news that we do not already know. I mean that it is only a matter of time until the Executives, the Coven, or whatever we choose to call them, realize what we are doing and how we've slipped through their grasp. They must suspect that we are using the bush as our avenue of escape and place of hiding."

Dante gave a short, irritable shrug of his shoulders. "Well, yeah. We've operated all over the island. I'm sure they have a rough idea of where we are and what we're doing at any given time. It's a matter of staying one step ahead. Without Singh on their little board of directors or whatever, though, it *does* seem like they've taken the gloves off lately. Things are probably going to get worse."

Eleanor disliked such talk, but she understood the reasoning behind it. It made sense to be prepared for the worst while hoping for the best.

They came to a residential urban village, beyond which lay the outmost exurbs in the hills—then, if one turned north, the forested wilderness, so much of which had been scarcely touched by human hands.

With an odd and droning air of nostalgia, Amahle continued, "I remember well this sort of conflict. When I was a revolutionary fighter in South Africa, we used the bush as our highway, ocean, and hiding place. We could move there as we pleased, avoiding the government forces or drawing them into traps. It worked...for a time."

Dante looked back at her. His affected skepticism was giving way to legitimate concern and curiosity. "For a time, eh? What did the government do when they figured out what you were up to?"

Amahle's eyes were cold. She was staring at something far away, beyond the horizon's distant curve. "They burned the bush down."

CHAPTER FOUR

Daria had poured drinks for everyone. As usual, she'd calibrated the strength and volume of each glass of vodka to the respective tolerance of each individual, going light for Eleanor, Amahle, and Gage; medium for Ty and Dante; and a strong double for herself. As a Polish Jew, she processed alcohol like other people processed lemon water.

Ty was the first to greet her. "Hi, Daria. Much appreciated." He picked up a glass of vodka on the rocks next to his usual place and drained most of it at once. "No refills, though. We might have to move again soon. We're only lying low here for as long as it takes to get our next course of action down pat. The operation today was," he sighed. "Pretty much a total fuck-up."

"So I gathered," Daria said. She looked at Eleanor, Dante, and Amahle. "I'm glad everyone made it back safely, however. Gage is here already, as well. He will join us in a moment."

Dante squinted as though he wanted to argue but was too tired. "It wasn't a *total* fuck-up, Boss Man. We learned some stuff and took out some of their people and equipment. We *know* more, and they *have* less. Still, I'll agree that it should have gone a lot smoother. It was my fault. Eleanor did everything right. It was my idea to blow up half the place with, um, an improvised bomb, we'll say. That's something we need to talk about."

He grabbed his drink and chugged it, letting out a nice gasp afterward that sounded like it might turn into a cough. He stopped himself at the last second, though.

Gage appeared from deeper within the house. "Hello, everyone. I overheard all that was said, and I listened to the radio earlier. I am aware of the situation. But, please, let us sit and talk."

The small Nepali man was probably the friendliest and most gentle-natured of them. In battle, he became amazingly fierce and ruthless, but under normal circumstances he had a way of putting people at ease, calming tensions, and making everyone feel that things might work out okay, after all.

Still, it was impossible to mistake the overall miasma of glumness and defeat that hung over the proceedings. Eleanor kept quiet, for the most part. She let Dante do the bulk of the talking. Despite his attempt to gallantly take the blame for the general chaos that had broken out, she still felt that things could've gone differently had she reined in her emotions better.

She kept seeing that girl in her mind. The awful, pitiable image refused to go away, and each time it impressed itself on her consciousness, it was as though a firebomb went off deep within her soul.

She picked up the light shot of vodka that Daria had poured over a pair of ice cubes for her, appreciating it, but wanting more. She didn't drink much, generally. After a moment's hesitation, she decided it would be enough. Getting fully intoxicated would solve nothing. She raised the glass to her lips and drank it all in a long, single sip.

The others listened, mostly quiet and intent but occasionally interrupting to ask for clarification on certain details as Dante regaled them with the account of what had happened at the clinic. Their faces were serious to the point of being grave.

Dante's boast that they had somehow struck a blow against their adversaries rang hollow.

Yes, they'd killed a few Coven lackeys. They disrupted the operations of a single facility, setting back the shadowy organization's plans and stymying some of the cash flow they made from catering to miscellaneous wealthy clients. In so doing, they'd inadvertently played into the Executives' narrative that the Executioners were now some kind of rogue guerrilla group wreaking havoc in the streets, more foe than friend to the average person.

Worse, in Eleanor's opinion, was the gnawing fear that if *that* were true, she'd escaped the proverbial frying pan only to land in the fire.

Everything they'd seen at the clinic had been able to happen, in part, because of things *she* had done in the past. Her long, loyal service to the Executives. Her willingness not to ask too many questions.

"So," Dante went on, "yeah, there were problems, but we exposed a lot of nasty stuff. Word about those experiments they're conducting will get out. We can use some of our contacts to spread the rumors. They won't get away with trying to pin all of this on us."

The others pitched in their two cents. Eleanor had enough. She stood, turned, and walked out of the room.

No one followed her, said anything, or tried to stop her. It was because she'd not made it too obvious that she was on the verge of a ranting outburst. She hadn't jumped to her feet but merely risen at a normal speed. She hadn't stormed off but simply moved at an average clip. Everyone would've noticed how sullen and perturbed she was, but years of self-control meant there wasn't enough evidence for them to guess what she was about to do.

It would be unwise to rush. Making too much noise, being in too much of a hurry, would incur her friends' curiosity. She didn't want to waste time, either. If she was going to do this, it needed to be while she was still angry.

Eleanor waited in the kitchen a moment so the other Executioners would assume that she only needed a minute or five to herself and stood in silent contemplation. She listened to the conversation in the living room until the voices rose and grew more agitated as her partners argued their respective cases or concerns.

Then Eleanor found the door to the garage, opened it with nary a sound, and slipped outside.

Jori Singh still sat there, tied to his chair, doing nothing whatsoever. He'd remained there for a month since his capture. The Executioners had given him food and drink, allowed him to use the bathroom, and periodically let him walk around a bit or perform his yoga stretches, but only under supervision. Otherwise, he'd been a prisoner in Daria's garage the whole time.

He was awake and alert. He looked straight into Eleanor's eyes with his usual mixture of serene calm and arrogant intensity. Although he was the captive, his expression made it seem like this was his office or his study, and she'd arrived for an appointment or interview that he'd been expecting all day.

It only made her that much more furious. Her nails dug into her palms as her fingers curled in, making fists of her small hands.

"Miss Cervantes," Singh greeted her, his voice soft but somehow theatrical. "It is always a pleasure to see you. How may I hel—"

Eleanor cleared the distance between them in two long, fast strides and sent her fist swooping across the man's face, her knuckles catching his nose and upper lip area and knocking his head to the side.

"Shut up," she snapped. "I was at your clinic today. I saw a little girl there, being experimented on by your precious friends as part of their wise and benevolent agenda." She spat the words. They tasted acrid and bitter in her mouth.

Singh made no move to look back at her. His face remained angled sideways, and a bit of blood leaked from his left nostril and part of his split lip. It was the only sign of distress in him. Otherwise, the tall, lean, dignified older man was no worse for wear.

Eleanor kicked him in the shins with the treads of her boots. "How long?" she demanded to know. "How long have you been doing these things? How long were you using *me* to do them? Answer me! If I was part of your crimes, I want to know."

Her fist lashed out again, this time slamming into the lower corner of the man's abdomen, hard enough to send a ripple of tension through his body. Otherwise, though, he didn't react to her abuse.

Slowly, he returned himself to an upright posture, facing ahead and looking at her. His appearance was one of mild annoyance or disappointment, at worst. The Executioners had found over the weeks that it was nearly impossible to fluster him much.

"As long as was necessary," he stated in a low, even tone. "I'm afraid I do not recall the exact dates, or the exact timeframe, of all the specifics of such things. You were always an integral and essential asset, Eleanor. Our operations always depended heavily upon you. Of course, you had no direct involvement in the affairs of which you speak—"

She cut him off. "I would've had *no* involvement if I had known you were doing *that*." She crossed her arms and glared at him. In a way, she was morbidly curious about what nonsense would come out of his mouth next, what ridiculous platitude he might use in the hope of calming her down but would only make her still more irate.

Instead, he calmly continued to answer her question in more detail.

"In particular, you were of tremendous help to us in establishing and protecting Zero Site. Your diplomatic savvy, your connections, your willingness to be discreet even in relatively controversial matters...and, of course, your excellent work in managing the Executioners. During the period when they were most useful, that is." His mouth rose into an understated yet nearly smug smile.

Eleanor's eyes bulged as the last of her patience and restraint evaporated all at once.

"Bastard!" she shrieked, pouncing on him. She clawed at his iron-colored hair, his ears, and eyes, and she kneed and kicked him in the legs, chest, and stomach, spitting on him as she thrashed and flailed. He made no sound, only closed his eyes and relaxed his body to accept what she did to it.

From inside the house, footsteps became audible, and someone called, "Eleanor? You okay? What's going on?" It sounded like Tyler or Dante, a male voice with an American accent.

Eleanor ignored them, focusing instead on the object of her rage. She picked up a broom with a plastic handle leaning against the wall and swung it like a cricket bat against the side of the man's face. It snapped in half at the point of impact, driving his head aside and leaving an ugly red welt along his cheek. Then with the broken upper half still clutched in her shaking hands, she jumped at him again, swinging madly at Singh's head, shoulders, and arms.

In the back of her mind rose the fear of losing control. She, who had always been so self-disciplined, lived with that fear constantly and in a way, yearned to be free from it.

There would be something *liberating* about letting go, giving in totally to her emotions, and beating Singh over and over again until he died. Allowing herself to kill him. Blood flowed from his wounds, over her hands, and she realized she was panting through bared teeth.

The voice from the kitchen shouted, "Hey! Something's going on in the garage. With Singh." Eleanor ignored it.

She raised the stick, noticing how sharp the broken-off point was, intending to drive it deep into the man's throat and end it once and for all. He barely seemed to notice her. He swayed in his chair as if drunk.

And then, in a single motion that seemed far too smooth and casual for how blindingly fast it was, Singh slipped out of his bounds and rolled off the chair. In a swooping circular motion, he came up beside the woman and snatched the jagged plastic stick with one hand while wrapping the other around her throat and shoulders.

Her mouth opened and shut. Her tongue writhed within it, trying to speak but producing only faint strangled noises. Total shock had impeded her anger and left her helpless to form coherent words.

She reached up and tried to yank Singh's arm away from her throat, but he slipped it farther down, pinning her arms to her sides with a surprising degree of wiry strength, like that of a steel cable. Then the point of the snapped-off broom handle pressed against the soft flesh beneath her chin.

The door between the kitchen and the garage burst open. Eleanor couldn't see much. Singh's body blocked most of her vision, along with her disheveled hair. The tall silhouette she briefly glimpsed had to belong to Dante. He leapt into the garage, and behind him were Amahle, Ty, and Gage. There was no sign of Daria.

"Hey!" Dante bellowed, pointing his left hand while balling his right into a fist. "Stop what you're doing right there, old man. Don't do anything fucking stupid."

Amahle stared at their prisoner from behind the physician's shoulder. "We will kill you, Singh, before we let you kill her. Just because we took you alive the first time does not mean we won't change our minds."

Eleanor's emotional breaking point was now behind her. Singh could easily cut her throat and puncture her windpipe before they could so much as hope to lay a hand on him. She should've killed him herself a moment ago when she had the chance.

"Singh, you bastard. Just do it!" Tears streamed down her face. "You already sold my soul without asking me if it was for sale. How many children did your people hurt because of me? Both of us deserve to die. Kill me and get what you deserve from them!"

Dante's face shifted from fury to alarm. "Hold on, Eleanor, no need for that."

Ty stepped out from behind the tall doctor. "No one touches Eleanor." His tone was low and icy, the way it got when he was a hair's breadth from taking someone's head off. "Let her go. You will not succeed in taking her from us, but we will take everything from you. You don't have time to negotiate, Singh. Drop the woman or die."

His right hand rested on the hilt of his wakizashi with an almost ginger lightness. Eleanor had seen him draw from the sheath before. Men had lost their hands before they could get their weapons halfway clear.

Gage moved around to the side, facing both parties obliquely and standing roughly halfway between them. "There is no need for anyone to die. All that is needed is for no one to be stupid." His face, too, was stretched with horror. Not only for Eleanor's sake—he didn't want to lose Singh, either. The scientist in him valued the man's vast knowledge too much.

Sensing that they would prefer not to terminate him, Singh intoned, "Oh, but I already died once. Do you not recall? What makes you think that you can keep me dead if you kill me a second time?"

Ty snarled, "No fucking way to reattach your head if I cut it off and dump it in the sea. The rest of you we'll take to the middle of the jungle. You won't 'magically' recover from that, Singh. Give it up."

Singh chortled. "Removing me from the Board was quite foolish, you know. I was the main thing standing between the rest of the Coven and their desire to crush you all like insects. They have become far more aggressive lately, haven't they? Release me, and I will talk some sense into them."

"No," Amahle stated. "Not until you begin to cooperate."

For a second, Singh's eyes burned with an emotion rarely glimpsed in him. Anger.

Then something flashed from the shadows, swift and silent enough that even Singh, for all his borderline inhuman reflexes, couldn't take note of it and counter it in time.

A baton crackling with electricity rammed into Singh's lower back. He let out a strangled groan as the voltage flowed through him, seizing up his muscles and drawing sparks from the point of contact. Eleanor screamed, still gripped tightly within his arms—the current passed through him and into her, as well.

Daria stepped out, driving the baton harder against the man. Eleanor's shrieks faded, and she slumped halfway to the floor in his arms, unconscious. Singh's teeth ground together as he struggled to resist the effects of electrocution. For all his mastery of yoga and other, more obscure techniques, he wasn't invincible. With a final rustling sigh, his eyes drifted closed, and he fell over, landing on the floor like a tipped scarecrow.

Before anyone could bother to suggest it, Dante had pounced on Eleanor, dragging her away from Singh and checking her vital signs. "She's going to be okay, I think." He gave a hard look at Daria. "Another second or two, though, and she might not have been."

Daria scowled. "In another second, he might have cut her throat. Better to hurt them both now than risk each of them ending up dead a little later." She moved closer to the crumpled form of Singh, holding the baton over him. If he returned to consciousness, it would be nearly impossible for him to do anything without striking it and getting the same treatment a second time.

Ty stepped forth, occupying the center of the whole scene. "All right. We have a couple of major failures here that need to *not* happen a second time. First of all, I thought Eleanor might be upset, but I didn't think she'd come out here and do this. I should've checked on her, and I'll take responsibility for that."

Daria pointed out, "We all *knew* she was upset, but that is fair enough, yes. She has always had such good self-control that it was hard to anticipate her doing something so foolish."

"Right," Ty acceded. "Second, we thought we had Singh under control, but evidently not. How the hell did he slip his bonds like that?"

Gage, ever the first to examine any question or curiosity of a technical nature, was looking over the chair and the cords they'd used to tie him to it. "I cannot tell. He didn't cut any of the cords, and I don't think he broke them either. He might have been able to untie enough to loosen the rest. Or perhaps he has some yoga trick that allowed him to contort himself in ways most people couldn't. He's also very thin..."

"Whatever," Ty grumbled. "Point being, he needs to be kept far more secure. In addition to tying him up, we have to start keeping him someplace that's impossible to escape from. A nice vault or prison cell would help, but we probably don't have access to one of those. Keeping him in one of the trucks might work. They were designed to function as holding cells if need be."

Amahle opined, "That should work as a short-term solution, but someone must watch him at all times. We aren't planning to stay here long, though, are we? I was under the impression that we were heading to the jungle soon. Surely we had intended to take him with us."

"Yeah," Ty affirmed. He knelt to help Daria pick up the man and re-tie him. If he somehow snapped back to awareness and slipped free again, he would have a far more difficult time of it with the entire crew surrounding him while he was at a disadvantage. Singh possessed abilities beyond the average person...but he was still only a human being.

As she worked on tying Singh's hands, Daria said, "It's one of many things we must finish discussing. We cannot rely on my house to remain safe for long. Frankly, I'm amazed that they haven't stormed the place yet, or blown it up from the air with a plane or something. The Coven is still operating with *some* discretion. After the scene they were willing to make in the city today, we must assume their patience has ended for good."

Gage shook his head. "Yes, I'm afraid so. The destruction of their facility a month ago must have been a most terrible blow to their ambitions. We might have set them back by a year, three years, or more. They could not have built such a device as we saw there in mere weeks. Plus, it would have cost them a great deal of money."

Dante had gathered up Eleanor in his arms and was staring at her with an expression of professional and personal concern, along with something else. He was biting his lower lip.

Gage cleared his throat. "I take it you will let her rest until she recovers? When she wakes up, we should ask her what happened between Singh and herself that made her so angry. It might be useful to know."

"Yeah," Dante responded, but he seemed distracted and was still staring at Ms. Cervantes's face. "Good idea. I'll, ah, take her to the bedroom." He wandered off, leaving the rest of them behind to deal with the problem of their prisoner.

As Ty and Daria lifted Singh and made ready to load him into the back of the nearest Autocutioner, Gage mumbled, "For such a brilliant man, even I will say he's been more trouble than he is worth."

Daria added in a strained voice, "He's also heavier than he looks. Feel free to help out."

CHAPTER FIVE

Eleanor awoke before her eyes were open, or at least before she could see. Everything was dim and hazy, and she felt as though someone had systematically bludgeoned almost every inch of her body with a rolling pin before depriving her of water for a whole day. She stretched, wincing and trying not to cry out from the painful ache of her limbs.

Her skin seemed sensitive too, as though burned by excessive sun exposure. She had no memory of where she was.

She opened her eyes. There was a ceiling over her head and a bed beneath her body, and it was dark. She was in a small room.

Coughing at the dryness of her throat, she gasped, "Daria's house. We came back here. Right?" Her memories were indistinct, as though something had scrambled her brain at the same time her body had taken a beating.

She swung her legs around, made herself stand, and struggled to remember it all.

Yes, it was coming back. Singh had threatened to kill her mere seconds after she'd nearly killed him. There had been a standoff. Then something else had happened, a vague recollection of pain, and that was all. But she was alive.

Eleanor was still wearing her clothes. She trudged to the bedroom door and out into the hall, seeking the bathroom, where she turned on the tap and used her hands to cup water into her mouth. When she had drunk her fill, she headed out into the hall.

Her friends were having a conference in the living room, but she didn't know if it was a continuation of the one she remembered or a new one. An hour might have passed, or a day. Maybe longer.

The talking stopped when she came to the threshold of the room. The other five—those who had so *willingly* become Executioners long before she had become one out of *necessity*—all stared at her.

She looked at the floor. "How long have I been out? What happened?"

Dante glanced at the clock. "A little under two hours."

Daria added, "I electrocuted you. My apologies. It was easier to do that than to risk Singh killing you, yes? We recaptured him, also. He is quite secure for the moment."

Eleanor gave a slow nod. "I understand. And...I am sorry for what I did. I compromised everything. I don't understand what came over me. Do what you must."

She waited.

When they'd inducted her into the order, she'd sworn the same oath as the rest of them. "Justice Before Mercy." Such was the creed of the Executioners, those who enacted judgment upon those who brought terrible fates to others.

By losing her cool, allowing her emotions to get the best of her, and utterly embarrassing herself in letting Singh get the drop on her, Eleanor knew she'd failed. Her luck was stretched thin enough to begin with. By rights, she should be dead, and Singh escaped to return to helping run the Coven. It was only chance and Daria's quick thinking that had spared them from things being worse than they already were.

More shameful still, the discoveries she and Dante had made at the clinic had cast into stark relief the wrongness of her past choices. Her actions had made possible the inhuman experiments that the Coven had been carrying out all this time. She'd misguided the Executioners on behalf of their former employers, thinking of her career advancement before she thought of anything else.

She wondered how her family would feel about all of this.

The best she could expect was that the Executioners would expel her from the organization. She would become a lonesome outcast, no longer welcome on Atlantica and probably returning to Mexico in disgrace. If she was bolder and more fortunate, she might go instead to the United States and try her hand at some modest business venture.

With all the harm she'd done, she would understand if her partners decreed that her life must be forfeit. She'd seen them carry out executions before. When done under formal circumstances, they at least made clean kills and allowed the condemned to retain as much of their dignity as possible.

It was, perhaps, better than she deserved.

Ty stared at her. He blinked. "What the hell are you talking about, Eleanor?"

She looked back up. The others seemed as confused as their de facto leader, squinting and trying to think of what she was referring to.

A lump formed in Eleanor's throat. "I have failed terribly," she admitted. "I had, ah, assumed...that I'd receive punishment for it." To her further embarrassment, she began to weep and buried her face in her hands.

Tyler let out a long, low sigh. "No, Eleanor, it's okay. You screwed up, yeah. Fine. Whatever. What did you think we were going to do? Kill you? Come sit down. We made some progress on the discussion here, but we need your input on what to do next."

Daria looked at Ty and snapped, "She needs a minute or two, it would seem before she will be much good for input, Mr. Katakura. Here. Dante! Hold her."

Dante stood and stretched. "I mean, if you insist."

Eleanor stood in place, saying and doing nothing, unable to sort through the tangled mess of emotions that bound her. Dante came over to her, his facade of cockiness fading and his expression turning serious and tender. He opened his arms and paused while his eyes sought hers, asking if she wanted him to do what Daria had suggested.

She closed her eyes and took one step forward into his embrace. His arms wrapped around her shoulders and she rested her head against his chest.

In a soft voice, he said, "We've all made slip-ups from time to time, and there's that saying about how the enemy always gets a vote. Sometimes we do everything right, but so do they. We're gonna be okay, though. We'll figure things out."

She sniffled. "Yes. I think we will."

The others gave them a minute before Gage inquired, "Would you like some tea, Eleanor? The water is still somewhat warm. It will only take a moment to get it hot enough again."

She drew away from Dante, and he lowered his arms, allowing her to separate, although they still stood close to one another. "Yes, please, that sounds wonderful."

Ty cracked his knuckles. "Okay, good. Sounds like you're feeling better. All of us have things in our past that we're not proud of, remember. We might as well call ourselves the 'Fresh Start Club' or something corny like that. Have a seat and let's talk about what comes next."

Eleanor wandered over and sat next to Ty. Her composure was partially back. She felt odd and vulnerable, as though she wanted to cringe away after they'd seen her in a fit of anger *and* seen her cry. She didn't, and strangely enough, her mood began to lift itself out of the depths. She was one of them.

"Tyler," she began, "I remember when we first spoke back in the labor town two years ago. You were a man who seemed to have little hope in life for anything, save perhaps that you would be able to help others and get by for a little longer before you died in battle along some muddy street. You spoke of being less than proud of your past actions.

"So, I believe you. Until things went wrong so recently, you became a respected man. Maybe there is a way for us to help each other back into a place where others respect us and where we can respect ourselves."

It felt awkward to say it aloud, and she half-feared they might laugh at her. Ty only gave a slow nod of the head—a bow, nearly. Then Daria, Gage, Dante, and Amahle did the same.

Eleanor let her eyes fall shut. Something had happened. She couldn't put a finger on exactly what it was, and despite the odd calmness and lack of emotion swelling within her at the moment, something situated itself in her mind with cold, firm, and unmoving certainty. She'd turned a corner with the Executioners. They respected and accepted her as a full member.

That she'd handled herself well on several missions had contributed, of course. Her words this evening, just now, were what had solidified it.

Gage was the first to break the moment of silence. "Yes, each of us has come far to be here, and the journey is often full of difficulties and mistakes. We have done well together. All of us."

Amahle looked at their newest member. Her face was serene, albeit slightly aloof. It was the expression she wore when she didn't wish to discuss personal matters but didn't want to be abrasive, which usually led to her trying to change the subject.

"Eleanor, you and Singh were speaking of something before we came in. What were you discussing? It might help us to hear about it."

Ty turned his eyes pointedly to Eleanor again, indicating that he was glad Amahle had posed the question. His black eyes burned with interest.

Eleanor folded her hands in her lap. "For the most part, I was asking him about how long the Coven had been…using me in ways that aided them, even when it meant things like what we saw at the clinic. But also…Zero Site. Yes, we mentioned it."

Dante raised his eyebrows. "Sounds important, whatever it is. I'd be willing to bet money that you know more about it than we do."

Daria scoffed. "She comes from a family of business people and wouldn't be so stupid to take a bet like that. Yes, Eleanor, tell us."

Eleanor shut her eyes, turning her mind toward the vast stores of information within her head, recalling pertinent memories and focusing on what was most important to the situation at hand.

"Zero Site is a location whose modern history dates back to the initial discovery of this island," she explained. "It is in a large mountain formation within the jungle to the north. The Executives originally planned for it to be the birthplace of a second major metropolitan area, one which would not grow organically but could be planned and constructed from the ground up to be run only by the Executives and would serve their purposes."

Dante asked the obvious question. "What purposes? Coven stuff, or something more prosaic?"

Eleanor wasn't sure if there was a clear answer to that question, so she simply elaborated more upon what she knew for sure.

"The idea was that it would primarily be an industrial zone, more so than Atlantica Metro. They could process raw materials after they brought them in, either from mining excavations on the island or from offshore shipments. Then, they could distribute their manufactured or refined products to the larger city or any other settlement on Atlantica. The place that controls the flow of important goods to other places, ultimately, *controls* those other places."

Daria swished the half-ounce or so of vodka that remained in her glass, then raised it to her lips and drank. Setting the glass hard down on the coffee table, she commented, "That is smart. When I was in smuggling, there was great respect for the suppliers of goods. To anger them or try to cheat them was to destroy one's own business."

Ty grunted, "Makes sense. Eleanor, go on, please."

She did. "Discretion was important. That's something they always said, always emphasized, and even when they didn't say it out loud, they implied it. You couldn't fail to understand that they didn't wish it to become common knowledge. Other powerful interests might become involved if they knew about it."

Shaking her head, Amahle quipped, "Of course. That could lead to war over control of the resources."

"Or," Eleanor pointed out, "at least a great deal of sabotage and trickery with money. The Executives were arranging to have huge amounts of money and material funneled to this place. It was one of their most ambitious projects. Yet, I had thought it all failed.

"It appeared that as the situation in Atlantica became more anarchic, they'd abandoned it to focus on other things. I was originally involved in the planning and management of Zero Site. Then I was reassigned—to assist with the creation of the Order of Executioners."

She noticed that Gage was looking at the floor, yet his face was creased in deep concentration. He was probably applying his scientific background to all she'd said, attempting to tie her outline of the Execs' intentions for Zero Site to their experiences at the water treatment plant and elsewhere.

Leaving him to his ruminations, she completed her account. "I had almost forgotten about that place and the entire project. It has been two years, after all. Now I'm not so certain that it failed or was canceled. I wonder if the Executives have kept it alive but directed it instead to fulfill the objectives of the Coven of Miracles."

She paused and gave a delayed shrug. "I cannot say for sure. Such is my best guess, based upon what I remember from those days and from all that I've learned more recently."

Dante opined, "It sounds like it's worth checking out. Even if they did abandon the place, there might be something there that could point us in the right direction."

Ty sat up straighter. "I agree. Eleanor, where is this site? Can you help us get to it?"

She frowned. "Yes and no. Unfortunately, I never went to Zero Site in person. It was somewhat remote at the time and the facilities they'd planned to install there weren't in running order. I also cannot recall the exact coordinates." She raised a finger. "Do not despair. I believe that I can find a means of figuring out where we must go."

She elaborated on how she was well-acquainted with a particular member of the Junior Board with whom she'd worked on the project in question. Furthermore, the individual was unique among the Executives in that he didn't come from a pure business background as most of the others did. He was more of an architect by trade, with some experience in project management and the like.

"His name is Zhu Dongfeng." Speaking the name aloud brought back several memories she tried not to dwell on. Such things were irrelevant to what they needed to do.

Dante stared at her in a strange' way, however. It was as though he suspected something.

Daria adjusted her hair. "I don't recognize the name. Do you know where we can find him?"

All eyes were on Eleanor. The fear she'd experienced after waking up had mostly dispersed in the warmth of reassurance, but she still felt the pressure of their expectations.

"Not for sure," she admitted. "I might have an idea or two. If we can get to him... From that point, I'm pretty sure we can find Zero Site."

They all seemed to sense what she thought. Namely, that it wasn't much—potentially no more than a wild goose chase. All the same, it might be their only hope.

CHAPTER SIX

Most of a day had passed. Everyone had gone to bed shortly after they decided to pursue Zhu Dongfeng and through him, attempt to gain access to Zero Site. They all suspected they would have another long, strenuous week ahead of them.

Eleanor sat on the bed in Daria's guest room. Spread out in front of her on a small folding table was an assortment of portable first-aid supplies, copies of building schematics, and a couple of boxes of .380 ACP ammo as well as spare magazines for her Walther pistol.

She loaded the cartridges methodically into the mags, idly wondering why someone hadn't yet figured out an easier and more efficient way of performing the task. Her thumbs were rather petite, and she didn't have much hand strength, so it was always unpleasant forcing the bullets down against the retention spring, particularly when it required her to press one round-edged object against another.

Her mind wandered to all that had happened over the day and all that would proceed to happen tomorrow. There was a lot to review.

Daria had checked in with a couple of her old smuggling

contacts to confirm Eleanor's leftover information on Dongfeng's whereabouts. They'd seen stuff with Chinese lettering on it and architectural publications coming and going from a particular skyscraper downtown. So it seemed a fairly safe assumption that their man was still based there.

Tyler and Amahle had gone ahead into the city to scout the place out. Their goal was to determine how best to gain access, what the building's security detail was like, and from where one or both of them might be able to take up a sniper position to cover the actions of whoever ended up doing the infiltration. Supposedly, they would be radioing back soon with their findings.

Gage and Daria remained at the house, drawing up plans, working on the vehicles, and fielding more information from people Daria knew. Dante hung around somewhere as well, working on weapons or something, although he'd made a short trip into town to speak to an acquaintance.

Eleanor had spent most of the day alone. The tentative plan, so far, was for her to pose as a prostitute to gain access to the building. Dongfeng's security chief often hired high-end call girls so it wouldn't be too suspicious. Still, she wasn't much looking forward to the task, especially since her little pistol would be the only weapon she could realistically conceal on her person. Having a submachine gun or a rifle would make her feel far better about the whole thing, despite not having a great deal of experience with weapons of that magnitude.

Outside in the hallway, someone was approaching. Eleanor listened for about two seconds and determined that it must be Dante. The strides were long enough that they had to belong to a person taller than Gage and heavy enough that they couldn't have belonged to Daria.

He probably wanted to check to see how she was doing again. She sensed that guilt consumed him after all that had happened to her, and he continued to blame himself for it despite them all agreeing that no single person was at fault.

There was something more, though. A desire simply to see her and be with her. He had been showing her an extra degree of special attention lately, and she didn't particularly mind.

A fist knocked on the door. "Eleanor? It's Dante. I wanted to make sure you were okay."

No surprises, then. She turned her head toward the entrance. "It's unlocked. You may come in."

As he turned the knob and opened the door, another thing occurred to her. She'd hoped he *would* come to see her again before the day was over. Whatever his faults, she found that she liked having him around. It was nice for the two of them to be alone under circumstances other than a dangerous mission. To be able to talk for the sake of talking, rather than solely because their objective demanded that they share information and tactics.

Feeling the way she did, though, reminded her of certain things. Things pertaining to what lay ahead of them.

Dante stepped in and closed the door behind him. He looked simultaneously tired and energetic, as though he were impatient to charge into something that he'd spent all day and night thinking about instead of sleeping. His shirt was half-opened. He might've forgotten to button it up after whatever else he'd been doing earlier.

He smiled at her. "Hello. How are you doing? Still feeling all right? It's not uncommon to have symptoms that recur from time to time after an episode like what you went through. Electrocution can potentially cause major trauma, but you came back from it pretty well, I'd say."

"Yes, I've been fine. Thank you for asking." She paused, hesitant to say more, and wondered if there was anything else *he* wanted to know. "If anything is bothering me, it's more that I'm worried about how our operation tomorrow will go. Still, I'm sure we can handle it. Especially with Ty and Amahle making the preparations in advance."

Dante came three steps closer. "Yeah, I trust them. Even when our plans go awry, we always seem to find some way to figure things out at the last minute. This time, though, we have more time than usual to get it right."

He wanted to ask something else. She felt it. Further questions burned in his mind, but he wasn't sure if he wanted to voice them yet.

She said, "I appreciate your concern for me. If there's anything else you wish to know, you may ask. It's best for us to clear the air now before we don't have time later."

He looked at his hands, and his face mildly contorted with something that was a half-wistful smile and a half-scowl of displeasure.

"I'm wondering what the deal is with this Feng guy," he admitted. "We're going after him so we can shake him down for information. It could get ugly. I don't know. It seemed like you knew him personally, so I'm hoping that doesn't...complicate things."

Eleanor's face hardened in irritation. "We worked together closely, so in a manner of speaking, I did know him. That was years ago. I will do whatever I must. Do not concern yourself with it."

"How will he react?" Dante insisted. "As in, will the fact that you two were so well-acquainted make him say or do something you wouldn't expect? How will you respond to *that?*"

His tone was mild, but she didn't like the implications of his words. It was as though he were questioning her loyalty to the Executioners or her commitment to their cause.

More aggravating still, he seemed to have guessed that the two of them had been more than mere coworkers. That was none of his business. Still, it was obvious, now—the notion in his head of Eleanor and Feng being former lovers was making him...jealous.

She snapped, "Dante, stop this nonsense immediately. None of what happened in the past involving him and me is your concern. It would be childish of you to pretend that it is. I've made it clear that I'm with you—with the Executioners, I mean—and will see things through to the end. You have no cause to question my willingness to do whatever is needed. All of our lives are on the line, and that is far more important than any petty personal issues."

Blinking and leaning back a half-step, he protested, "Now, wait a minute here. I never said I doubted you. All I want to know is, are you prepared to deal with your feelings? Have you thought about what you'll do in different scenarios?"

"Of course," she replied hastily. "I will do whatever seems smartest, and that leads to our success. I can tell that what you're really asking is if I was in a relationship with him. Yes, I was. Does that satisfy you to know? Well, it's over now. Have you thought about what *you* will do? This time perhaps it would be better not to blow up a building on a whim."

As soon as the words left her mouth, she knew they were harsher than necessary, and she cursed herself for it. Yet getting it all out made her feel better, in a way.

Dante sighed and sat at the end of the bed. "Since this all started, Eleanor, I've been the only one on your side."

She tensed up again. That wasn't what she'd expected to hear from him. "What do you mean?"

He shook his head. "Everyone else was so suspicious of you at first. Not me. And that's only the beginning."

She reflected on the day she'd been de facto expelled from her position. The night when she'd finally told the Executioners about how the Coven of Miracles had infiltrated the Executive Boards and probably taken them over, and the Coven had responded in kind by sending armed men out to kill her.

Dante had spoken on her behalf while the rest of them had behaved as though she were a spy. He'd continued to support her the whole time since. Whatever mistakes he'd made during their earlier misadventure at the clinic, he'd done all he could to protect her. She also knew that after the shock baton had knocked her unconscious, Dante had been the one to pick her up and carry her to the guest room, caring for her in his capacity as a doctor, as well as—

"Dante, I..." she began, unsure how to put her feelings into words, "I'm usually in control of myself and my emotions. I don't react to things in foolish ways. I feel that I'm capable of facing whatever I must deal with. Perhaps that is not true. You've been extremely helpful. You have my thanks for that."

He gave a light, half-sarcastic chuckle and rolled his shoulders. "You're welcome." Sensing that she wanted to say more, he waited.

Eleanor swallowed a lump in her throat. "Now, everything seems so uncertain. I find out, more and more as time passes and events grow stranger, that I have my limits, like anyone else. The situations we've been through aren't only things which I could never have imagined; they're also things which I would never have...condoned. I feel so terrible about it all."

She didn't want to say what she meant explicitly—the little girl at the clinic. Men were sometimes dense when it came to reading between the lines, but she hoped that Dante would grasp what she meant.

He nodded. "Yeah, I know what you mean. It's all been hard to believe. Sometimes things aren't what we thought they were. It can be hard to live with, knowing you might have contributed to it without meaning to."

He turned on the bed to angle toward her, and the distance between them shrank. Eleanor leaned back a bit and turned to face him in kind.

Dante added, "There's a bond between us, though. We've both been through it. Us, and the other four. I think when we can come to grips with the uncertainty of what we're dealing with, we'll find our strength. We have to understand that this is the only way forward, even if we feel unequal to the task."

Over the course of the conversation, their hands had drifted closer together, and now Dante put his atop Eleanor's, holding it gently. She did nothing to stop him. Its strength, weight, and warmth felt good after everything they'd been through in the last forty-eight hours.

"Apart, we might not be able to beat this," the physician said, his voice low but oddly hoarse with subdued emotion. "The odds against us are pretty stiff. But together...maybe, just maybe, together we have a shot."

Eleanor held his gaze, her dark eyes opening ever so slightly wider. "You mean as a team, as Executioners?"

He hesitated. In his expression were simultaneous flickers of self-satisfied amusement and awkwardness, but he didn't lose his cool. "Is that what you want me to mean?"

"Well," Eleanor allowed a coy, borderline playful tone to creep into her voice. "What else could you be thinking about?" She arched one of her finely-shaped eyebrows and waited for his reply.

There was an instant, brief but undeniably present, in which something passed between them like an electric current drawing them together. Then Dante leaned forward and kissed her.

Their lips met, and their noses brushed. Dante's hand rose from where it had laid atop Eleanor's and cupped the back of her head, strong without being forceful, then moved down to her neck and shoulder, drawing further tingles of warmth and electricity as her hand went to his jawline, keeping his face against hers.

After lingering another minute, Dante drew back, but only a little. "That's more like what I was thinking about." He smiled. The shadow of hesitation was gone, leaving only the confidence.

Eleanor's mouth lay half-opened, and her pupils dilated more as she looked at him. "Do you think it's going to be enough?"

"It's a start." He left the rest unsaid. His hand moved down her shoulder to her back.

She took his wrist, not to stop him, but to guide his hand on its course. "Well, I think I want more than just a *start*."

Their mouths locked again, more passionately this time as Dante's other arm wrapped around her body. She raised a leg and pressed her knee against the side of his waist, drawing him against and atop her. They fell together below the line of sight of the window but were past caring about the presence or attention of anyone but each other.

CHAPTER SEVEN

The next morning, around eleven, one of the Autocutioners—newly disguised as a brown parcel truck thanks to Gage's efforts last night—pulled up to the nearest empty lot near the building where Feng dwelled. Gage rode shotgun while Daria was behind the wheel. In the rear compartment were Eleanor and Amahle.

Everyone had their task and their position laid out. The operation, like a machine, had several moving parts which all had to perform the necessary activities at the right time in conjunction with one another for the whole thing to work.

They'd picked Amahle up about a mile away and spent the short period it took for her to change into the new clothes and redo her hair and makeup. Eleanor was already in costume.

"Amahle," she began in the kindest and most encouraging tone she could muster. "You look splendid. Classy, I would say."

The South African's jaw muscles rippled as she clenched her teeth. "There is no such thing. I don't see why someone else couldn't have done this. You would be better off with me in Ty's place. And, perhaps, him in mine."

Eleanor managed a short, dry laugh at that but shook her head. "No, I'm afraid that Mr. Qiangguo only likes women. I learned more about him than I wanted or needed to know while working for Mr. Dongfeng. At least it has proven useful to us now."

Chen Qiangguo was Feng's head of security, responsible for his small but skilled team of bodyguards. The man was a long-time friend of Feng's family, which was the main reason he tolerated him. Eleanor had always had the impression, without Feng having to say it, that he despised Qiangguo and would rather dismiss him. Due to familial connections and the dangers of faux pas that governed Chinese society, he was obliged to use the man for what he was good at and turn a blind eye to his indiscretions.

Gage looked back over his shoulder. "Are you two ready? I will leave first. Then Daria will take us up front, where you can get out. It would be better if we do not all disembark from the vehicle at the same time or in the same place."

Amahle made a low growl in her throat. "To the extent that anyone can ever be *ready* for something like this, yes, I am."

"Good." Gage adjusted his workman's cap. He also wore suspenders and had a toolbox he'd be carrying in. As a supposed maintenance worker, it wouldn't be overly suspicious for him to be poking around with wiring in the basement. Still, with the tense atmosphere in the city, it never hurt to be cautious. As such, Eleanor gathered that a certain amount of money may or may not have changed hands with one of the building's janitors, who would help ensure that no one detained the Gurkha on his way to his job.

Bidding them goodbye and good luck, Gage hopped out of the truck and strolled across the street to the rear of the skyscraper, disappearing around the corner en route to the basement. Once he was safely gone, Daria took them back onto the street and made a loop around the block before returning and heading for the front entrance.

Eleanor took a moment to admire the surroundings, not least the handiwork of the man they intended to trap and coerce.

Fittingly enough, the high-rise was of Zhu Dongfeng's design. Eleanor hadn't been privy to all of the details of what had happened. Still, she gathered that the Executives had agreed to assign Feng the project, allotting him office space of his own within it in addition to his usual fee. Of course, the rest of the Execs expected certain services, perks, and kickbacks in return.

It was the third-tallest building in the city. It had been second, but another skyscraper had gone up on the other end of downtown that had knocked it down a peg. Still, at eighty floors, it remained impressive. Slightly taller than the Chrysler Building in New York, if Eleanor recalled, but not as tall as the Empire State Building.

Feng's office lay on the seventieth floor. This posed a substantial challenge for the task of installing an overwatch sniper nearby. Not only for the sake of getting Ty high enough to where he could get a good vantage point but also because Eleanor found it difficult to recall which side of the building the office suite lay on. Eventually, she remembered that it was on the south side, something to do with *feng shui*. There was a slim chance that the man had relocated since she'd last heard from him.

Under her breath, Eleanor said a brief prayer in Spanish, hoping that this would work.

She thought of Dante, of the night they'd spent together, and how much she wanted to see him again. He alone among the group had stayed behind to guard Jori Singh. Despite the earlier talk of keeping the man locked in an Autocutioner, they'd ultimately decided to store him in Daria's cellar. There was only one point of egress and no way a mechanical failure could occur like a truck.

Plus, if by some chance he *did* escape from one of the reinforced back compartments, he would already be in an escape vehicle. In a basement, he would have a harder time getting away except on foot. Dante, the youngest and strongest Executioner, would be sitting in his way with a shotgun across his lap the whole time.

"All right." Daria parked across the street out front. "It's show-time, ladies. Remember that no one will be too suspicious of women in your supposed profession who look like they secretly don't want to be there. Of course, you must still behave your-selves until the time is right."

Eleanor blanked her mind of any thoughts save those pertaining to the mission. "Of course. We will speak again soon."

Amahle looked like she would break into a sudden angry rant, but she held her tongue. "Yes. Let us get it over with." Muttering under her breath, she got up and opened the back door.

Both women hopped down, and when it was safe, strode across the street. They were wearing tightly fitted dresses, short enough at the bottom and low-cut enough at the top to draw men's eyes, but not to the point of being tasteless. As the classier type of prostitutes, they didn't want to look too brazen or trashy. Amahle also had a fine leather handbag, and Eleanor had added some faux pearl earrings to her ensemble. Most importantly, Eleanor had bundled her dark hair up beneath a blonde wig.

When they stood before the front doors, Eleanor asked her partner, "Are you sure you can do this? We must not make any mistakes. Dongfeng might be our only chance."

"I can do it," Amahle growled. "But if I must tell the truth, I would rather be dangling from a tree for three days, peeing down my leg with a branch up my ass."

Eleanor stared at her, mildly dumbstruck. Then she snickered. "Well, that was colorful. But, easy now—save the dirty talk for the *pendejos*." Then she turned to the door and pushed it open with Amahle close behind her, and both prepared to do whatever it took.

CHAPTER EIGHT

The lobby matched the building's exterior. It was fine quality and beautifully furnished but in a minimalistic, less-is-more way. Very modern. From what Eleanor recalled, Feng had an especial interest in taking the so-called Modern style that was popular a decade ago and helping it evolve further to meet the changing tastes and demands as the sixties drew closer to their end.

There wasn't much in the way of a waiting area and no chairs. Presumably, this was the type of place where visitors needed an appointment, and if they had one, they wouldn't have to wait long to be attended to and shuffled off to wherever they were supposed to be. The lobby was there to make a good impression, not provide comfort.

A single broad desk of bright, polished oak stood out front between two elevators. Behind it was a crisply dressed young man with a lantern jaw, who undoubtedly doubled as receptionist and security guard.

"Hello," he greeted them in a cool and slightly skeptical tone. "May I help you, ladies?"

Eleanor smiled at him. It hardly needed to be agreed in words that she ought to do most of the talking. Amahle could simply tag along and speak only when necessary.

"Yes," Eleanor began. "We are here to see Mr. Qiangguo at eleven-thirty. We are from Hertz Personnel Solutions. Surely they informed you that we would be interviewing for assistant positions?"

The man looked them both over, his eyes going rapidly from top to bottom. "Ohh, yes. I recall now. Mr. Qiangguo interviews a lot of young women for positions like that. Let me send the word on up to him, and I'll buzz you through."

While the guard slid back in his rolling chair toward an in-house phone, Eleanor casually examined their surroundings in more detail. There were no metal detectors, which came as a pleasant surprise. If there had been, surrendering her gun wouldn't have been overly suspicious, though. Many Atlanticans were armed wherever they went.

It was difficult to hear everything the guard said into the telephone receiver. He spoke in a low voice and seemed to switch back and forth between English and Mandarin. Eleanor had learned a few phrases of the latter tongue while working alongside Feng but hadn't had time to attain anything remotely like fluency.

Amahle, meanwhile, stood in place and stared blankly at a point beyond the elevators. Although making no particular effort to be charming, at least she was keeping herself calm and being professional.

After a moment, the guard hung up and looked at Eleanor. "Okay, you're clear, but don't try anything funny, all right? We've got cameras on every floor and a tight security system here. If someone causes problems, it's dealt with right away. And yes, I'm required to say that to everyone, so don't take it personally."

Eleanor tittered. "Of course not."

The man pressed a button, and the doors to the right-hand

elevator opened. "Go on in. No need to press any buttons. It'll take you where you need to go."

Amahle quipped, "A good system, then." She and Eleanor walked into the compartment and waited as the doors closed in front of their faces.

There was a console of sorts within, but there were no buttons to press, aside from a single red one with the word "EMERGENCY" printed below it. A crude digital readout said that they were currently on **Floor 01**. As the elevator lurched up, the readout changed to reflect each floor that passed. At length, it slowed down at sixty-nine and stopped at seventy. A pleasant *ding* sounded, and the doors opened.

Beyond them was a short hallway that ended at another security desk, attached to a chest-high gate of sorts that blocked the hall off from the rest of the floor. Behind the desk sat a beefy, dark-faced man who had been humming to himself and barely seemed to notice the pair until they came up to the gate.

"Hellooooo, ladies," he drawled and laughed. "Looking mighty fine, I must say. It seems like Mr. Qiangguo is broadening his horizons. That's a good thing, though. What you got in the bag, little lady?" He stared at Amahle.

She forced her mouth to smile. "My makeup, perfume, and one or two other things which are private," she declared. "I'm sure you understand."

"Oh, I do, I do." The man chortled. "I got to have a look anyway. Make sure you aren't hiding a weapon in there. If you are, you'll get it back when you finish. Fear not, fear not. But no guns or knives go past this desk."

Eleanor cursed mentally. She ought to have anticipated something like this. Her pistol was concealed against her inner thigh, as high up as she could get it, to the point of being uncomfortable. But it meant that a man would have to get awfully *familiar* to find it.

Amahle wasn't so lucky. Scowling, she handed over her handbag. The man opened it at once and stared within.

"Well, well." He plucked out her little Iver Johnson .32 revolver. "Private, eh?" He guffawed. "I'll be holding onto this, then. Like I said, you come ask me nice later, and you'll get it back."

Amahle glared. "Oh, I will."

When the guard turned to Eleanor, she claimed to have no weapons on her. "I do not like them. We usually rely on her gun to protect us both. It is enough, yes?"

The man stood. He was taller than he'd looked while sitting. "Better let me check, all the same." He reached out and patted down her shoulders, under her arms, around her waist, and up her thighs with his big hands. He missed the Walther by barely a centimeter. Then, staring at her chest, he swiped a hand through her cleavage as fast as he could.

She made a show of gasping in horror. "How could you? Is this how you always treat women who come for interviews?"

He threw his head back and laughed. "Interviews! Is that what they're calling it now? Okay, well, you're clean. Go on ahead through. Remember—talk to me nice when you finish. You'll get your little pistol back."

Neither said anything as the guard pressed a button and opened the gate. They stepped through, ignoring him. Amahle stopped abruptly, though, and swiveled on a heel toward the man, her hands balled into fists. His back was to them, and he didn't notice at first.

Eleanor's eyes widened. She sprang forward and grabbed Amahle's wrist. "No. Come along. Let us, ah, conduct the interview and maybe get paid, yes?"

Amahle resisted. Larger and stronger than Eleanor despite still being lithe, it would've been exceedingly hard for Eleanor to drag her away by force. Still, after a second she spun. Her timing was impeccable. The guard had begun to swivel in his chair to have a look at them. All he saw were their backs as they resumed their course down the hallway.

With the danger of an outburst from her partner abated, Eleanor noticed something odd about their surroundings. The seventieth floor no longer looked like the combination of corporate office and artistic studio it once had. New walls had been added, turning it into what almost looked like part of a police station. She wondered if Dongfeng still had his business quarters here or if he'd converted the floor to a security checkpoint and moved his sanctum elsewhere.

The remainder of the floor was divided into a cluster of small rooms behind doors to their left, an open lounge-type area to their right, and a large room at the end of the hallway. From what Eleanor could recall, the room at the end had remained the same. It used to be Feng's office. A soundproof glass wall still surrounded it.

Chen Qiangguo appeared behind the glass. Noticing them, he waved, leered, and held up a hand to indicate he would need a minute. He began to loosen his tie and stepped away and out of sight, behind a stack of drawers and other furniture.

Amahle gestured. "That is him? Feng trusts him with security?"

Shrugging, Eleanor explained, "He owes loyalty to his family. Feng tolerates him because he is good for thuggish pursuits. He turns a blind eye to Chen's tendency to send away for prostitutes as a noontime snack. It helps that Chen is jealous of his boss and wishes to impress him one day. He knows his limitations and is aware that he would have few opportunities outside of what his boss uses him for. Chen can be a dangerous man, but not a hard one to manipulate, I think."

"Good," Amahle stated, her tone grim and hard.

Together, they advanced toward the room with the soundproof glass walls. Now that she could see things better, Eleanor determined that the extra walls and wings added to the floor were a good thing. Provided they could get Chen out of the direct line of sight from the hallway, they could deal with him without the stupid guard noticing.

The downside was that there was no indication that Dongfeng still used the floor.

Chen reappeared, now wearing a bathrobe and slippers, and unlocked the door, holding it open as the two ladies moved coyly in.

"Good day," he said, grinning and then shutting the door behind them. He was a rather large and jowly man, well-groomed but still with something distinctly bestial and unpleasant about him. Eleanor had always been vaguely uncomfortable in the past whenever he'd shown up.

On the plus side, he'd also seemed to forget who she was half of the time, so she was confident that he wouldn't recognize her today, particularly with her hair and makeup in a different style. Feng had mentioned something about how Chen had difficulty telling women apart who weren't East Asian.

Chen gestured at a large couch, out of sight from the hall, which stood in front of a thick shag carpet. Eleanor and Amahle seated themselves and crossed their legs.

Chen nodded as he appraised them. "Get comfortable. You want drinks? I make them."

"Please," said Amahle.

As the man turned and went to his bar, pulling out a variety of bottles and glasses as well as a dish of ice, Amahle turned to Eleanor and whispered, "I bet we can entice him to let us tie him up. Want to try?"

Eleanor almost laughed out loud. "Yes, I think I do. But if he becomes suspicious, we stop at once." Given his security work, Chen could be the paranoid sort. But then again, he was not overly bright.

Their host returned with two glasses loaded with a drink that Eleanor could not identify on sight. It was a pale greenish-yellow, and she would probably have to taste it to tell what it was. For the sake of keeping up appearances, she took the glass and accepted a sip. Some or another amalgamation of soda, lime, and vodka. "Ah, thank you."

Amahle did likewise. Then she gave the big man a suggestive stare, tilting her head to the side. "You look like a man who likes to try new things." She fluttered her eyelashes.

Eleanor looked at her, then back at Chen. "Yes. Of course, there are always the *usual* things, but those aren't so much fun, and everyone always does them anyway. Would you care to try something adventurous, Mr. Qiangguo? We are so bored with the *usual* things."

Chen was staring at them, his gaze drifting back and forth between the two, and his mouth hung slightly open. "What new things? Adventurous?"

"Yes," said Eleanor. "We will let you try something special...and for the same price. Only so we can do something different today. Please?"

Gradually, they made it clear to the man that they wanted to try a domination scenario where he, naked, was tied up and teased for as long as possible before they finally gave him release. At first, he looked skeptical, but his interest grew by the minute while the two women described everything in as much detail as they could stand.

At last, grinning and shuddering with excitement, Chen disrobed and told them to do their worst.

Amahle came up behind him. "Oh, we will." She planted a foot on his rump and pushed him down on the couch, then pulled his hands behind his back and bound them at the wrists with his discarded necktie.

Eleanor tied his ankles together with his shirt, leaving enough slack for him to shuffle forward with small, tight steps. Then Amahle went into the man's desk drawer and produced a wide roll of masking tape. "Here." She ripped off a length of it and pasted it over Chen's mouth, binding it tightly but leaving his nostrils free to breathe.

Amahle stood Chen up and pushed him toward the individual bathroom attached to the office. "Now we will bend you over the toilet," she suggested. "It will be dirtier that way."

She sensed the tension in him, as though he were suddenly afraid of what they might do, but his curiosity was greater. He complied, inching closer until Amahle opened the bathroom door and tossed him in. He struck the edge of the toilet with his shins and fell to his knees without them having to ask.

"Good," Amahle told him. "Wait there, please."

Eleanor wheeled the chair out from behind the desk, pushed it into the restroom, and tipped it over at an angle so it blocked Chen from being able to stand without smashing into it and getting himself entangled. His eyes widened in confusion verging on alarm.

Amahle slammed the door. "The desk," she said. "Help me push it."

She and Eleanor ran around to the far side and heaved the desk forward. It scraped along the floor, screeching unpleasantly, and they gave thanks for the soundproof glass. The door shuddered as Chen threw himself against the chair, but with his limbs bound, he couldn't do much. The edge of the heavy desk banged against the door, holding it in place.

"All right," Eleanor gasped, surprised at how tired her arms were all of a sudden. Nonetheless, she dashed over to Chen's discarded shirt and pulled out a security card from the front pocket. "We must find Dongfeng. He's probably on a higher floor, perhaps the penthouse."

Amahle glanced around. It took only a second before she pointed at the far end of the office, near the bar. "Over there. Looks like an entrance to a private staircase, or maybe an elevator."

They ran to it while Chen continued to *thud* uselessly at the door. Eleanor hoped the hall guard wouldn't be able to feel the vibrations through the floor. If they moved fast enough, it might not matter, anyway.

Beyond the door lay a short hall that contained both a compact elevator—big enough for two, maybe three people at most—and a stairwell that went both up and down.

Eleanor slid the security card into a slot next to the button and struck it, sighing in relief when the elevator *dinged* and opened. She and Amahle stepped in. Unlike the one the front desk guard had directed them to from the lobby, this one had a traditional console, but it only seemed to go between floors seventy and eighty.

She punched in the topmost floor, reasoning that it would be easier to work their way down than up. There came the familiar stomach-churning sensation as the elevator began its ascent, and then it was smooth riding.

Sensing her thoughts, Amahle remarked, "If we go to the top, and he isn't there, it will be easier for him to escape downward if he's on the seventy-fifth floor or something."

"*Mierda*," Eleanor cursed. "I didn't think of that. But I know Feng. If he moved, it's probably to the penthouse so he can look down on the whole city at once. Unless he's not in the building..."

Amahle shrugged. "All these layers of security mean he probably is here. Or if not, something valuable is above us."

The elevator stopped at the top story, its door sliding open to reveal a broad, open space encompassing nearly the entirety of the floor. Much of it resembled spacious and modern living quarters, with clearly defined lounge and kitchen areas, but more than half of the available room was an architectural design studio. Miniature buildings lay on tables, and sketches and diagrams were attached to easels and drawing boards.

In the far corner, near the edge of the kitchen and before a smaller closed-off area that likely encompassed the bedroom and bathroom, a man stood talking on the phone. He faced away from them. The two women froze, fixing their eyes on him and moving forward with soft, slow, gradual steps.

Amahle tugged on Eleanor's arm and gestured with her chin and eyes toward the space behind a rack of books. She wanted to hide and ambush their quarry.

Eleanor shook her head. Before Amahle could try to begin a silent argument, Eleanor slipped free from her grasp and stepped right toward Zhu Dongfeng in the most obvious fashion possible. Amahle threw up her hands, rolled her eyes toward the ceiling, then inhaled sharply and followed her friend into the chamber.

The man was average-sized with a full head of hair graying at the edges. He wore a robe not unlike Chen's, but had regular clothes beneath it. He glanced over his shoulder at the pair of guests, not yet recognizing Eleanor, and said into the phone, "Excuse me for a moment."

Eleanor and Amahle stopped. Feng did a lazy scan of them, as though acknowledging the presence of a tea refill by an unobtrusive waitress. "If you are the call girls that Chen requested, I'm afraid you are on the wrong floor. Please go back down to seventy. Thank you."

He raised the phone back to his lips and was already starting to turn.

"*No.*" Eleanor stepped forward, her voice loud and insistent, and her hand rose to tear the wig from her head. Her eyes bored into his. This time, when he looked back, he truly saw her for the first time.

His mouth opened a little and stayed that way. "Pardon me," he said into the receiver. "I must call you back later. This is important, I'm afraid."

Someone on the other line began asking if he was all right, but Feng ignored them and hung up. He stared at Eleanor, then turned his eyes briefly to Amahle and back. "Ms. Cervantes. It's a pleasure to see you again, although a most unexpected one. However I might feel about it on a personal level, the first thing I must say is that you cannot be here. If someone finds you, your life is in great danger."

"Yes, I know this, Feng. My friends are nearby, and we have taken steps to minimize that danger. All the same, I wouldn't have come here unless I thought you were the only one who could help me."

She let a slight vulnerability creep into her voice and eyes. It was to her brief but stinging shame that there was no need to fake it. In many ways, she'd never felt so lost, exposed, or helpless as she had these past several days.

He shook his head as he lost himself in her eyes. "Eleanor. I would like to help you. There may be limits to what I can do, considering all the mistakes you've made and all the trouble you've brought upon yourself. But, tell me. What is it you want from me? I can promise nothing. Nothing except that I will listen to what you have to say."

Amahle watched the man, wary but not alarmed. He seemed kinder and more gracious than she'd expected, yet there was every reason to believe that he was in league with the Coven and might betray them if he had the opportunity.

Eleanor drew a deep breath. "I think you already know why, to some extent. I've discovered the terrible things that the Executives have been doing and that I was a part of it, in my way. They've tried to kill me for following my conscience. There is no recourse for me now except to stop the worst of their evil actions. There are certain things about which you would know better than anyone."

The pair argued back and forth, largely in low and respectful tones, but the flares of temper underlying their words were obvious enough. There were raw, wounded feelings on both sides. Eleanor continued to insist that Feng could only help her by divulging the information she sought. He, in turn, tried to convince her to leave the building and flee Atlantica for her own sake.

Eleanor wouldn't relent. While Amahle listened, feeling half-guilty for hearing so many references to their personal history as a couple, each of them brought up things from the past that hurt the other. At the same time, it drew them closer together in the memories of what they'd shared.

They'd remained lovers in an on-and-off fashion for a good six or seven months after Eleanor's transfer from the project. It made it harder to meet, harder to find time to spend together. Still, the bonds of attraction and care were still there.

All the same, there were ever-increasing pressures on their relationship as time went on that exceeded those imposed by their professional assignments. Zhu had become more secretive and reclusive, sharing fewer and fewer of his thoughts and feelings. At the same time, Eleanor grew discontented with the actions and methods of the Executives. Her tendencies in that direction only grew stronger as the role of the Coven of Miracles came more clearly into focus.

"Eleanor," Feng repeated, "you cannot stay here long. Whatever you did to reach my penthouse, they will find out soon. I can order Chen and my bodyguard to stand down, but Executive Security obeys an authority that goes beyond mine. We must—"

"Why?" Eleanor cut him off, stepping closer and looking at him with imploring eyes. "Why do you never tell me what you mean anymore, or what is truly going on? Did you join the Coven yourself? Did you hold back from telling me about it because you knew I wouldn't approve?"

Once more the image of the little girl on the operating table intruded on her thoughts. She wished it would go away, but to forget it would be worse than remembering it, in a way.

Feng looked away from his former paramour, and his eyes caught the dark and burning intensity in Amahle's gaze. He hadn't bothered to ask who she was, but he probably knew anyway. The Executives had all received briefings and photographs on the rogue organization known as the Executioners.

He realized there would be no escape from the truth.

"The Coven of Miracles is a highly ambitious but imperfect institution. I learned this quickly." He sighed. "If you must know, I don't agree with all of their actions or methods, and I have spoken to them about this before. They do offer the best path forward. Atlantica, and indeed the world, faces problems that the existing power structures are incapable of dealing with. There must be a new way. Someone must take the reins to guide us into the future."

Eleanor took a slow step back, trying to ignore the slowly rising sense of revulsion at what she'd heard. She didn't doubt his sincerity or his good intent. However, what he'd said sounded disturbingly familiar.

"Feng. This is the same kind of talk that led to your family's destruction! Your parents, starving in Mao's famine. Your cousins, killed by the Red Guards as enemies of the state. You told me yourself. You came here alone because nearly everyone you cared about in China was dead.

"This attitude of 'the ends justify the means' is one of the reasons why you swore never to go back—until you could change things for the better and in the right way. Don't you remember that?"

Feng stared at her, and his expression was abashed, as though she'd slapped him. The women doubted that none of this had ever occurred to him before. Rather, it was as though he'd lived in fear of someone saying it aloud.

He looked aside, his nostrils flaring while he struggled to get himself under control, thinking over his next response carefully. When he looked back, the anger had passed, but the hurt remained.

"What do you want to know? You must leave soon and never come back. Perhaps I can give you...something."

She looked into his eyes and gave him a slow nod of understanding. "Zero Site. Where is it? I need the exact coordinates."

He shook his head and told her. His tone was reluctant, as though he sensed that bad times were ahead but had accepted there was little he could do about it.

Eleanor thanked him. "It might be that this is the best thing you've done in a long time. We shall see, perhaps. They will find out we were here and blame you once they know our intentions. Say that we beat it out of you. Or that you didn't give it up, but we found it in your office."

"That is a good idea," he murmured.

Amahle strode over to the desk where Feng appeared to do his business paperwork. "Allow me to help." She kicked over his fine, leather-backed chair. Then she tossed papers on the floor in heaps, threw a lamp at the wall, pulled open drawers and left them hanging out of their slots, and scattered his office supplies.

Feng stood watching the spectacle with a dismal look of resignation. When it was over, Amahle came over to him. "We should rough you up a little as well, then."

The man shrugged sadly. "So be it."

Eleanor kicked him in the back of the leg as Amahle punched him in the stomach. He doubled over, and the South African threw him to the floor in such a way that he crashed against an end table and its legs left scuff marks against the floor. It also tore his robe.

As he slowly drew himself back to his feet, Amahle added, "Sorry. I'm sure you understand our reasoning."

"Yes," he replied in a flat tone.

Eleanor's heart ached for a second, seeing this man she cared about in such a broken state. "Feng. Thank you. I won't forget this."

He brushed himself off. "I imagine you won't. Good luck, Eleanor, and you too, Ms. Nikoze. Oh, one final thing that might interest you."

Eleanor's eyes widened. "Yes?"

Feng turned halfway toward the massive southern window, through which almost the entirety of Atlantica Metro was visible, and beyond it, the shimmering sea. He had folded his hands behind his back, ignoring his bruises and torn clothes.

"It often seems to me, lately, that the dream of Atlantica might die shortly before it was finally to be born. Time is running out."

Eleanor squinted at him and moved closer to his side. "What do you mean?"

"The Third Atlantica Conference," he proclaimed. "The date for it has, at long last, been finalized. We knew the approximate year when it would arrive, but that was all. Now we have reliable information that the conference will take place on January 5, 1972. Not a terribly long time, is it?"

Eleanor's mind buzzed as she fit the new information into everything she already knew. Things began to fall into place. The approach of the date was the likely reason why the Coven, and the Executives, had gone into overdrive, hurrying and making sloppy mistakes as they grew more crude and brutal in their methods. They needed to accomplish as much as possible before their plans were upset by whatever might happen at the conference.

She squeezed his shoulder before saying goodbye. Then the door burst open.

Amahle threw herself to the side, jumping and rolling behind the desk as men stomped in. Eleanor, standing out in the open, simply drew herself closer to Feng—hoping that he would provide cover but ashamed at the thought that he might not.

Chen Qiangguo was out in front, his clothes thrown sloppily back on and his hair a mess. There were red welts all over his face and body from having the tape torn off as well as his efforts to dislodge himself from the bathroom by brute force. At his right elbow was the smirking, dark-faced guard from the seventieth-floor hallway, and behind them were two more men in the uniforms of Executive Security. The two in the rear held rifles. Chen and the hall guard had drawn handguns.

"I heard!" Chen bellowed, pointing at his boss. "I heard enough. You told them. You're helping them, aren't you, Mr. Dongfeng? You want to save your skin. So you've betrayed us. I would make a better Junior Executive than you anyway, don't you think?"

A nasty leer spread across his face, and Eleanor's hopes that they might get out of this in one piece dwindled to nonexistence. She cursed herself for not heeding Feng's advice that they get the hell out of there immediately. The thought faded right in time for the first gunshot.

CHAPTER NINE

The first to shoot wasn't Chen, the hall guard, or either of the two Exec Security men. It was Amahle.

When pulling open the drawers of Feng's desk, she'd found a .357 Magnum revolver badly hidden under a handkerchief. She'd neglected to take it at the time. Doing so might have alarmed Feng, not to mention it was his property anyway. If there'd been a chance for them to escape quietly and peacefully, she would've been content to leave it to him and not have to deal with the complications of having a second gun on her when going through the security checkpoints.

Those chances had evaporated. Now, their only way out was *through* Chen and his goons.

Amahle raised the gun, snapping it up into a strong double-handed stance and squeezing the trigger while holding the muzzle on the head of one of the men with armor and rifles. Their weapons and protective gear made them far more dangerous than Chen or the hall guard.

Her aim was true. The revolver didn't kick as much as she'd feared it might, suggesting that Feng had probably loaded it with .38 Special instead of Magnum rounds. Although less powerful, they were still capable of getting the job done. The slug Amahle fired went straight into the man's unprotected ear.

He crashed sideways into the wall, spasming briefly and dropping his rifle, making no vocal sound as his body shut down. He was dead at the same instant he slumped to the floor.

"*Fuck!*" the leering hall guard exclaimed, waving his .45 pistol madly around in a circle as he tried to figure out who'd shot first in his sudden panic. "What the *fuck!* You..."

Eleanor grabbed Feng's shoulder and pulled on him with all her might. She wasn't very strong, but adrenaline did truly amazing things. "Get down!"

The surviving Exec Security goon opened fire with his rifle, squeezing off a short burst of four or five rounds that sailed narrowly over Eleanor's and Feng's heads as they fell to the floor. Behind them, plaster shattered, glass cracked, and the wind whistled.

Chen haphazardly fired one shot from his Chinese clone of a Tokarev pistol at Eleanor and Feng before pivoting to shoot in Amahle's general direction. The hall guard did likewise, the two of them peppering the desk with handgun rounds.

When Eleanor hit the floor, she felt Feng collapsing on top of her but rolled aside in time to avoid getting pinned in place. Everything was happening too fast for her to get a clear idea of where the guards were or how soon they would be able to shoot again. The painfully echoing din of gunfire and the howling of cold winds from the shattered windows didn't help, either.

She looked around, frantically grasping the first thing that came to hand. The imitation Ming vase had tumbled to the floor in the general chaos, but had miraculously remained unbroken. She picked it up with one hand, whipped it over and around, and flung it at the three men by the door.

It struck the security guy on his hands, knocking his rifle aside right as he was about to perforate them both with another burst of 7.62 projectiles. The vase also cracked into three or four pieces. One got stuck atop the rifle and fell against his wrist. He stopped himself from blind-firing and instead shrugged off the debris while readjusting his position. He was fast, but the moment's hesitation was enough.

Eleanor grabbed Feng's arm and dragged him up and away. The pair sprinted across the open floor to hurl themselves behind the partial wall that separated the bedroom area from the rest of the penthouse. The guard opened fire with a pair of short bursts of two or three rounds as they ducked out of sight. Most of them punched easily through the wall, but its material sent the bullets slightly off-course. They veered high or low, missing the man and woman by mere centimeters.

On the other side of the dividing wall, Amahle had folded herself in half while pressed against the floor behind the thickest and heaviest part of the desk. The wood was enough to stop a few pistol rounds, barely, but she didn't have much time. Feng's rolling chair was in sight, but it still lay on its side amid piles of randomly-strewn papers.

Cursing in her native tongue, she stuck her hand into the open area at the middle of the desk, where Feng's feet would've had room to extend, and fired two shots from the revolver at the legs of the three men. There wasn't time to determine if she'd hit anything, and she only needed to cover herself for a second, anyway. Chen and the hall guard stopped shooting and jumped back toward the door to the elevator.

Amahle sprang out, grabbed the chair, and somehow managed to heave it upright and shove it at the guards in the same motion. The leering, dark-faced man from the hallway was out in front, and when he raised his pistol, the chair struck him in the knees and groin. His gun went astray, and he popped off a useless shot at the wall.

Amahle jumped up and ran toward them, bellowing a war cry and emptying the last few rounds in the revolver as she dove for the fallen rifle of the goon she'd killed a few seconds ago. One shot struck the hall guard in the arm. He yelled in pain and stag-gered back against the wall, struggling to switch his gun to his other hand.

The other two shots missed but at least kept Chen and the last man pinned down while Amahle snatched the rifle, rolled, and sprinted toward the dividing wall. When she saw the other rifleman emerging to shoot at her, she fired a couple of rounds sideways to discourage him.

It irked her that she was spraying so much lead without rendering kills each time, but close-quarters, fast-paced combat wasn't her forte. She could handle herself, but such things were Ty's specialty. She should've been the one in the sniper's nest. Unfortunately, Ty would've failed to pass as a call girl.

As she ducked behind the wall and more gunshots rang out behind her, she wondered where Mr. Katakura was and what he was doing. He must have heard all the commotion by now. Entire blocks of the city probably had. Still, they'd set him up on the assumption that the seventieth floor was where they'd be, not the penthouse.

In a lull in the noise, Amahle found Eleanor and Feng trying to crawl into the bathroom. "No! Get up. Don't get trapped back there. We can shoot our way out of this." She hefted the rifle in her hands to emphasize her point. In the back of her mind, she knew that more armed thugs would be along shortly, but if they acted fast...

Then another sound rose behind them, coming from some-where outside. With the windows broken, a cold wind was whipping in from outside. At first, they thought it was simply the air itself. But no, it was something mechanical, growing louder with each second. Amahle fired a few shots on semi-auto through the wall to discourage Chen and his minions from advancing. Then she crept closer to the void that lay beyond the jagged glass.

A helicopter rose through the air as it drew closer to the

building. It would've been naïve to assume that it wasn't headed straight for them.

Eleanor got to her feet. "Shoot our way out, then, as you said!" she insisted. She'd retrieved her hidden pistol and braced herself to shoot when Amahle did.

Amahle switched to full auto. She had no spare magazines and would have to bank upon finishing their enemies off with one final, powerful burst. She leaned around the corner, gun aimed and ready, and fired half of what remained in one go, destroying much of the wall around the door by the elevator. Eleanor emptied her magazine too. It sounded like someone yelled in anguish, but it was hard to be sure.

"Come on!" she called, and the three of them sprinted back into the main area. Behind them, the chopper grew louder.

Off to the left, the wounded hall guard appeared from behind an overturned bookcase. He'd switched his pistol to his weak hand. Amahle was about to shoot him when the other guard with the rifle also sprang out from the blasted doorframe. Then all three of them hesitated, for a second or less, as the helicopter pulled up alongside the long main window.

Eleanor cried, "It's *them!*"

They had all assumed the chopper was Executive Security. It wasn't.

Within it were four men, including the pilot. All wore modern armor accessorized in ways better suited to medieval Europe or feudal Japan, with frightening demonic features added to the masks and various grim symbols painted on the chests and shoulder plates. They couldn't see them at the moment, but Eleanor and Amahle knew that all of their weapons would sport a contrasting yet complementary decoration scheme full of holy and angelic iconography.

Prominent among them was Augustus Freeman, a young, fresh-faced black American man, the commander of the Hell-breakers. He was operating a belt-fed machine gun, probably an old World War II German model, aimed out the helicopter's side door directly at the building's penthouse. A huge toothy smile spread across his face.

"Down!" Amahle barked, throwing herself to the floor.

Eleanor tried to drag Feng down with her, but something in his leg seized up—a side effect of the injury she'd given him earlier—and he was too slow, freezing briefly in a contorted, half-kneeling position. Beyond him, the hall guard stood paralyzed in terror. The other rifleman swore and threw himself back through the door toward the elevator.

The air itself was ripped open by the din of Gus' machine gun. The belt zipped into the device and empty casings sprayed from the other side, raining down from the heights into the city streets below. A bloom of flame leapt from the weapon's muzzle as it spat lead at tremendous speed.

Feng cried out as bullets tore through him, puncturing him in at least three or four places and knocking him the rest of the way to the floor. Gus swept the machine gun around in a wavy line, hosing the entire penthouse as though he were trying to cause as much destruction as possible and simply kill everyone within.

The hall guard who had found it so amusing to frisk Amahle and Eleanor blubbered stupidly as twenty rounds ripped him to shreds, rendering him an unidentifiable reddish mass that was half-buried by blasted debris from the walls, floor, and furniture.

Amahle had landed on her back, and she brought the rifle up between her legs, aiming it at the helicopter and unloading the rest of the magazine. It wasn't as long of a burst as she would have liked, but enough of the rounds sparked off the helicopter to spook the pilot. More importantly, at least one or two struck the machine gun itself, jamming or disabling it.

While the pilot tried to pull them around the corner to a safer position and Gus, frustrated, attempted to get the weapon working again, Amahle got to her knees and crawled over to Eleanor and her former lover.

Eleanor cradled Zhu Dongfeng in her arms. He was still alive, but she knew it was hopeless. Gus had punched holes the size of small fists through his lung, stomach, and shoulder, and he was bleeding everywhere, too profusely to stop it with a rag or tourniquet. He coughed, and his eyelids fluttered.

"Feng, thank you. I will see to it that what you've done for us matters. I promise."

He gurgled. "Eleanor. I'm..." His eyes rolled backward and turned glassy as a death rattle went through his body. Eleanor lowered him to the floor.

Amahle took her by the wrist. "We can mourn him later. We need to *move*."

The two women got to their feet and ran for the door. Amahle paused briefly to pick up the .45 that the hall guard had dropped. She popped out the magazine and weighed it by feel, trying to recall how many times he'd fired. She guessed there were only two or three rounds left in it, but that was better than nothing.

As they stepped over the threshold, the second security officer sprang out and pressed his rifle across Amahle's throat, pinning her to the wall. Before he could draw his sidearm and finish them both off, Eleanor kneed him in the groin and kicked him in the back of the knee.

He faltered, and Amahle twisted the rifle from his grasp, striking him in the face with the butt. "No!" he exclaimed, tumbling sideways and falling down the stairs to the right. The elevator was already descending—Chen must have reevaluated his priorities and beat a retreat.

Amahle started down the stairs, keeping a bead on the guard as he rolled to the first landing. As soon as he stopped, she shot him twice in the chest. He squawked and lay still. Then she plucked a spare mag from his vest and slid it into the belt that encircled her waist.

Eleanor paused to take the man's handgun as well, a Browning. She saw no extra mags for it, but since he hadn't fired it, she assumed it remained loaded with a full thirteen rounds of nine-millimeter. She hoped it would be enough to get them out—at least to where the other Executioners could reconvene with them.

Though they were moving down rather than up, ten stories' worth of stairs was still enough to take its toll on their stamina. Eleanor wondered if it might have been faster to wait for the elevator. Then again, doing so would restrict their mobility. They would be sitting ducks for Chen once they reached the bottom.

Outside, they heard the Hellbreakers' chopper buzzing around the building, but there was no gunfire. Eleanor had no idea if this was because Gus had failed to get his machine gun working again or because they were waiting until they knew who and what they were shooting at. The weapon had an incredible rate of fire, and their ammunition could hardly have been unlimited.

They reached the landing for floor seventy. In theory, they could've tried to keep going all the way down, but it would've taken too long. With Gage in the basement, there was a chance he'd be able to help them if Executive Security tried to meddle with the elevators or otherwise prevent them from escaping.

Amahle kicked open the door and sprang out, her rifle ready to fire at an instant's notice. Eleanor came up to the side of her with her pistol at low ready, knowing she should act as support rather than trying to duplicate her partner's front-line role.

They emerged into an open space off to the side of the glass-walled office. Amahle could barely see someone in a security uniform hiding around the corner of the hallway area.

She didn't bother waiting for them to spring the trap. She unloaded most of her magazine on full auto, spraying the hallway and punching through walls, creating a wall of lead that few things or people waiting ahead of them would be able to escape unscathed.

The guard who'd been waiting right around the corner fell to the floor, his head and shoulders visible and his face permanently frozen in an expression of anguished and horrified shock. Someone else, out of sight, was grunting and cursing.

Amahle used her head to gesture at the glass office. While she covered the hall, Eleanor moved behind her, opened the door, and checked for anyone hiding in what had become Chen's den. She found no one and so returned to her friend's side.

By now, Amahle was slowly advancing into the hallway. She fired a single shot to finish off another guard she'd wounded in the earlier barrage. Eleanor kept about four paces behind her.

Then two things happened at once. One of the office doors close enough that Amahle had been about to check it opened and disclosed another Exec Security officer. The woman grabbed Amahle's rifle and knocked her into the opposing wall.

At the same time, another door ahead opened, and out sprang Chen. He fled straight ahead, jumped over the desk where the other guard had frisked them earlier, and made for the elevator.

Eleanor cried out in alarm, jumped onto the female guard's back, and tried to pull her off Amahle. The woman tried to elbow Eleanor in the face and half-succeeded. The blow came in at too oblique an angle to do much damage, but it still *clonked* her jaw and knocked her partially off-balance.

It also gave Eleanor a better angle to aim at a gap in the woman's armor on the side. She punched the muzzle of her pistol into the weak point and fired three times. The guard screamed. Amahle shoved her away and kicked her in the chest, so she fell back into the office she'd emerged from, trailing blood the whole way. The rifle stayed in Amahle's hands.

"Come on!" she snarled and started after Chen. Eleanor was right behind her.

The elevator doors were closing as Amahle stuck the rifle's barrel into the gap. She was about to fire, but Chen stepped aside. As the doors reopened, he hit the muzzle with the palm of his hand to knock the gun aside.

Eleanor and Chen both raised their pistols and fired at the same instant. The flash and noise made it briefly impossible to determine what had happened, but when Eleanor's vision cleared half a second later, she saw Amahle and the big man struggling over the rifle. Eleanor herself seemed to be unhurt.

Eleanor plowed into them, and all three stumbled into the elevator as it closed again. A *ding* sounded, and the compartment descended, the usual lurch into motion throwing them all off-balance for a moment.

Chen's face twisted with a mixture of fear, anger, and what almost looked like crazy elation. He muttered to himself in Mandarin and periodically barked at them in English.

"Stupid! You are terrible hookers. I will be an Executive next. Stupid!" He punched Amahle's face, mostly missing, but he was slowly overpowering her with his greater size and strength. The rifle was aimed at the ceiling, not fully controlled by either.

Eleanor raised her gun arm to shoot the man, knowing that the noise would be excruciating in such a small space, but Amahle and she would both die otherwise. Chen mule-kicked her in the stomach before she could pull the trigger. Grunting, she fell against the front wall.

The elevator was still descending. It had a long way to go. The red "EMERGENCY" button was right in front of Eleanor's face. She smashed it, not sure what would happen as a result.

A low, buzzing alarm sounded, and the elevator slowed before stopping at the next floor. Something was off, though. When the doors slid apart, the next hallway was two-thirds of the way up from the elevator car's floor. Below that lay the edge of the open shaft.

Eleanor pounced at Chen again, this time dodging his attempt to backhand her and pistol-whipping him in the back of the head. He made a spitting sound and staggered a step or two to the side. It was enough for Amahle to get away from him, but the rifle stayed in his grasp, not hers.

Amahle shoved Eleanor toward the opening. "You first."

Eleanor reached up and grabbed the edge of the floor while Amahle held her legs. She crawled out, turned around, and extended her arms to help pull her friend out too.

Behind them, Chen had recovered and advanced on Amahle. He was about to ram the gun into her back, either to ensure a hit or to shove her into the gap that led down the shaft. She half-pivoted and kicked him in the face, turning the motion into a short hop that let Eleanor pull her up to the hall floor.

As he stumbled, Chen inadvertently squeezed the trigger. Thunderous gunfire reverberated within the compartment, but the two women escaped the absolute worst of it. The rounds went high, blasting through the elevator ceiling and damaging the cables and mechanism above. Sparks rained down, and there was a disturbing metallic groan.

Eleanor shouted, "Get back!" and pulled Amahle's arm, drawing her away. They briefly glimpsed Chen's eyes widening in alarm as the compartment tore loose from its moorings and plummeted down the shaft, leaving only empty air where it had been. They didn't know which floor they were on, but they couldn't have been any lower than thirty, maybe twenty.

A moment later, the compartment crashed to the bottom. It had been a pretty long drop.

"Well." Amahle inhaled and brushed herself off. "It looks like we must take the stairs the rest of the way, after all. Or find another elevator."

Glancing at the signs as they advanced into the hallway, they saw that they were on floor twenty-seven. No security goons sprang out to meet them. They saw a few white-collar employees cowering in an office and left them there. Outside, the Hellbreakers' chopper still buzzed and roared as it scouted the surrounding airspace for its prey.

Amahle and Eleanor found a door leading to the main stairwell. Bracing themselves, they jogged down twenty-seven flights, both feeling the pangs of fatigue despite being in excellent physical condition. When they reached the bottom, Eleanor pointed at the fire exit.

"It will not be locked no matter what, for safety reasons, and they might have secured the lobby." When Amahle nodded, Eleanor pushed the bright red bar, triggering another alarm, and they stepped out onto the streets.

It was a cool day and had grown more overcast since they'd left the penthouse behind. The streets still bustled despite the obvious violence and chaos that had taken place within the building. Some local gawkers pointed at the devastation near the top of the high-rise, and others speculated about what the helicopter was doing.

"Now, where the hell is the cavalry?" Amahle grumbled. "They must be expecting us. All we have is that." She gestured at Eleanor's handgun. "We're in little condition to fight any serious opposition."

Seconds after she spoke, the helicopter buzzed around the far side of the building and came straight toward them. "Fuck," Amahle added.

Then two gunshots rang out, and sparks fell from the chopper's hull. It swayed to the side, almost swiping the building as the pilot struggled to get out of the line of fire while still maneuvering in the limited space between the downtown towers.

Eleanor's heart swelled. Their companions were still working to get them out of here. "It's Tyler. It must be."

"Probably," Amahle agreed. "Come." She jogged across the street, making for the lot where Daria had first parked, and Gage had dismounted, which was their Plan A meeting place once the mission was over. If the Autocutioner wasn't there, the Plan B location was another block down the street. It might have been a better option if there wasn't an aircraft after them.

By now, the civilians had begun to squawk and cringe at gunfire breaking out in the streets. Most of them fled in all directions, leaving the road relatively clear. The helicopter pilot had recovered from his slight shock, and the craft itself wasn't seriously damaged. It looped around and chased the two women again.

Eleanor glanced up and saw, to her horror, that Gus Freeman was leaning out the passenger's side of the chopper with an AR-10. He motioned for the pilot to bring them lower to the ground while still advancing on the Executioners.

"Oh, no," she muttered and picked up the pace.

The air was split again by bursts of gunshots. Gus fired a whole magazine at them but didn't hit much due to distance and the inherent difficulty of shooting from an unstable position while in midair. He still laughed and whooped like an enthusiastic spectator at a football game.

Someone cried out. Eleanor and Amahle looked behind them and saw an older man fall to the pavement with a hole in his leg. The chopper was gaining, but it looked like Commander Freeman was momentarily absorbed in reloading his rifle.

Amahle dashed over to the man. Against his pained protests, she dragged him aside where the corner of a storefront offered him partial cover. Then she tore a strip from her dress and pressed it against the wound. "Keep pressure on it."

Eleanor aimed her pistol at the helicopter, knowing it wouldn't do much, but it was better than nothing. She squeezed off all the shots that remained in the magazine, and about half of them struck the frame or windshield. None hit Gus, who seemed unconcerned with taking fire.

Amahle grabbed Eleanor, and they ducked around the corner toward the Plan A parking lot. Leaving the wounded man behind didn't feel right, but he would live as long as someone else helped him to a hospital soon. Plus, the Hellbreakers weren't after *him*.

Both women's spirits sank when they saw that their getaway vehicle wasn't in the lot. Either Daria had gone ahead to Site B, or she was driving around somewhere trying to intercept them.

Eleanor cursed herself for not insisting on wires and transistors for the mission. It would've made things far easier despite the risk of discovery.

They jogged on, shouting at lingering pedestrians to get out of the way and take cover. The helicopter rounded the corner behind them.

Eleanor looked and saw the chopper wheeling laterally so Gus could get a better shot at them. He'd pulled the machine gun back in, abandoning its use for now, and was relying only on his rifle. When it looked like he was about to fire, another man within the aircraft stopped him.

Eleanor squinted. She couldn't recognize him, but the only Hellbreakers she knew by name were Gus and his right-hand man, Nic, anyway. This other individual, whoever he was, had grabbed his commander's arm to stop him from firing into the crowd. It looked like they were shouting at each other, arguing vehemently. The noise of the chopper made it impossible to hear their words.

Gus paused as though thinking. Then with an abrupt jeer of scorn, he smashed the butt of his rifle into the side of the other man's head before hurling him out of the cockpit altogether. Eleanor gasped, watching the body tumble nearly ten meters to land atop a parked car, crunching its roof and shattering its windows.

Amazingly, the man wasn't dead. With movements that varied between stiff and spasmodic, he crawled off the top of the car, pulling himself across the rippled steel, down to the pavement, and reeled in pain as he rolled to the ground.

Amahle slowed and turned. "What happened?"

Before Eleanor could point out or explain, two black vans rounded the other corner up ahead, speeding toward them. Further complicating the situation was another chopper. *This* one, they felt sure, belonged to Executive Security. It appeared to be headed straight for the Hellbreakers' craft, intending to intercept and neutralize it while the ground forces swept up the Executioners.

Daria's Autocutioner suddenly roared out of an alley in front of them. Daria leaned out the window and frantically motioned for them to get into the back. It looked like Gage was next to her in the seat, toting a rifle.

Amahle hopped into the opened rear compartment at once. Eleanor hesitated.

The Hellbreakers and Execs' men were momentarily distracted by one another. She had a minute, at most. She hoped it would be enough.

Sucking in her breath, she sprinted toward the damaged car and the injured man crawling away from it. "Here!" she shouted at him and waved her arm so Daria would see her and bring the truck around to the man's position.

Behind her, it took a few seconds before Daria advanced. They all might have been arguing about what to do. Eleanor focused on the individual ahead of her. Big and tan-complected, he seemed dazed by his wounds and was simply moving by instinct down the street, probably with no real goal in mind.

Eleanor crouched by his side and took his arm. "Wait. We're here to help. Stop. Let us get you somewhere we can take care of you. Yes?"

He shook his head, coughed up a spot of blood, and did nothing else.

The truck backed up to their position, cutting across lanes. There was no other vehicle traffic in the immediate vicinity since the locals had finally gotten the hint that they needed to be somewhere else. Above them, Gus and the Executive chopper were shooting at each other and attempting to outmaneuver one another in the relatively tight space above the streets.

The Autocutioner's back door was still open. Amahle stood braced within it, her lips drawn back as she stared at Eleanor with a combination of fury and amazement. "What are you doing? He's one of them!"

Eleanor looked up. "He tried to stop Gus from shooting. He might know something. Here, help me get him in."

"You're crazy. We should put a bullet in his head." Nonetheless, Amahle hopped down and grabbed the man's collar with one hand, putting her other arm under his shoulder to pull him up over the bumper while Eleanor pushed from behind. He tensed up and moaned a couple of times. He almost certainly had broken bones. Still, they managed to get him off the street.

Daria snapped, "Do hurry up, please."

Gage leaned out the window and unloaded his rifle at the two approaching black security vans. He popped a tire on the lead one so the vehicle skewed, slowed its approach, and blocked off the other. It gave the Executioners enough time to close the back door while Daria took off at high speed in the opposite direction. They passed almost directly underneath the helicopters, but the two aircraft were still fighting.

Eleanor looked down at their passenger. He was still dazed, and each time he coughed, more blood flowed over his lips. He probably had a pierced lung. "We must get medical attention for him. We should take him to Dante."

Amahle glared at her. "He's a member of a group that tried to kill us. Even if he doesn't attack us once he comes to his senses, he'll spy on our operation and report back to his own. The best thing we can do is dump him in the parking lot at Atlantica General."

Eleanor looked past the South African. "Daria. It's your house. What do you say we do?"

After navigating another turn and passing a couple of honking motorists who seemed bewildered by why things were so chaotic, Daria sighed. "Let me think about it."

CHAPTER TEN

Eleanor sat on the couch, sipping tea. It should've occurred to her, she realized, that suggesting they take their captive back to Daria's house meant that someone else would end up getting the guest room.

Ty, sitting across from her, said, "I understand, but if he makes one wrong move, it's over. If he reaches for something too fast, I'll cut his hand off and won't bother to provide him with a tourniquet. If he tries to run for it, Amahle will put a bullet through his spine. In the type of situation we're in now, we *cannot* afford to take major risks with people we can't trust."

Amahle sat next to him, and her grim nod confirmed that she and Ty were in complete agreement on the matter.

Eleanor sighed. "Yes, I see. He is not Jori Singh—he doesn't possess strange powers beyond those of any strong young man who has combat training. He's badly wounded. He won't be able to go anywhere or pose much of a threat to us as long as we're smart. If he agrees to talk, there is a great deal of help he could give us."

Focusing on the issue of what to do with their guest helped take her mind off Zhu Dongfeng. In the desperate rush for escape and survival that had followed the helicopter attack, there hadn't been time to mourn him or reflect on what had happened in general. She knew that she *should* mourn him, but she didn't yet have her mental and emotional strength back up to the point where she could do so and remain functional.

Daria sat next to her. Although still somewhat wary, she was the only one, so far, who'd expressed open support of Eleanor's ideas. Since her house was still their hideout, she had a certain amount of clout in such matters. "Eleanor has a good point. Of course, he might not be *able* to talk anytime soon."

They all nodded. Dante was working on the man after they'd restrained him in the guest room's bed. He'd sedated the Hellbreaker with painkillers, which wouldn't make him much good for delivering detailed accounts of his group's activities.

There was no guarantee that he would survive anyway.

Eleanor glanced toward the kitchen, where the light was on as Gage sat at the table with a map of Atlantica and a chart and compass, attempting to plot out the location of Zero Site per Feng's instructions. Then she looked back at the others, particularly Ty and Amahle, and cleared her throat. She'd been trying to refine and expand upon her basic argument, and now that things were getting calm again, the time was right.

"We thought the Hellbreakers were all fanatics. That to a man, the absolute belief in their cause and the thirst for blood consumed them, even if it's that of innocents. Certainly, this is true of Augustus, as well as some of the others."

Ty and Amahle narrowed their eyes, but they were still listening. They didn't object or try to cut her off.

"What I saw suggests to me that this isn't the case for all of them. The man we saved tried to stop Augustus from shooting at us. I'm not sure if it was out of concern for myself and Amahle or because he was worried about them hitting bystanders. An older man took a bullet in the leg while Gus was spraying his gun at us a moment before."

Ty countered, "It could be a purely pragmatic concern. I've known people who didn't give a shit about innocent casualties on a moral level but were smart enough to understand that they made everything a lot more complicated later."

"Yes," Eleanor conceded, brushing hair from her face. "I know. It seemed more than that. He appeared upset. When Gus threw him out, how did the others in the helicopter feel about it? I wonder. Perhaps some of them could be...put on a more constructive path if they had better leadership. We might be able to turn some of them to our way of thinking."

No one responded at first. All paused to consider the idea. Their experiences with the Hellbreakers a month ago hadn't been particularly encouraging.

Daria was first to comment. "Yes, I support the idea, in a general way. We could always benefit from having more allies, but they must be stable and reliable. That, of course, is why the Hellbreakers failed as our allies so quickly the first time.

"You might be right that young Mr. Freeman and a handful of his most ardent supporters are the real problem. The rest could perhaps be rescued from Freeman's madness and come to be worthwhile allies against the Coven."

Ty glowered and flexed his hands. "Let's just say that I see your reasoning, but I'm *very* skeptical about it working out. If it does, what would we gain besides two or three extra guys? That could help, but it takes time to integrate new people into a working team. Right now, I think we're better off with a small group of people we know we can trust and who know how to get things done together."

Eleanor frowned, thinking of how it wasn't so long ago that Ty regarded her as a questionable asset at best. Still, that was in the past. She'd proven herself.

Amahle added, "I say again, he might play along to gain our trust, but slip away and tell Gus all about us as soon as he can. We cannot allow that to happen. We have enough problems dealing with the Coven without also having to fight those idiot Hell-breakers."

Daria cocked her head toward the kitchen. "Gage! I'm sure you've overheard most of this. How do you feel about it all?"

The Nepali replied, "I am reserving my judgment for now. I will support the group in whatever decision it reaches. I'm busy at the moment with mapping. Please, let us discuss this more later."

Daria snorted. "Your refusal to act as tiebreaker will be remembered and not forgiven, of course. We'll hear from Dante when he gets back, then."

Ty chimed in with, "How's that coming, Gage? What's the overall situation look like as far as how we get in and out, what our strategy will be depending on how well-defended the place is, and all that?"

Gage drew a deep breath. "Well, it will not be easy, I'm afraid. As Eleanor suggested before, Zero Site is near a mountain in the deep jungle. The terrain is quite rough. Approaching on land will not be easy. Since there is no access to the sea or from a lake or river, land will be our only option. Or air, perhaps, but that comes with difficulties of its own."

Eleanor added, "I don't know what the Executives do or don't have at this place, but it was always important to them. It would be unlikely for them to leave it unguarded."

"Indeed," Gage affirmed. "So, not only will we face the rigors of the terrain, but we should also count on having heavy defenses arrayed against us. It may prove to be the type of mission where the only realistic options are extreme stealth or overwhelming force. Or both, if at all possible."

Daria looked at the First Executioner. She'd wanted to offer her advice but thought it better to defer to a warfighter. Her expertise lay in the subtler arts.

Ty scratched his ear and stared a good thousand yards into the distance, reflecting on his vast store of knowledge of things he might rather forget. "If you have a well-defended, fortified position on high ground, storming it is always going to be a nightmare. The traditional, smartest way would be to bombard the place with lots of heavy artillery fire. Then, if at all possible, coordinate an air-drop of ground forces as close as you can get to overwhelm and secure the target."

"Yes," Gage agreed. He was also a veteran of formal military campaigns. "There is, however, the slight problem posed by our lack of artillery. I suppose we could think of something to get around that. It does restrict our options until we address that. Oh, and we also don't have any aircraft."

Daria shrugged. "This is Atlantica. Everything is for sale if you can afford it and know where to look. Artillery would be hard to get. Aircraft, though, can probably be arranged. I will talk to people I know. They can surely help, but I cannot say how long it might take."

Ty nodded. "Do so. As for not having artillery...we could possibly get by with a big, loud, colorful distraction. It might not do as much damage as a nice barrage of explosive shells, but at least it would serve the purpose of keeping them busy while we slip our people in. Of course, an aerial drop would still be dangerous. They always are."

Eleanor had an idea. "As we were discussing moments ago, there is the possibility that the Hellbreakers, or at least some of them, could aid us with this. They have access to at least one helicopter, do they not?"

She knew the others would probably reply in much the same way they already had, with a mixture of skepticism and cautious optimism. Still, having them as allies would alleviate some of the hardships they faced. No one could argue with the fact that they had an aircraft ready to go—unless Executive Security had successfully destroyed it during the battle near Feng's high-rise.

Amahle gave a slow headshake. "As we said, Gus must be removed from leadership for any such thing to work. He seems to inspire the other men in the group, for whatever reason, but I wouldn't trust him to drive a taxi or teach a child to fire a pellet gun, much less lead a band of armed renegades. Do we have the time for that? Do we have the resources, and can we risk it with so much else going on?"

Eleanor hated that she was right. "Those are good questions to ask ourselves," she admitted in a glum tone. "Still, it might be that the answer is *yes*."

Tyler interjected, "Let's hear what our guest has to say when he's able to talk again. That will clear things up. For now, we need to draw up plans for how to approach Zero Site, helicopter or no."

While he, Gage, and Amahle focused on that after Gage brought his maps into the living room, Eleanor and Daria drifted into the kitchen where Daria poured a drink for both of them. She kept the vodka content low in Eleanor's case and relatively moderate by her standards for hers, in either case mixing it with a minimal splash of seltzer and juice.

Eleanor downed the mix in a single gulp. "What do you think, Daria?" Her voice was thinner than usual as the alcohol fumes rose through her mouth and sinuses. "What should we do?"

The other woman's mood was pensive and neutral. She sipped her drink idly and looked out the window.

"We don't have enough information to make a final decision yet. Be patient. Sometimes with these sorts of things, there is no way to know what the right choice is until the last minute. It's important to be able to adapt and change one's mind. What is right and wise at one moment might not be at the next.

"As things shift around us and new possibilities open up, we might have to adjust to them as we go along. So, do not worry too much yet. In the morning we will likely have a better idea."

Eleanor rinsed out her empty glass and left it on the counter. "I hope you're right."

As they drifted back into the living room, footsteps came

down the hall, and Dante emerged from the shadows. He looked tired but noticeably resolute, as though he felt like he'd accomplished something and was determined to move on to the next task. Eleanor wanted to wrap her arms around his neck and kiss him but now wasn't the time.

Ty was the first to greet him, albeit in his usual no-nonsense style. "Welcome back, Dante. Report?"

The tall physician stopped at the edge of the room, leaned against the wall, and put his hands in his pockets.

"Well, he's doing better. For a guy who fell out of a damn helicopter, he wasn't doing too bad to begin with, but he needed some care. I patched up his broken ribs, put his shoulder back in its socket, and gave him some anti-inflammatories for the strains and abrasions. He should be ready to talk pretty soon. Obviously, I sedated the hell out of him. For the pain, and also to make sure he couldn't try anything and escape."

Amahle asked, "Will he be able to walk? Or should we all go into the room to speak to him there once he wakes up? Allowing him to roam around on his own wouldn't be a good idea."

"Agreed," Dante riposted, his tone a tad irritable. "Therefore, I propose that in about an hour, at least half of us go in there, see if we can wake him up, and interrogate him that way while he's still in restraints."

Ty snapped his fingers. "Good idea. You, Amahle, and Eleanor can handle that. He might recognize you, which could help get information out of him. Daria, Gage, and I will focus on the logistical and tactical aspects of the rest."

When Dante asked exactly how they meant to "interrogate" the man and what sorts of info they wanted to extract, Eleanor piped up. She repeated her idea about trying to sway the more moderate or sensible members of the Hellbreakers toward their cause to unseat Freeman and gain the rest of the group as allies.

Dante listened carefully to all she said, then spread his hands in a gesture of reluctant acceptance. "I'm not so sure that will work. Still, it's worth a try, and we don't necessarily have many better options, do we?"

Daria remarked, "You're correct. Gage, do you have any other comments?"

The Nepali exhaled slowly and adjusted his glasses. "As I said before, if the Hellbreakers have access to helicopters, they would prove to be most useful friends. Air support would be vital to our success unless we wish to put ourselves in even greater danger. I do have another idea that I wish to work on, however."

As he hesitated, seeming to reflect on the best way to explain himself, Ty prodded him. "Yeah? Say it."

Gage stood. "It will require me to talk more with our *other* guest. Meaning Jori Singh. I will have to run some tests. To say this idea of mine out loud, right now, might, ah...might not sound good. It would be better to wait until I know more. Please trust that I will fill you in on it soon."

Amahle arched an eyebrow. "*Might not sound good?* You cannot say that without expecting us to grow only more curious, Gage."

Gage chuckled. "Well, I would not want you youngsters to think that I have finally gone senile. Be patient."

CHAPTER ELEVEN

"His eyes fluttered." Dante pointed in case the two women beside him hadn't seen in the dim light. "Usually a good sign."

Amahle, leaning against the wall with her arms folded, quipped, "Yes, usually a person's eyes open when they wake up from sleep. Thank you, Doctor."

Dante smoothed his hair. "Don't mention it."

Eleanor stood quietly, watching the big man who lay before her. The bed barely contained his form since he was both tall and wide. Dante and Ty had lashed him in place with an assortment of ropes, zip ties, and bungee cords. He wasn't going anywhere, no matter what sort of mood he might be in when consciousness fully returned.

Their captive squirmed, twitched his limbs, and tried to move from side to side, but the resistance of his bonds stopped him. It was difficult to tell if he was attempting to roll over on his side or if his body had the automatic stretch reaction many people experience upon awakening. His eyes drifted open.

"Uhhh..." he moaned, blinking and continuing to wriggle in place, as though trying to figure out where he was and what was going on.

Dante had placed a glass of water on a nightstand next to the bed. He walked over and took it in hand. "Good morning. Or evening. You might remember falling out of a helicopter. We picked you up and took you into our custody. I'm a doctor, and I got you all patched up. You're going to stay tied to the bed until we have a little talk first. Do you think you can handle that?"

The man turned his head on the pillow and stared at Dante, his vision coming back into focus and his brain returning to normal functionality as sleep and the sedatives wore off. "Yes," he stated.

"Good." Dante approached him, lowered the glass to his mouth, and allowed him to drink half of the water before pulling it away. "You'll get the other half after you answer a couple of questions."

The man frowned and made a faint growling sound in the back of his throat but only said, "Sure, whatever, mate. Ask away."

He had an Australian accent. From what Dante could recall, the Hellbreakers were mostly American and Aussie troops who had been in Vietnam but deserted their posts to come to Atlantica, originally as mercenaries for the Executives. The man was well over six feet tall, even taller than Dante, and looked almost twice as wide, mostly owing to his broad skeletal build and substantial musculature. Awake and moving, he seemed far more powerful. He had moderately dark skin, hair, and eyes, and Dante suspected that he might be of mixed heritage, probably Australian Aboriginal and English.

Dante exchanged a glance with Eleanor and Amahle, who nodded at him. Looking back at their prisoner, he inquired, "First of all, what's your name?"

The man didn't hesitate to provide an answer. "Walter Oxebowe. Everyone calls me Ox." He tried to swallow, but despite the few ounces of water he'd ingested, his throat seemed dry and his mouth sticky. "Hard to talk, mate." Though clear-headed, it was also obvious that he was still groggy.

Dante let him drink the rest of the water. "I was going to hold it off until you'd told us a couple more things, but I feel generous. Anyway, nice to meet you, Ox. I guess you know who we are."

Once he'd emptied the glass and Dante had taken it away, Ox replied, "Yeah, I do. You're the Executioners. We were tryin' to kill you. I suppose I don't deserve for you to have scraped me off the sidewalk like that and give me medical care and all, besides. But...thanks. I appreciate it."

Eleanor took a step forward. "I saw what you did. I saw why Mr. Freeman threw you out of the helicopter. That's one of the things we wish to talk to you about."

Coming closer, she saw how badly messed up he was. In addition to the myriad bandages Dante had put on him, there was also a nasty laceration on his face—cruciform, she noted, with vague discomfort. The results of having been bashed in the face with Gus's rifle stock. Like many of his followers, Commander Freeman had added religious iconography to his weapon. In this case, a cross embedded in the butt of the gun.

Ox cleared his throat. "Yeah. I don't know what came over me. Might have been a stupid idea, though. After all, look how I ended up." He turned his eyes sideways toward Dante. "Doctor. How bad am I? What are all my injuries? I can't tell. I'm only feelin' a dull pain all through me. Can't trace it to any one place, you know?"

Crossing his arms, Dante stated in a soft but dispassionate tone, "You had a dislocated shoulder, four broken ribs, a sprained ankle, and a whole boatload of bruises, abrasions, and lacerations. You're lucky you're not crippled or dead.

"Since you seem to be in good health, my prognosis is that you'll make a full recovery, but you're not going to be having too much fun for a while. Of course, you're not leaving that bed until you answer the rest of this nice lady's questions." He gestured at Ms. Cervantes.

Pouting a bit, the man looked back at Eleanor, who resumed her interview.

"You said you don't know what came over you. Why? What made you feel that way and caused you to act as you did?"

She tried to avoid any major insinuation in her word choices or too much of an urging tone. She didn't want the man to guess that she hoped for a particular answer. If so, he might simply play the game of telling her what she wanted to hear. What they needed was pure honesty. Only with that could they accomplish a proper assessment of his mental state—and that of the rest of the Hellbreakers, perhaps.

Ox closed his eyes, and his mouth wrinkled up as if he'd bitten into a lemon. When he opened his eyes again, his gaze darted around. It was as though he assumed someone was listening in and that Eleanor's questions were a trap designed to tease out any semblance of disloyalty or incorrect attitude.

"Commander Gus," he began. "He...was firin' into a crowd. Hittin' innocent people and the like. I couldn't stand to see it. That's not how soldiers are supposed to fight. You kill the enemy, not regular spackers who got in the way, is all. I tried to stop him and talk him out of doin' all that sort of thing. I guess he didn't agree, did he? He's not good about takin' criticism. Thinks anyone who speaks up is either a coward or with the enemy."

Eleanor gave a slow nod in response. "That is what I would've guessed, based on what I saw. You grabbed his arm. Then the two of you were shouting and arguing. That was the last thing before he knocked you out of the chopper."

Ox's jaw muscles tightened and, abruptly, his whole demeanor changed. He was steeling himself for something, growing stoic and defiant.

"So, the other thing you need to know is that it wasn't the first time he did somethin' like that. Before, I didn't try to stop him, but I should've. I'm guilty of lettin' him do it. And here you are—the Executioners. 'Justice Before Mercy,' that's your saying, isn't it? So, pass your judgment, and be done with it, I say."

Amahle let out a soft, dry chuckle. "Maybe later, Ox. We're not in that business right now. In case you hadn't noticed, the Executives have washed their hands of us and they no longer use us to do their dirty work. We're now working for ourselves. Whatever crimes you might have committed in the past, or allowed to happen, are not our present concern. We have other things to worry about."

Ox stared back at her for what felt like a full minute, then he looked at Eleanor and Dante in turn, assessing their reaction, their honesty. None flinched or said a thing.

The big man relaxed. Slightly. "Aye, I suppose you do. The Coven wants us all dead. That much is for sure. So why exactly did you take me alive and try to nurse me back to health? Doesn't seem like you'd do it purely out of the goodness of your hearts."

Eleanor began pacing beside his bed, walking the short distance between Amahle and Dante, then turning to repeat it.

"What we wish to know Ox, is how you feel about the rest of your comrades. To be more specific, I suspect that you might not be the only one uncomfortable with some of what your organization has done. Surely, not every man in the unit is as callous and maniacal as your commander. I understand that you're motivated by religious faith to stop the Coven. What I ask you now is this. Does *every* member of the Hellbreakers believe that they can do good in the world by killing everything that moves? Or are you the only dissenter?"

His face scrunched up a bit, and his steely, standoffish demeanor returned. "Why do you want to know that?"

He couldn't have been such a fool as to fail to guess the general motive behind their inquiry. He wanted to stall, Eleanor concluded, and find out more about the Executioners' intentions before he revealed too much. Whether this was out of loyalty to his former partners, or spite, or simple self-preservation, she couldn't be sure.

Eleanor ceased her pacing, about halfway between her partners, and folded her hands behind her back. "Let me approach the issue from a different direction, Mr. Oxebowe. Can you confirm, or deny, what I'm about to say?"

She didn't wait for him to respond since he didn't know what she was getting at anyway—yet.

"You men came to Atlantica from your terrible experiences in Southeast Asia. You sought work with the Executives, hiring your guns to them without realizing the trouble that would result or the depth of corruption in their organization. You discovered the existence of the Coven of Miracles and were horrified by it, vowing to destroy its power. So you went rogue."

That much was affirmatively true, according to everything they'd heard from Gus himself. By restating what they already knew, she hoped to lull Ox into a sense of complacent inevitability and get him to cooperate.

Ox only stared back at her, sullen and feeling his injuries, by the look of it. She had expected as much.

"Once you left the care of the Execs, you had few friends and a great many enemies. All around us, it seems that Atlantica is falling apart and things are changing for the worse. There is more tyrannical authority in some places and greater chaos and anarchy in others. In such an environment, you men desired leadership. So you accepted Augustus Freeman as your commander."

Dante gave her a sly look. He understood what she was getting at.

Eleanor went on, "Gus was charismatic and had the courage of his convictions, being willing to fight along with his men and with a great thirst for victory. Yet, as you said only a moment ago, he rules with an iron fist. He seems to care nothing for the harm he causes to innocent people in pursuit of his goals. So I ask you, Ox—have I described the situation within the ranks of the Hellbreakers accurately?"

He glared back at her, then relaxed and let out a long sigh. "Yes."

"I see." She started pacing again. "It's understandable that you would want an unyielding person as your leader in such difficult times. Now that same man has tried to kill you simply because you urged him to exercise greater sense and compassion."

Ox looked down at his chest. He still gave off a cantankerous, hesitant vibe, but there was a growing sense of resignation and openness about him at the same time.

"Yeah, that's right," he muttered. "Never thought I'd see it come to that. With Commander Gus... A lot of us feel indebted to him. He started the whole thing. The rebellion against the Execs was his idea. He organized us and gave us somethin' to fight for when it seemed like we would either have to run away from this damn island or do things that went against our beliefs."

Amahle remarked, "Well, it's good to have principles, is it not?"

Getting the point easily enough, Ox continued, "He keeps gettin' more and more...indiscriminate, shootin' anyone who gets in his way and not wantin' to be bothered with figurin' out who to shoot and who *not* to.

"Oh, a few Americans mentioned somethin' about a massacre over in Vietnam that he was involved with. Helped wipe out a whole village or somethin' like that. It's part of why he left the U.S. Army. They were about to investigate it."

The others stayed quiet as the mood darkened, and Ox wrestled with some invisible foe. "We started this for the sake of doin' the Lord's work. Maybe the Hellbreakers have been misled by a devil this whole time."

Then his voice changed, growing more formal and sonorous, and he intoned, "*Every kingdom divided against itself shall be made desolate: and every city or house divided against itself shall not stand.*

And if Satan cast out Satan, he is divided against himself: how then shall his kingdom stand? And if by Beelzebub cast out devils, by whom do your children cast them out?"

Eleanor recognized the passage at once from the Book of Matthew. She responded and was at first surprised to find Dante echoing her in unison, but he, too, had been raised Catholic and would've been taught the same things.

"But if I by the Spirit of God cast out devils, then is the kingdom of God come upon you. Or how can anyone enter into the house of the strong, and rifle his goods, unless he first bind the strong? And then he will rifle his house. He that is not with me, is against me: and he that gathered not with me, scattereth."

The big man looked at each of them with widened eyes. There was something new growing within them. Respect and understanding, Eleanor thought, although she couldn't be sure. Amahle stood at the rear of the room, holding herself apart. She had no religious beliefs that Eleanor was aware of. Still, she seemed to appreciate how much such things mattered to some people.

Ox drew a long, slow, deep breath. "All right, mates. Maybe I can trust you after all. You understand why we're doin' this. It's to stop the Coven. So, if you can trust me, I can get you in. If we're all lucky, maybe together we can get Gus to step down or kick him out."

Dante added, "With the Hellbreakers and the Executioners working together again, and being smarter about it this time...the Coven will have a much, much harder time of things. I'd almost feel bad for them if it was anyone else."

Amahle had taken a seat beside Tyler and rested a hand on his arm, both to soothe him and to better judge his reactions. She'd opted to leave the bulk of the "presentation" and the persuasive element of the speech to Eleanor and Dante, who were better at such things than she was, anyway.

In addition to Ty, Daria and Gage were also present. Everyone had gathered in the living room except Ox. Dante had left him in bed for now, but with the promise that he'd be free soon enough.

As Dante and Eleanor finished their sales pitch, the vibe in the room wasn't as warm as one might have hoped.

Ty shook his head. "I don't know. What he said makes sense, but it could be a ruse. Or he might have a change of heart. We don't know this guy. We know nothing about him or his track record. I don't remember seeing him with the Hellbreakers before, but I gather that they had reserves the whole time and didn't bring their entire force to the water treatment plant. I mean, it could be a great opportunity. There's also a lot of ways it could go seriously wrong."

Daria looked at Ty and nodded before turning her face back to Eleanor and Dante. "Yes, while I support Eleanor's proposal in theory, we must consider the details. If it fails, it could well be worse than if we had not tried at all. As Mr. Katakura says, we haven't had time to observe how this man behaves and how honest he might be."

Eleanor and Dante looked crestfallen and exasperated. Their shoulders slumped. Observing them, Amahle could imagine the frustration they must feel at having put so much effort into their pitch only to encounter the same doubts from the others.

Amahle spoke up instead. "Yes, it is risky. I believe this man Ox is sincere. Nothing told me that he was lying. At first, he tried to say as little as possible because he didn't trust *us*. He opened up as time went on. I think he is a good and honest man at heart."

Ty gave her a skeptical glance, but the set of his mouth suggested that he was warming to the idea.

Gage interceded. "I trust Dante and Eleanor to work with this man and bring our plan to fruition. Yes, things can always go wrong. It sounds as though our chances are better than we'd feared. Besides, we must face the harsh reality that we are only six. We could benefit greatly from backup."

Sighing, Tyler said, "Okay, we'll give it a shot. But we can't put everyone on the job at once. We're going to have to divide up duties. There are a *lot* of preparations to be made if we have any hope of getting into Zero Site."

"Yes," Gage agreed. "Dante and Eleanor, I am afraid that you must handle Ox and the Hellbreakers alone. It sounds like he has reason to trust the two of you more than the rest of us. I must have the help of two other Executioners to acquire some, er...resources and materials...from the Metro area. The last of us must stay behind to watch over Jori Singh."

Daria pursed her lips. "Good idea. Any volunteers for guard duty?"

Amahle raised her hand. "I will stay. To be honest, that fight in Mr. Dongfeng's building wasn't easy, and I would rather have time to recover. I will be vigilant. He will not escape on my watch."

Singh had been quiet and given them no trouble since the ugly incident with Eleanor. They checked on him every hour or two and found nothing amiss. They all knew well how unwise it was to underestimate him.

Ty looked at everyone in turn. "All right, then. Sounds good. We have our assignments. Now, we make it all happen."

CHAPTER TWELVE

It seemed far too dark for this time of day. Such was the nature of things in places like this—places found in any large city, which had been all but forgotten about by most of the populace. For those few who remembered, such districts were generally agreed not to be forgotten but forbidden.

"Man," Dante mused, his voice low and breathy. "This has to be one of the oldest parts of the city. I bet it dates back to the island's initial discovery. Not in the war, I mean. After that. Which, come to think about it, was only like what, ten years ago or less? Nothing compared to New York. But still. It sure *feels* old compared to the rest of the town."

They'd taken one of the disguised Autocutioners, with Dante behind the wheel and Eleanor in the passenger's seat. Behind them, Ox stood, filling the narrow space before the rear cab with his massive body, yet still gripping the seats for support.

Dante's professional opinion as a doctor was that the man should've stayed in bed for at least a couple more days. However, they were operating under extraordinary circumstances, and they needed his help. To his credit, the big Australian had agreed.

"Aye." He gestured weakly. "Keep goin' straight ahead. There you go. Up by that fence at the back of that lot there, park the truck. We'll have to go on foot the rest of the way. Too narrow for this big truck. We'd make too much noise, besides. I want us to get in a fair distance before anyone starts a commotion."

Eleanor grimaced. "I trust your judgment, Ox, but we won't have much cover or protection on foot. I hope you know what you are doing."

"I do," he insisted. "If we walk in like you're my prisoners, there won't be no problems. Ought to get us in deep enough to talk to the commander. Of course, that's where things will get rough."

The Autocutioner crept ahead toward the dirty, abandoned lot. All around them were storage lots, built quickly and cheaply in the first days of Atlantica's development to hold shipping containers and construction machinery.

Surrounding the lots, or in some cases rising amid them, were blocks of low-grade housing intended to give the workers someplace to live for a few months, or maybe a year at most, while they labored on various projects. Most had since abandoned them, but it looked as though poor itinerants or members of the island's often transient working class had reclaimed a third of them. They then slowly left the blocks behind again when maintaining their poor-quality materials and barely adequate utilities became too challenging.

Dante slowed the truck to a stop, parked, and patted himself down. He had his 1911 pistol hidden in his waistband and two spare magazines. It wasn't much but far better than nothing. He and Eleanor didn't dare take long guns.

Ms. Cervantes had her Walther. She'd considered taking the Browning she'd acquired at the clinic given its greater firepower, but she was too petite for it to be easily concealable on her person.

Ox alone had a serious weapon. Since the Hellbreakers often used the same AR-10 rifles that were the standard main firearm of both the Executioners and Executive Security, there was nothing particularly suspicious about his having borrowed one from his new friends' private armory.

Dante looked at his partners. "All right. Let's go."

He and Eleanor dismounted first, with Ox following and making a show of holding his rifle on them. The plan was to use a cover story whereby Ox had captured the two Executioners and was now bringing them back to Gus to trade their lives. In return, he would ask for the restoration of his good standing...until such time that they could depose Gus and usurp his authority over the Hellbreakers.

Ox gestured for them to walk around the fence and deeper into the maze of empty lots and decaying buildings. The structures grew taller and the walking space narrower as they pressed on. The whole area seemed to be deserted, save for rats and birds. Atlantica's animal wildlife had largely abandoned the metro area since people were quick to eliminate pests, but rats always found a way to survive *everywhere*.

Total silence reigned save the slight noises of the scampering vermin. Otherwise, they could hear little but their footsteps. Although it was barely noon, the sun faded as the dense mass of dilapidated buildings closed in around them.

Something felt wrong. Dante and Eleanor both noticed it, an eerie sensation of not being as alone as they thought they were. It faded from time to time, only to flare back up a moment later.

Dante glanced off to the side, moving only his eyes while keeping his head motionless and aimed straight forward. He saw a flitting dark shape, a clear blur of motion. If the brief impression of what little he could discern was accurate, the dim light glinted off a pair of eyes.

There was no longer any doubt. Someone was watching them.

"We're not alone," he whispered. "People are hiding all around here and keeping an eye on us."

Eleanor did much the same as he had—she observed her surroundings without moving her head. "Yes. I think you're right. I had a feeling that someone was looking at us as soon as we came into this place. Ox, what do you think?"

The big Australian didn't reply at first. He only kept striding ahead, attempting not to limp or stumble as he worked around the painful limitations of his injuries, guiding them deeper into the ramshackle labyrinth of shadows.

"Yeah." His voice was a low rumble, like distant thunder. "They watch things closely. Most of my mates have experience scouting, doing guard duty, stuff like that. They know we're here. And we're surrounded. No getting out of it."

Dante cleared his throat. "That's not encouraging, Ox. Not at all. If your plan to dupe them into thinking you captured us works, great. If even one crack appears in it and they all swarm us, we're fucking dead. You realize that, right?"

He gave a slight twitch of his good shoulder, which they supposed qualified as a shrug. "Aye. It's the only way, though. Don't have any other chance, really."

Eleanor felt the gnaw of anxiety grow sharper, and part of her wanted to turn and bolt back the way she had come, running wildly out of this forgotten slum and hoping the others would be smart enough to do the same.

When she turned a faux-casual glance toward Ox's face, she immediately felt the worst of her panic calm itself and fade. Something in the man's eye was curiously reassuring. Confidence that verged on the lazy, even if he, too, was tense with the knowledge of how dire things might turn.

He knew it was going to work. Or so it seemed.

Speaking past him, Eleanor said to Dante, "Try not to worry. Ox knows his comrades well. If they wanted to kill us, they've already surrounded us, have they not? They could have done so by now. They wish to wait and see why we're here."

Dante blew the air in his lungs out between flapping lips as his jaw muscles rippled, then tightened. "I'm glad the two of you seem to know something I don't. Since I'm not feeling too good about this. If I had known the bastards would be thick as fleas as soon as we stepped in, I'd have at least liked to bring my shotgun."

Ox said, "Trust me."

Ahead, beyond a half-collapsed fence and penned in by a temporary housing block on two sides and a defunct radio tower on another was a large storage shed, or perhaps a garage. It looked utterly abandoned. No lights burned in the windows, no cars were parked outside, and the debris that had drifted there over the years appeared largely undisturbed.

Ox gestured with his chin. "There. That's where we're going."

"If you say so, pal." Dante sighed. "I guess it would make a nice hiding spot since it sure as hell doesn't look like a whole military unit could fit inside it."

The big Australian gave a faint wave. "Keep your voice down."

He led them along the side of the building, bypassing the main, vehicle-sized door for a standard human-sized one. To the surprise of Dante and Eleanor, a modern keypad hid next to the knob under a clever small awning and some strategically placed boards.

Ox punched in a few numbers on the pad. When he finished, a tiny green light flashed, and something *clicked* on the other side of the door. No sooner had Ox twisted the knob than someone else yanked it the rest of the way open and a rifle's muzzle aimed at his face.

Eleanor gasped, expecting a flash of fire, a thunderous *crack*, and an ignominious end to all they'd worked so hard for. The guard within the building held back. Still, Ox froze. At an urging from the man within the shed, he stepped aside. Then two more sentries rushed out of the building while a fourth man appeared from a hidden position somewhere behind them.

Dante and Eleanor raised their hands as men surrounded them. The guard who'd pointed his rifle at Ox and the one who'd lain in ambush nearby were fully armored. The other two wore only casual clothes. Rather than AR-10's, one had a pistol while the other had what looked like a sawed-down bolt-action rifle, perhaps an Obrez Mosin-Nagant.

The man who'd opened the door was about Dante's height and had a bushy brown mustache. He chortled. "Well, Ox is back. We kinda thought you were dead. Of course, Gus isn't exactly going to be happy to see you since you dying was the whole point of what he did. Who are these two? Wait, let me guess."

The guy with the sawed-off rifle said, "Executioners. The doctor and the receptionist lady who worked for the Coven."

Eleanor snapped, "I was not a receptionist."

"Whatever," the man responded. "Burk, we taking them in?"

The mustachioed man nodded. "Yeah. Got to hold onto them until a decision can be made about what to do with them. By better minds than ours, right? Ha."

The guards guided the trio into the large shed, which looked as dilapidated and unused on the inside as it did from without. Once the door was closed behind them, Burk and Sawed-Off held their guns on the prisoners while the other two frisked them for weapons. To Eleanor's consternation, they found both her pistol and Dante's with ease.

Ox told them, "Sorry about that. I snuck into their truck and ambushed them there, didn't have time to disarm them, especially since there's only one of me. Figured you spackers could handle it when we got in here."

"Oh?" Burk's tone had a jeering note. "You captured them? Bringing them back as a peace offering, is that it? Well, who knows what Gus will say. I guess you're smarter than you look. I have to take your rifle, though, until he gives the order to give it back."

Ox scowled, but when the men didn't relent, he complied.

With all three now bereft of firearms, Burk led them to a pile of rusted tin sheets out in the middle of the floor but not far from a wall. He kicked the sheets aside to reveal a hidden hatch leading underground. The guy with the pistol opened it and led the way while Burk had Ox, Dante, and Eleanor climb down next. Then he and the other two guards followed.

Eleanor's breath drew sharply in when she saw everything that lay beneath the surface. The Hellbreakers had hidden well. All of them.

The basement was at least three times the size of the shed above it and probably stretched below the housing complex next door, as well. It had sparse furnishings, but it did have a generator and several bare lightbulbs hanging from the ceiling, which provided bright yellow light in the gloomy depths.

The whole space smelled of sweat. The reason was obvious. In addition to the damp warmth of the air, people crammed the cellar. Eleanor estimated around thirty besides the four who had captured them. All were a rough-and-tumble bunch, lacking in polish, but with the killer eyes she would've expected from hardened ex-soldiers.

The Hellbreakers' numbers were greater than she would've guessed. They had only a handful left after the debacle at the Coven's so-called water treatment plant, but as her friends had intuited, they'd only taken a partial force, leaving many of their other men in reserve.

Furthermore, gun racks and crates of ammo on the far side of the chamber, along with a smattering of explosives and other tools and gear, suggested that they'd been busy gathering supplies. They lacked the lavish funding that Exec Security received. In a clash with the Coven's servants, they would still be able to make a good fight of it.

Three dozen equipped with a respectable arsenal was far better than half a dozen, Eleanor reflected. If they could force Freeman out of his role and gain the rest as allies...

She shook her head. It was important not to get ahead of themselves. She and Dante were only two people, and if they could trust Ox, they had three now versus thirty should things go badly for them.

Given the Hellbreakers' numbers and how heavily armed they were, it was clearer than ever that the Executioners couldn't hope to take on them *and* the Coven at the same time.

Someone shouted, "Hey! It's the Executioners! Ox brought 'em back."

Another man added, "Fuck you! Lapdogs of the beast. Turncoats!"

Someone threw something, a small piece of rotten wood. Eleanor turned her head and avoided being struck across the face with it but felt it tear through the lower part of her hair and nick her shoulder as it passed.

Another couple of guys spewed off curses and tossed an empty can at Dante. He deflected it with his forearm and ignored them as they made a mixture of religious condemnations and crude insults.

Eleanor tried to ignore it all. The anger in the air was thick, and it was always painful to be hated in such an unashamed way. She would have to get through this if they were ever to resolve the larger situation.

One thing she noticed that impressed itself upon her attention amid the flood of verbal abuse was that Augustus Freeman was nowhere in sight.

Burk prodded each of them with his rifle. "Go stand in that corner and wait. When Gus gets back, we'll decide what to do with you."

One of the other Hellbreakers near the rear of the crowd yelled, "That's a load of shite, Burk. We know what he'd do, might as well get started ourselves, aye? Pull their damn bloody finger-nails out and bash their heads to paste."

Two or three others laughed and cheered. The rest seemed uncertain, but a disturbing number of them smirked at the thought.

Someone else said, "Nah, we could always stab 'em each in the gut, tie a rock to 'em, and dump them in the canal with their hands and feet tied. If they're still alive when they go in the water...too bad. Won't be for long."

"Let's beat the shit out of them," another grunted. "See if they can take it. I heard they're tough. Might as well put it to the test."

By now, all three were in the corner, with Burk and two other armed guards standing over them. The sea of roiling bodies and angry faces beyond made no move to attack them. Yet.

Eleanor tried to remain calm. She'd been through a lot, but something about the thought of being tortured by a mob after being already rendered helpless was nearly unbearable. She couldn't think of anything to say because it took all her self-control to avoid panicking, breaking down, and pleading for mercy.

Burk turned away from the trio and strode back into the crowd, grumbling, "Yeah, yeah, shut up, you bunch of punks. Gus will make the final decision..." He didn't seem overly committed to enforcing it, though.

Someone else, a wiry but dangerous-looking man of about twenty-five with wild eyes, stepped forth. "Ox, what are you doing back? If Gus tried to throw your ass out of a chopper, you don't belong here anymore. And *they* sure don't, either."

Ox stared back at the man. His face was still bandaged, as was his chest, and he had been moving slowly and carefully to account for his injuries. They barely diminished the sense of power he conveyed. "We wait for Gus," he stated.

The wild-eyed man looked at Dante. "Not if that fuck keeps looking at me like that! *Hey!*"

While Dante braced himself, the wiry man sprang forth.

He didn't get far. Ox stepped in with greater speed than would've seemed right for a wounded man of his size. His sledge-like fist lashed out, catching the attacker across the face and spinning him a good two hundred and seventy degrees around. He crashed into the opposite wall and then fell unconscious to the floor.

The room went silent. Ox looked at his comrades, his jaw set and his eyes blazing.

"Why you protectin' them, Ox?" asked an Australian. "Thought you *captured* their arses."

Ox grunted, "I did. But not 'til after they saved my life. After Gus knocked me out of the chopper, they patched me up and sent me on my way. I owe them at least a fair judgment. If Gus can even give one after what *he's* done. Which means none of you lot are goin' to hurt or kill them until we hear from the commander."

The guy with the Obrez sputtered, "What the hell? That's a load of crap."

Ox ignored him and instead pointed at a particular man, one of the youngest of the group, midway back in the crowd. "You. Szymanski. You were in the chopper. You saw what Gus was doin'. And what I did that made him hit me and throw me out. Tell everyone else."

A hush fell over the chamber as Szymanski swallowed a lump in his throat. He looked nervous and uncertain, with sweat rolling down his forehead and temples. "Ah," he stammered, "I don't really remember."

Ox turned to another. "Chavez. You too. Tell them what you saw."

Chavez, a portly man of around thirty and one of the oldest of the group, shifted and looked at the floor. "As you say, Ox, we wait for Gus to get back. Ask him then."

The big Australian snorted. "I'm disappointed in the lot of

you. Here, look at this." He raised a hand and yanked off the bandage on his face. Everyone's eyes fixed on the wound and the unmistakable cruciform outline in his flesh. "You think that just happened? For no reason, eh?"

Szymanski exhaled, then confessed, "Yeah, it's coming back to me. Gus was...shooting into a crowd, trying to hit the Executioners. Ox tried to, uh, talk him out of it. They fought, and Ox fell out."

Chavez added, "The commander tell us, Ox is as good as dead, no? Said we would get the same if we told about it and made him look bad. Too important for him to have the respect of everyone here. Ox was the one who did wrong, he said."

Ox took a half-step forward, causing the guy with the Obrez and the others to tense, but they didn't stop him yet. Raising his arms, Ox announced, "I'm tired, mates. I'm tired of servin' out of fear, of havin' Gus threaten us all the time and make us do terrible things. He doesn't care who he kills, as long as he gets to kill. Don't pretend like you don't know I'm right, either."

Eleanor saw and felt the unstable mixture of emotions. Dread of what might happen to them for having such a conversation in the first place, anger at Ox's apparent disloyalty and defiance. Most encouragingly, vague yearning for what it might mean if he were right, after all.

Ox went on, "That's not why I came here. That's not why any of us came here. We wanted to get away from all the senseless murder going on in Southeast Asia, didn't we? Do somethin' good, instead? With the Hellbreakers, we joined up to stop the Coven, not to be as bad as they are. I'm tired of runnin', and I'm tired of seein' good men dyin' for bad causes. If any of you is as tired as me, then I say it's time we start livin' up to the principles we claimed to uphold, back when we bloody well started this little outfit."

Eleanor's heart thumped, and her spirits rose. Although it was a hard sell, Ox was making inroads with them. Nearly all of them knew, deep down, that he was correct. At the very least, they were questioning themselves and the course they were on.

They had a chance. Some of the Hellbreakers might recognize what had to happen.

Then the hatch opened.

Szymanski spun and froze. "Oh, *shit*," he hissed.

CHAPTER THIRTEEN

Clanking and rustling sounds filled the basement as men, four of them from the looks of it, descended and immediately took up positions near the back of the chamber. All were in full armor and armed with rifles, as though they'd been on patrol or come back for a battle. Or, maybe, as though they'd expected to *enter* a battle.

At the head of the quartet was Augustus Freeman. His round, dark, boyish face held its customary confidence and intense energy. Yet, there was something around him, emanating from within him, like an electric charge—vicious anger, a cruel contempt.

His eyes scanned the whole room, slowly taking in each individual, and he reacted no differently to any one person than any other. The presence of Ox, Eleanor, and Dante neither perturbed nor shocked him more or less than the more expected presence of his men.

Gus handed his rifle to the man by his side. Then he extended both arms, cupped his hands, and began applauding with slow, deliberate motions, the clapping sound the only thing audible.

"Who knew," he intoned, "that big dumb Ox was an orator? I

sure didn't. Did he rehearse that speech? Did the Executioners write it for him? Did the beast write it for him and whisper it into his ear? *That's* what I'm wondering, friends.

"What kind of man would try to sabotage us? Why would he do such a thing? When what we're doing is so, so important. And when I'm the only one who's helped us all to pull through, time and again."

He paused as half the men hung their heads in half-ashamed discomfort. Eleanor suspected that the ones most affected were those who had been on the proverbial fence. Those loyal to Gus were merely glad to see him, whereas those who had made up their minds to defy him were unaffected.

It was impossible to be sure what anyone was feeling, who might or might not declare for Ox and the Executioners if things got ugly. There were too many ways in which the whole affair could descend into a melee of chaos.

Ox stood firm, shaking his head. "You organized us at first, Gus, and we followed you because it seemed like you had all the answers and would get us to where we needed to go. Over time, you've turned into a madman. You don't know what you're doin' anymore, mate. You kill for the sake of killin'."

Eleanor watched the reactions. Some of the men were moving closer to Ox, closer to the rear corner where he stood, and Dante and herself behind them. In addition to the three bodyguards he had with him, Gus had also drawn about half a dozen in his direction. The others languished in the middle of the chamber, waiting to see what happened.

Gus pointed at the Australian. "No, Ox. I know *exactly* what I'm doing, which is taking the fight to the beast. We've seen a level of evil—pure, shameless, unadulterated evil—that cannot be compromised with or forgiven. We must destroy it at any cost. Anyone who aids the beast is just as bad. We'll shed no tears for them.

"People who are not involved, furthermore, need to get out of the way. Our mission is too important to abandon because someone took a stray bullet. The entire world is at stake here, Ox!"

Faces looked back and forth between the two of them. Emotions were high, but there was no indication that a specific mood or conclusion dominated the crowd. Everyone was waiting to see how the battle of wills between Walter Oxebowe and Augustus Freeman played out.

Ox crossed his arms. While Gus was already growing shriller and more dramatic, Ox remained calm and stoic. "No. The Coven has to be stopped, yeah. We all agree on that. But killin' innocents is the worst possible way to go about it, Gus. Deep down, I think we all know that, and I think a lot of us have been wonderin' why it keeps happening so much."

"Shut up!" Gus shouted. "Ever since we left our posts, I've steered us in the right direction. You owe everything to my leadership. No one ever debated my role as commander. I've taken care of you all. Look at how many victories we have! We've struck multiple blows against the Coven in a matter of months. Their days are numbered. Stick with me, and we'll finish them off."

There were cracks in his confidence. He asserted his importance so loudly, Eleanor saw, because part of him doubted that it was true.

As he ranted, Gus and his bodyguards kept moving closer to the back corner. The other men parted, giving him space to advance.

Ox held firm. "We've had a loss for every victory. A lot of our mates got wiped out at that facility a month ago. Lost a few men the other day too, if I remember right. The regular people in Atlantica, all of them are goin' to remember *us* as the people who sprayed bullets everywhere. What do you suppose they think about that, eh? Think they'll turn to the Coven to protect them?"

Gus stormed forth, clearing the last of the distance between them with two long strides, and Eleanor tried not to gasp as the young commander drew a pistol from his side and aimed it at Ox's face. It was a Colt 1911, much like Dante's, and it trembled slightly in Gus's grasp.

"You're too stupid to understand," Gus asserted. He barely seemed aware of Eleanor and Dante. "Do you think there aren't reasons why I was elected commander, and you weren't? Hmm?" He waved his free hand. "You're a soldier. Do as you're ordered. Don't fucking question me. I should've shot you after I threw you out. You're endangering the whole campaign!"

Eleanor expected Gus to pull the trigger at any second. She braced herself for the worst. Without Ox, their chances were practically nil.

The big man didn't budge or betray any sign of being more than mildly annoyed. "Remember this, boys," he declared in a measured tone. "See me, now? See where I am and what he's doing? Well, tomorrow this will be you when this madman forgets that he's not in Pinkville anymore."

Gus's eyes bulged, and a wave of malice surged off him. Eleanor read his intention at once.

"No!" She leapt forward, driving her hands up against the underside of Gus's right wrist, knocking the gun up at the same instant he squeezed the trigger.

The pistol went off, its report cracking apart the still air and leaving everyone with painfully ringing ears. Dante flinched aside, out of the line of fire.

Ox flinched too. Everything happened too fast for him to judge the exact trajectory of the shot, and no amount of stoicism could keep him from reacting to a gun blasting off nearly in his face. The bullet went high and to the side thanks to Eleanor's intervention. It grazed his temple, drawing a line of bright red blood, then blew a hole in the wall behind him.

Pandemonium erupted. Gus's bodyguards tried to shoot Ox and the Executioners, but the other Hellbreakers tackled them, seizing their weapons to disable them or pull them aside. Someone else, farther across the basement, took a shot and seemingly hit another man in the leg, only to be dogpiled. Fists and feet flew. Men lashed or fell to the floor, wrestling and choking.

Ox's arms pistoned forward, his fists slamming into Gus's chest. Thanks to his armored vest, the commander took no real damage, but the sheer impact drove him stumbling backward. His arm got tangled around Eleanor's elbow, and he pulled her back. She cried out in alarm, barely keeping her balance and afraid he would grab her and throw her down.

Dante let out a throaty rasping sound that nearly resembled a word. He pounced toward the entwined pair of Eleanor and Gus, trying to separate them.

Ox stepped forward to intervene. Before he could, one of Gus's loyalists pulled a submachine gun on him. Someone else slammed into the man from the side, and he lost his sight alignment. That gave Ox an opportunity to knock the weapon from his grasp and headbutt him, knocking him to the floor.

Gus lashed out mindlessly at everything around him, now crazed and desperate. The back of his hand caught Eleanor across the face, badly stinging the flesh and swatting her aside so she slammed into the wall. Then he raised his pistol once more as Dante waded in to engage him.

Dante punched him in the face. Gus barely seemed to register it, showing no pain or confusion. His usually pleasant face was almost inhuman with fury. Still, it was enough to slow him. Dante grabbed his arm and twisted it.

Gus moved in the same direction Dante did, ruining his leverage, and swung him around toward the same wall where he'd knocked Eleanor. He kicked the physician hard in the stomach, doubling him over, and clawed at his face.

Dante managed to duck and avoid the worst of the blow. Otherwise, the fierce, grasping strike might've taken half the flesh off his face. His fist pummeled Gus's lower abdomen and groin but failed to connect with anything tender enough. Gus simply ignored it all, pressing forward, consumed with the need to kill.

Eleanor saw what was happening. She pounced on Freeman and gripped the gun by its slide, twisting it and putting her weight into it so it finally ripped free from his grasp and spun into the crowd, vanishing amid the general disorder.

Undeterred, Gus pulled a knife. Before he could use it, Ox moved toward him, giving him pause, but one of the other Hell-breakers jumped onto Ox's back and wrapped his arms around his neck. While the two struggled, Gus turned back to the Executioners.

"We could've taken them on together!" the young commander protested, his tone oddly whiny. He flicked the knife at Dante's face, deliberately pulling it short but seeming satisfied with the way the doctor tensed and stepped back. "Oh, no, but you had to get cold feet, just like everyone else does. I'm taking all of you out! Nobody is getting in the way anymore. No one has the right to stop us!"

He turned and slashed at Eleanor, who ducked and tried to grab his leg, hammering her small fists into the back of his knee. It wasn't enough to drop him, but he faltered, momentarily off-balance.

Dante dashed in and clamped his left hand around Gus's right wrist, immobilizing it, though the young man's strength was almost terrifying. He was marginally smaller than Dante, yet it took everything the physician had to keep the knife-arm in place. He clawed at Gus's face, but to no avail.

As Eleanor came back at him, Gus's leg came up and kicked her in the stomach. She let out a sharp groan and doubled over, falling to the floor with the wind knocked from her lungs.

Then the harsh yellow electric light that bathed them all darkened as something rose to block it out, a tall, broad figure that could only belong to one man. Facing him, Eleanor and Dante noticed the change at once.

Gus did not. He was so deep in his crazed bloodlust, so single-mindedly fixated on killing the enemies right in front of him, that he didn't think to look behind when something as obvious as the light changed all around him. Avenging the wounds to his ego was the only thing that mattered.

Dante tried to keep his eyes off Ox so he didn't clue Gus in. He gripped the other man's wrist tighter, knowing he only needed to hold him off for another second, two seconds at most. His muscles ached with the effort, and sweat poured down his whole body. The knife's blade was a thin flat rectangle, nearly a straight line at the angle from which he could see it, lighter against the general darkness that had fallen over them. It was getting closer.

One more second. The big silhouette was moving. Then—

Ox sprang forward without warning, all the momentum stored within his massive frame behind him. His huge hand clamped around Gus's neck as he crashed into him. The smaller man was knocked off his feet and lifted into the air at once, expelled from the space he'd occupied like smoke blown before the wind. He let out a strangled yelp of shock and rage.

Still moving forward, Ox hauled his former commander up and over Dante before slamming him into the floor as hard as he could. The vibration went through the surface and shook the walls. No one could hear any bones breaking under the general din, but it was hard not to assume that they had.

Gus's knife fell from his grasp and clattered aside. It landed in a bare patch of floor between two small groups of men, whose struggles slowed to nothing as they all realized what had happened and turned to watch.

Ox loomed over the fallen Commander Freeman, his hands balled into fists, snarling down at him. Gus looked back up with clenched teeth and tears streaming from his eyes. Rather than plead for mercy, rather than come to his senses, he clawed at Ox's groin in a last-ditch attempt at an attack.

Ox stepped aside and swiveled, dodging the strike and bringing his leg up in the same motion. Then with a loud bellow as pained as it was angry, he stomped down hard on Gus's neck and twisted his foot with a heavy, grinding motion.

This time, everyone *did* hear the breaking of bone, a faint crackling snap. Gus let out an inhuman squawk as his eyes bulged. His body seized up in a single spasm and went limp, succumbing at last to death after a final shuddering convulsion.

All the other scuffles had come to a halt. Silence reigned. Ox stood in place, his foot still on the ruined neck of his former leader. He withdrew it with a slow, almost ginger motion and stood normally, straightening his posture as he looked up and around.

The handful of men who'd remained loyal to Freeman were at a significant disadvantage. They were outnumbered and badly positioned, scattered across the basement, and most had guns pointed at their faces or torsos. Now, with their commander dead, they gave up. The brawl was over.

The guy with the sawed-off Mosin-Nagant was among those who'd stayed in one piece, although the melee had knocked the gun from his hands and he had no idea where it might be. He had, after careful consideration, decided to join those who supported Ox's coup d'état.

"Well," he announced, "I guess that settles it. We need new leadership, though. Back in the military, it would be whoever's next in rank, but this ain't the military. We're more like a barbarian tribe now, aren't we? Or a knightly order back in medieval times. Trial by combat and all that. So that makes Ox the new commander, doesn't it?"

A few of the men locked eyes with one another, if only briefly. For the most part, everyone looked at Walter Oxebowe. Dante and Eleanor, brushing their clothes and faces off and trying to reassure themselves that they were probably safe now, stood back and didn't interfere. This was a matter that the Hellbreakers would have to decide among themselves.

A couple of guys said, more or less in unison, "Yeah. Commander Ox."

Someone added, "He's good enough for now. Maybe we can have another vote later. But I vote for him."

The wave spread, its momentum coming to a head as most of the room voiced their affirmation of their new leader.

Ox blinked and looked a little sheepish at first. It was as though he'd never stopped to consider that he might end up in Gus's place and had no mental plan in store for how to deal with the responsibilities of command. He shook it off after a moment, standing up straight and trying to look authoritative.

"All right then, mates. First of all, anyone who wanted to follow Gus, you're still allowed in the organization as long as you don't make trouble or try to sabotage us, anythin' like that. Understood?"

The handful of Freeman loyalists nodded or grunted their assent. At no point had Ox suggested they change their core mission—overthrowing the Coven. He'd only taken issue with Gus's methods. Thus, there was no ideological reason for the holdouts to oppose him automatically. With Gus dead, their loyalty to him was rendered pointless.

"Good." Ox inhaled deeply and looked at Eleanor and Dante. He and the other men appeared to remember that they were still there for the first time in several minutes.

Dante gave a brief salute. "Congratulations on your promotion."

"Yeah," Ox grunted. "Let's focus on what's important. What can we do to help you?"

CHAPTER FOURTEEN

The afternoon was waning, too early, it seemed, but then again the whole day had seemed unusually dark. Eleanor and Dante had spent a couple more hours at the Hellbreakers' secret headquarters before they returned to the Autocutioner to take their leave.

"This time," Eleanor offered, "I will drive. It is only fair." Her midsection still hurt after Gus had kicked her. Dante had looked her over and determined that the attack hadn't broken any of her ribs but was concerned that she might have a hernia.

"Probably not," he'd reassured her. "Still, you need to avoid anything too strenuous for a little while, okay?"

Now, as the lot where their truck lay came into sight, he waffled, chewing on his lower lip. "I don't know about that, Eleanor. You'll likely be fine if everything goes smoothly and normally, yeah. But if you have to brake suddenly or twist around, and if you *do* have a hernia, that would be bad."

She sighed. "Yes, I'm sure it would be. You are not in much better shape, really, and I almost feel like this whole episode has been more stressful for you than it has for me."

"Yeah, because I've been worried about you this whole time."

Eleanor came close to missing a step. Her feelings sometimes ambushed her, usually when she was trying to avoid acknowledging them, and they weren't always clear at first. She was unsure whether to be furious with Dante for his seeming lack of faith in her ability to handle herself...or touched that he cared so much.

She thought back to the night they'd spent together recently, yet it seemed so long ago with all that had happened since then crowding into her memory.

Eleanor breathed in and out. "Dante. I appreciate that you want me to be safe and well. Truly, I do. Few people have shown such care for me since I left my home in Mexico years ago. But we are Executioners first, and we have a job to do, yes? Let me drive. You can take over if you must, but otherwise, you should rest. Unless of course, you need to shoot."

His sigh was long and ragged. "I'll concede that you're *mostly* right. Plus, I don't feel like arguing. Just be careful, okay?"

They climbed into the truck, checking to ensure that no one had stolen anything. All seemed to be in order. The Hellbreakers' presence in this neighborhood must have been perceived by most of the local population, if only dimly. It was hard to deny when dangerous men had taken control of an area. That would've deterred most petty thieves from hanging around and trying to loot things from parked vehicles.

Eleanor started the engine and piloted them out of the lot, trying to recall the exact route that Ox had directed them to take on their way in. She made a couple of minor mistakes, but the only consequences were having to make one or two extra turns and perhaps losing a minute or so of time.

Once they were back out on the road, Dante said, "All things considered, that went a hell of a lot better than it could have. We succeeded at what we set out to do. The Hellbreakers are our 'mates' now, as Ox would put it. We'll have to trust that they know what they're doing and don't go back to being addicted to killing as soon as they get onto the battlefield."

Eleanor nodded. "With Ox as their new leader, I think all will be well. He might not have the driving force of personality that Gus did, but he is strong and steadfast and has good judgment. He will keep them on a tight rein."

The one problem, obvious to them but remaining unspoken, was that they still didn't know the entire plan. Gage hadn't yet revealed the nature of his mysterious objective, and Daria and Ty still had things to do and conclusions to reach as well.

Thus, they had agreed to contact the Hellbreakers again once they possessed more information and things began falling into place.

The drive back toward the dock district was uneventful, aside from one minor incident when a stupid driver attempted to pull out of a side street too quickly and Eleanor had to brake and swerve. She managed it but winced in pain as her abused stomach muscles seized up. Dante nearly made her pull over so he could examine her, but she refused.

"There will be time when we're safe at home." To the extent that anyplace was safe anymore. And Daria's home wasn't technically Eleanor's.

It was an overcast day, hastening the onset of darkness as the sun crept toward the horizon. As such, it wasn't until they were well at the fringe of the neighborhood adjacent to Atlantica Harbor that they noticed the plume of black smoke rising in the sky.

Dante sat up. He'd been lounging in his seat, on the verge of falling asleep, but he perked up at once. "What the hell is that? It's right in the direction of Daria's house."

Grimacing, Eleanor speculated, "Perhaps someone had bad wiring or knocked over a kerosene lamp. I know there's a fire brigade around here and plenty of water. That would be terrible, all the same."

Many of the people who lived here were on the poorer side, and most of the houses were wood. There hadn't been enough rain lately. A fire might spread fast, dispossessing hundreds of people even if it claimed no lives.

Part of her, honed to a keen edge of cautious suspicion throughout her time with the Executioners, doubted that the smoke's cause was anything innocuous. As they drew closer to Daria's house, the number of *other* places the plume could come from narrowed.

Dante held up a hand. "Slow down. I don't think we should approach directly. I know of a couple of side routes. One leads up the slope, inland. We'll get a slightly better vantage point to check on Daria's place before we barge right in on it."

Eleanor protested, "If the house *was* attacked, shouldn't we help?"

Dante almost cringed. "Yes. But if we get killed or captured, we won't be in any position to help anyone. I hope Amahle and Singh were the only ones there. Amahle could probably get out before the bad guys got in. As for Singh...the hell with him. He hasn't been much help to us, has he?"

"He could be a help to the Coven, though, if they should recover him."

Nonetheless, she followed Dante's instructions, taking the truck uphill, around a curve, and into a series of narrow lanes amid various bungalows and hostels where there was a partially obstructed view of the little cul-de-sac where Daria's house lay.

Both their hearts sank at once. The column of ugly smoke was rising from a blasted hole in the ceiling of Daria's living room, with the flickering orange light of small fires illuminating the damage. Swarming all over her property were Executive Security officers. It was difficult to guess how many of them, but there were two black vans out front and possibly more parked elsewhere.

Dante muttered, "Shit. We *should* try to rescue them if they're still there. Amahle and Singh, I mean. But that might be—"

A loud grinding sound cut him off, and from behind a pole barn up ahead a Jeep rolled out, with two men sticking out the top hatch and operating a belt-fed machine gun. Another was behind driving, and a fourth in the passenger's seat had a rifle aimed out the window.

Eleanor exhaled. "This couldn't go any worse, could it?"

Two gunshots rang out, but they came from somewhere above and farther back toward a copse of trees near the end of the ridge. The first shot went through the head of the triggerman behind the machine gun, killing him instantly. The second bullet struck the weapon itself, cracking its chassis and sending the second man dropping back into the cabin for safety.

Dante shouted, "Get 'em!" Adrenaline had replaced rational thought. He snatched up his shotgun and bounded out the door, charging the Jeep on foot and blasting toward the windshield.

Eleanor had only a fraction of a second in which to be shocked. Then she seized a rifle and aimed it out the side window, squeezing off a few shots that sparked off the vehicle's hood. The AR-10, while a powerful and state-of-the-art weapon, kicked too heavily for someone of her size, and she knew she'd failed to hit anything important in her haste.

The hidden sniper fired another shot that pinned down the man about to lean out the side of the cab and open fire with his rifle. Dante unloaded on him with buckshot, and at least one of the pellets found its way into his throat. He screamed and toppled over.

Eleanor jumped down to the ground, putting her back against the Autocutioner's hull to brace herself as she opened fire on full auto, aiming for the windshield. The gun roared and climbed in her grip, though she fought against it enough to keep it firing in the general area she wanted. The windshield shattered and the driver was shredded, collapsing over the steering wheel.

The last of the guards in the truck tried to flee out the back, sweeping his rifle around, not knowing where all his foes were. The one who remained hidden had the advantage and took it. A rifle cracked again, and he fell over, bouncing once against the pavement before lying still.

Dante held his shotgun at low ready, looking around, while Eleanor ejected the empty magazine from her rifle and set the smoking gun aside, drawing her pistol instead.

A familiar voice called, "I'm safe, but none of us will be for long."

"Amahle," Dante yelled. "Jesus. Thanks. Where's Singh, though?"

Eleanor scanned the horizon, and all the shadowed nooks and crannies around them, for any sign of further danger, though she kept one ear on the unexpected conversation between her friends.

Amahle didn't answer Dante's question yet. "Wait a moment, please."

Someone, a man from the sound of it, grunted as branches swished and snapped. A bundled humanoid form fell out of a nearby tree, hitting the ground and rolling through the grass. As it passed through a shaft of light, Eleanor recognized it as Jori Singh, still tied up as well as gagged.

Then Amahle hopped down. She struck the ground feet-first and did a single smooth tumble before springing back up into a standing position, her rifle firm in her hands.

Eleanor looked her over. "Are you hurt?" She appeared to be fine, but with daylight mostly gone it was dark enough to make certainty impossible at first glance.

Dante had rushed over to Singh to check him for injuries and ungagged him so the man could respond to his questions. Since Amahle had probably kicked him off or thrown him, there was more chance of problems in his case than in Amahle's. Then again, his yoga skills and other strange powers meant he might well be perfectly fine.

Amahle had spent a moment scanning around them, much as Eleanor had done, but then her gaze snapped back toward the other woman. "Yes, I am well. Were you followed? Have you heard from Ty and Daria? We must not stay here long."

Annoyed at the flurry of inquiries and remarks, Eleanor nevertheless lined up quick replies to each of them. However, she clenched her hands and had to call upon her long experience dealing with impatient and pushy clients and superiors to remain fully calm.

"Good. No, we were not. No, we have not. And I agree." Before Amahle could say anything else, Eleanor added two questions of her own. "How did they find us? What happened here?"

Amahle topped off her rifle with a trio of cartridges from a pouch at her side, which she'd kept tightly buttoned until now. "I'm not sure. In all honesty, I think it was a stroke of bad luck more than anything else. Nothing unusual happened before they came."

Eleanor glanced over at Dante and Singh as the physician rose to his feet, taking the older man's arm and bearing him to stand, as well.

"Singh's fine," Dante reported. "No great shock there. We should all hope to be in such good physical condition at your age, Mr. Singh. How do you do it? Besides all the uncanny powers you get from ancient artifacts and shit."

Despite being tightly bound and having rolled through grass and dirt, the older man looked serene and none the worse for wear. "Attention to detail," he quipped in an emotionless voice. "And self-discipline, of course. Mind over matter, as the Westerners say."

Something about his demeanor seemed odd, Eleanor thought. As much as he generally had himself under control, she wondered if his long imprisonment was finally getting to him.

Amahle interrupted her ruminations on such matters, though. "There was a coastal patrol. Nothing about it seemed out of the ordinary. Executive Security sends its patrols sweeping along the water all the time, mostly to check the harbor. Today, for whatever reason, they came inland. They didn't stop to search each house, building, or alley along the way but moved directly toward Daria's house to investigate it and it alone. I do not know why."

Dante glared sharply at Singh. "Any doing of yours, bud?"

Singh only shook his head slowly. He seemed to consider it unnecessary to say anything since they all knew he'd been tied up in the basement the whole time.

Amahle continued, "I had little time—only enough to hide Mr. Singh and myself in the farthest and darkest part of the basement before the coastal security team broke down the door and began to search the house. They stumbled around, rifling through cabinets and looking under beds, I would imagine, but they didn't seem able to find us. At first."

Eleanor glanced past her, toward the smoking, glowing wreckage of the bungalow. More people would soon drift in to see what was wrong. The gunshots had traveled all through the harbor district, as well as the fire becoming ever more visible.

Amahle went on, "Unfortunately, one of the fools stumbled onto some of our stored weapons on the first landing of the basement stairwell. He started to call it in on his portable radio before I could get to him. I took him out and the others as well, which bought me some time. They had reinforcements nearby, so I had to act quickly.

"I grabbed whatever I could as far as supplies and gear, then took Singh out to hide him in the brush behind the home. Next, I set up Daria's boat to sail off by itself out into the waves. I thought the security people would see it leaving and draw their attention out to sea while we escaped on land. The ground team arrived more quickly than I would've thought."

As she spoke, she began moving at a steady pace back toward

the Autocutioner, and Eleanor followed her. Dante came along in the rear, guiding Singh by the arm and keeping a close eye on him.

"They were moving in from three directions at once and doing a careful sweep of the surrounding area. I knew they would catch me if I didn't create a different diversion right away. The only thing I could do was light a fire inside the house. I'm sure Daria won't be *happy* about that...but I should think she would understand. I hoped the fire wouldn't spread to the whole house. I believe it has only gutted the sitting room and left the rest alone."

Dante quipped, "Well, what's a burned-out sitting room among friends? She kept most of her books and photo albums in her bedroom, anyway."

Eleanor looked at him. "How much time have you spent in her bedroom, anyway?"

He replied nonchalantly, "Enough, when helping clean or checking on her when she had the flu."

Pinching her mouth shut, Eleanor kept walking as Amahle finished her story.

"There is one other thing, very important, which you must know. Before I left and hid Singh and myself in that tree, I heard a message over the radio from Tyler. They are meeting again in the town of Northvale."

It made sense, Eleanor reflected. Northvale was a community of working-class laborers located in the foothills northwest of Atlantica Metro. Ty had settled there after first coming to the island, when it had been little more than a shantytown, acting as their resident protector-warrior in exchange for basic accommodations.

The town had grown larger and far more refined in the intervening years. Many of its residents remembered First Executioner Katakura and all he'd done for them. Meeting there, they would be among friends—people who would cover for them and aid them.

Eleanor piped up, "Then let us not waste time. Security must be looking for us. They might know about that place and think to send their people there after us."

Amahle stopped before the hood of the Autocutioner, waiting for her partners to open the vehicle. "Indeed."

Eleanor first opened the back compartment, so Dante could lift Singh in and keep guard over him. Then she and Amahle climbed into the front and started the engine. So far, they were lucky that their enemies hadn't shown up.

As Eleanor pulled away from the smoldering house and tried to take the most circuitous and counterintuitive possible route away into the city, the anxiety lingered. She couldn't dispel a crawling sensation between her shoulder blades that something bad was going to happen, that they'd used up part of their luck and could expect things to only get worse from here on.

At first, things seemed quiet as they reached the edge of the harbor district, with the lights of the city proper stretching beyond. Eleanor's misgivings quickly proved justified.

"Stop," Amahle exclaimed. "Stop and pull over."

Eleanor hit the brakes. Not hard enough for them to squeal or to risk being rear-ended by a car a ways behind them, but she didn't hesitate. Amahle was sharp-eyed, and Eleanor trusted her.

As she turned the steering wheel to the right, pulling onto the shoulder and into the mouth of a dark alley, Amahle pointed past her through the windshield.

"There is a roadblock. Two black vans. Now they're moving toward us."

Behind them, Dante, who had overheard, rasped, "Goddammit. Nothing can ever be easy, can it?"

Since the road was a divided highway with the two lanes on their side of the concrete median being one-way, there was no way to turn around and go back without attracting undue attention and risk crashing into the various cars that continued to stream down the asphalt. Worse still, the alleyway ahead of them was a dead end.

Eleanor's hands twitched and danced nervously over the wheel. "This is bad. We might have to fight. Or, it might be better to ram them aside." The Autocutioner was larger and heavier than the vans used by Executive Security. The stuff Gage had added to its exterior to disguise it would act as rudimentary armor, to boot.

Amahle watched. "They're going car to car, checking inside each vehicle. And—oh. That is interesting. They even looked in a parked one. Turn off the engine, Eleanor."

She obeyed, her understanding of what Amahle had planned growing by the second. After a short discussion, they agreed to temporarily abandon the vehicle, hiding in a nearby building or behind a dumpster in the alley if necessary. If they were lucky, the Coven's men would simply see an abandoned vehicle, ignore it, and move on.

Dante threw in his own two cents. "Do they know what our truck looks like? Because if they ID it as ours, they're not going to leave it there."

Eleanor shook her head. "We don't have time to worry about that. Get Singh up and let's go."

Jori Singh had remained silent through the whole discussion. He offered no resistance as Dante pulled him through to the front compartment. The two men then followed the women out the passenger's side door.

They ducked around the side of the truck toward a nearby empty hardware store. One of the vans crept closer, driving against traffic—which was slowing down anyway as it became clear that no one was going to slip through the roadblock checkpoint.

Amahle was first to the door of the shop. "This doesn't look like a place that would have an alarm. I should be able to pick the lock. Then we can hide within and disturb nothing unless we—"

With one bizarrely fluid and quick motion of his arms and body, Jori Singh slipped out of his bonds and stepped away from Dante as though he'd never been a prisoner at all and could flee at will.

Dante spun in shock. "Fucking yoga! Hey!" He started after the man, but Singh moved with astonishing speed on his long legs, darting to the rear of the Autocutioner and seeming nearly to prance around the corner. He was heading straight for the security team, presumably intending for them to rescue him.

"No!" Eleanor gasped and made ready to go after Dante. She didn't much care about Singh escaping beyond the fear that he would divulge where they were going. The thought of Dante putting himself needlessly into the line of fire...

Amahle caught her shoulder and held her back in an unyielding grip. "Stop. You must not!" She yanked her back and held her against the front wall of the shop, where they stood together in a shaft of shadows between the beams of the streetlights.

Fortunately, Dante realized the danger he would be in if he went into the open. He stopped behind the truck, flailing his arms in frustration and silently cursing as Singh slipped away.

The slim older man bolted out into the middle of the street, raising his arms over his head. "Good day! Are you pleased to see me again?"

One of the security officers responded, and he didn't sound pleased in the slightest. "It's Jori Singh! *Open fire.*"

Before anyone could react, including Singh himself, four guns boomed and *cracked*. Bullets skidded and streaked past the Auto-cutioner, ricocheting off the asphalt. Those that found their mark tore holes through the astonished man, who spun backward under the barrage and hung suspended, braced on one leg. Then he toppled over, a faint red mist hanging in the air as he struck the pavement and lay there.

Eleanor clamped a hand over her mouth. She had no idea why they'd done that. It would've made sense for them to recover Singh—the Executioners had based everything they'd done in keeping him hostage on the assumption that the Coven wanted him back.

Then boots moved forth, their clomping steps growing louder against the damp pavement.

A man said, "Truck looks empty. I don't think he was in it. Must have slipped out from that alley or something."

Before the team could check in detail, though, a woman who had been in one of the civilian cars up ahead screamed in fury. Someone farther away shouted, "We got a situation here."

The goon who'd blown Singh away turned and ran back to the car, momentarily abandoning their search of the area around the Autocutioner. Dante saw his chance. He ducked out, grabbed Singh's arms, and dragged him back onto a dark patch of asphalt near the corner of the alley and the hardware store.

Amahle's grip relaxed, and Eleanor sprang free of it to kneel next to the dying man. Dante was already working to save him, but it looked like it might well be futile. Singh didn't have his protective bracelet. His talent as a yogi wouldn't be enough to undo the damage of so many holes through his body. Blood was streaked all along the ground on the path from where he'd fallen. There, it glistened in pools.

Dante frantically tried to stop the bleeding while plugging the sucking wounds in the man's chest. Singh stared up, drooling and gasping. That he was still alive at all was another of his strange accomplishments. But probably his last.

He chortled, the sound weak and hollow. "We only wanted...to make a better world," he groaned. "We, the only ones. Only ones who could do it. So much...time, spent, trying to..."

Then fate cut off his last words, his breath whistling away to oblivion as his lungs collapsed and the last of the blood drained from his body, his heart ceasing to beat. Dante let his head drop, staring.

"Dammit. *Dammit,*" the physician grunted. His bloody fists shook.

Eleanor took him by the arm. "Come. Leave him. They'll think he crawled over here by himself."

They sprinted to the storefront, where Amahle pointed out, "We must get out of here. I think we might have to abandon the Autocutioner, although I don't like to do it. Dante. Can you hotwire a car?"

He frowned. Having failed to save a life—his primary vocation—the last thing he wanted to think about were his *other* skills. "Don't remind me. Yes, I can."

CHAPTER FIFTEEN

Northvale's drive-in movie theater lay on a natural terrace or small plateau adjacent to the town proper, rising amid the low hills at the far northern end of the community. Friends of Ty Katakura got in for free. Eleanor, Dante, and Amahle arrived driving a 1961 Dodge Lancer rather than anything identifiable as an Autocutioner, so it took a couple of minutes longer than usual. Ty had to come over and clear them personally.

Once past the gates, Dante drove to their usual meeting place, which lay in the far rear corner of the little plateau, with a cliff near its back. Few of the usual patrons parked here since the view of the screen was bad. As near as Eleanor could tell, though, the movie showing tonight was some sort of World War II caper involving a secret mission during the conflict in North Africa.

Everyone was present. Ty, Daria, and Gage were all there. So was Ox, along with one of his subordinates. The Hellbreakers were too numerous, too rowdy, and hard to control for all of them to be present. Ox had vowed to act as a good representative and an effective leader. What they decided here, tonight, would get passed on to the others as firmly and accurately as possible.

Dante parked next to the other Autocutioner. Which was

now, they realized, the only one they had left. He killed the Lancer's engine, and they all stepped out.

Ty was first to ask the obvious questions. "All right, I'm glad the three of you are here, and all in one piece. But why the *hell* are you driving that thing, and where's Jori Singh?"

Eleanor and Dante were about to answer in their ways, but Amahle, standing between them, put her hands on their arms. "I will explain," she said in a calm, soft voice.

Eleanor let her handle it. There was a bond of sorts between her and Ty. She wondered if it might be a romantic attraction, but so far there was no specific evidence of such. They simply operated on a similar wavelength and had that closeness that sometimes arises between people who have been through the same difficult experience together. It went back to the jungle misadventure that had brought Amahle into the order of Executioners to begin with, Eleanor knew.

Amahle told Ty everything. Daria and Gage, standing behind him by their truck, followed. Daria's face went pale and strained with tension at the mention of the damage done to her house, but she didn't interrupt or protest. She'd spent many years of her youth in Poland orphaned, living as a fugitive from the Nazis and the Communists. Then the dangerous life of a smuggler had hardened her to any excessive attachment to places or possessions.

While the markswoman related all that had happened to the other Executioners, Eleanor and Dante kept an eye on the two Hellbreakers. Besides Ox, there was a young white man of average height with shaggy auburn hair. Eleanor vaguely recognized his face from the hidden basement but knew nothing about him.

She would have to trust Ox. He hadn't let them down so far. She only hoped that he was as good at choosing his friends as they were.

Amahle came to the end of her story, the part where the three had engaged in a short foot race against the Executives' thugs, ducking into a side street to steal and hotwire their new car before high-tailing it to Northvale.

She added, "Oh, when this is over, we agreed that we should return the car to its owner, or at least compensate them for it. We can find that information from the VIN and license plate, I'm sure."

Ty waved it off. "Yes, and it's good you thought of that. There's a lot more important stuff to focus on. Executive Security has run us out of our hiding spot. Daria no longer has a home; none of us do. Our other Autocutioner is in their hands, which means they also got some of our weapons, armor, supplies, and the like."

"And the Atlanticore crystal matrix that powers the vehicle," Daria added,

Gage was the most distant of the three. His eyes were downcast, and slowly he shook his head, his hands in his pockets. "Jori Singh is truly dead, then? I thought him dead once, and he was not. But I did not see his body for a time. Also, I'm not a medical doctor."

He let out a long, wistful sigh. "Perhaps he was an evil man, as bad as the rest of them. Still, he seemed most knowledgeable. Now we will never learn all that he knew, whether that is for better or worse for the world."

Ty looked at him and nodded. "Yes. It's sad. It also means there's something we *have* learned. Namely, the Coven is willing to kill anyone it fears might be a liability or able to compromise them. Even their members. Hell, *especially* their members. A full inductee would have a lot more beans to spill than someone out on the fringe of the inner circle like Eleanor was."

There was a moment of silence among them all. When it had gone on for what seemed like long enough, Ox strode over. His attitude was hesitant, bordering on deferential. Not so much in that he was uncomfortable or underconfident, but simply in that he felt he should tread lightly when the Executioners all seemed to be doing their best to manage their emotions.

Eleanor looked at him. "Ox, it's good to see you again. What can you tell us about what you've found in the meantime?"

"Aye, thanks," he responded. "I've got some news for you, that's sure enough. Oh, and this is my new right-hand man, Berger. He's a pretty good mate of mine. Keeps his mouth shut for the most part but gets the job done, and he wasn't no fan of Gus' mental way of doing things."

Berger raised a hand in greeting. "Good to meet you all," he declared, in a Midwestern American accent. "We're sorry that our two groups had to be enemies for a while. We're better off as friends. Anyway, um, I know that what you really want to hear about is aircraft."

"That's correct," Dante said. "What happened to that helicopter Gus took to the Feng building? The one Ox fell out of. I didn't see it anywhere at your headquarters."

Ox explained, "It got damaged. Won't be much use to us. That leads us straight into the good news. We got intel, you see. A few of us used to be Exec Security, and we know where some of their oh-so-secret facilities are. They've got an airfield in the middle of the badlands north of the city. A couple of planes and a whole fleet of choppers."

Gage perked up. The technical problem-solving of how to approach Zero Site, and the role his analysis would play in that, had piqued his interest and redirected his thoughts away from Singh's unfortunate death.

Berger elaborated further in a sedate and matter-of-fact way. "Our idea is to launch a raid on the airfield and commandeer several of these helicopters. As many as we can. The idea is to have two separate flights. Dr. Gurung already told us the rough outline of your strategy, and he also revealed his secret weapon. With a whole squadron of choppers, we can put everything we have to good use and have a shot at winning this."

Eleanor recalled what Gage had said, something about the "resources" he needed to gather with Ty's and Daria's help, and his mysterious idea for how to breach Zero Site that he'd refused to reveal until he had more information.

Ox picked up where his subordinate had left off. "So, there's two flights. One will head more or less straight for Zero Site. That's the simple part. The other one, well, it'll circle wide around the place and come in from the coastal side. Harder approach that way. Then it's the one that delivers the payload."

Eleanor couldn't take it any longer. "What is the payload? Gage, what is it you've been keeping from us all this time? Have you told the others already?"

He smiled. "Yes, I couldn't help but tell them for them to work with me on retrieving it, of course. The 'payload' of which Ox speaks couldn't have been procured by me alone. Tyler did procure it by himself initially, but he had two drivers, and it was in better working order."

For the first time in what seemed like far too long, Ty smiled as well. "That big, beautiful APC, the one that the Ashcroft twins had lounging in their garage. Remember that thing? Well, it's back from the dead."

Eleanor stood dumbstruck. She recalled the vehicle in question and assumed they'd lost it with Executioner HQ. Although morbidly curious, in a way, she didn't want to know what the three had done to recover it.

Dante clapped and laughed out loud. "Ha, ha! That's great. I missed that thing. Wait, you're going to tow it with a *helicopter*? It must weigh a couple of tons at least. I don't know if that's in the cards. Not to burst anyone's bubble."

Ox said, "No, we're going to use *many* helicopters, mate. Ought to work as long as we can commandeer enough of the damnable things. And, well, as much as we're all uncomfortable with the works of the beast, they tell me we can at least turn those same works against the bastards."

Eleanor looked at Gage.

He bobbed his head slowly down, then up. "Yes. You see, we recovered the APC some months ago, and I had stashed it away in a hiding place within the city. Not too far from Daria's house, but far enough that it would be safe if ever the Coven were to discover us. Which, sadly, they have."

Daria remained stony-faced. Eleanor wondered if she was grateful that everyone had lots of other things to discuss, the better to keep her distracted from losing her home.

Gage went on, "The vehicle was originally equipped with a device, powered by Atlanticore, which caused it to fall most slowly when driving off a cliff. Tyler said that it was as though it were defeating gravity itself.

"I didn't think such a thing would be possible, but I believe that I have repaired it and the anti-gravity component will work again. Therefore, it will lessen the burden on the helicopters. And dropping the APC into the compound will be far safer."

Dante shook his head in wonderment. "I thought that thing burned out. How the hell did you manage to get it working again?"

Gage shrugged. "In my spare time. I tinker with things when I'm bored."

Amahle let out an abrupt, snorting laugh, then turned it into a cough and lowered her eyes. "Excuse me... Um. I didn't think *anyone* had 'spare time' lately, but it sounds like it's a good thing you found some, Gage."

"Hopefully, it *will* be a good thing, yes," Ty interjected. "The bad part is that we don't have much time to test it in advance. Now let's discuss our strategy in more detail."

He knelt on a patch of bare earth and made crude drawings in the dirt with the tip of his finger. "Here's an extremely rough outline of the mountains where we'll be."

Daria nodded. "Extremely."

He ignored her and went on. "The helicopters towing the

APC will move in to the heart of the base and land us there. We'll be in the APC, by the way." He looked up at his teammates. "All the Executioners. That's our role in this."

Amahle grimaced. "If they shoot us down, they'll take out all of us in one fell swoop. I suppose this crystal flotation device will help with that, though."

Ty swiped a hand through the air. "It can't be helped. We need the full six to get the job done. We won't exactly be on our own. Once the APC touches the ground, we go on the offensive at once and try to create as much chaos as possible, thus diverting and destabilizing whatever defenses the Coven might have available."

Dante quipped, "Pretty sure I can see where this is going, and I'm not from a military background." He interlocked his fingers and flexed his hands, cracking his knuckles.

"Well, the danger is that they, too, will figure out what we are doing," Daria added. "Which is what concerns me most."

Gage raised a finger. "Yes, that is most worthy of consideration. But if we strike fast enough and keep our forces coordinated, we should be able to overwhelm them before they can put two and two together."

Ty nodded, reasserting control over the conversation. "Exactly. This leads me to the other prong of the attack. At the same time that the choppers are dropping us off in the APC, the Hellbreakers' ground forces will come at the facility from the jungle side. They'll press forward, infiltrate any entrances, scale walls, whatever it takes, while the defenders are busy dealing with us.

"Meanwhile, the other fleet of helicopters—the one from the coastal side—will remain airborne and fight that way, providing mobile support and guaranteeing air superiority. We don't know if the Coven has any planes or choppers of their own at Zero Site, but you can never be too careful."

Berger, Ox's lieutenant, said, "Well, they've got a whole

airfield that we'll be taking shortly so it's safe to assume they might have more flight-worthy vehicles besides what's there. Still, if we can pull off this raid, we'll probably be in a good position to crush the bastards from above."

Amahle looked at the two Hellbreakers. "Your people might take casualties if their defenses are heavy. Of course, so might we. There will be enormous risk for everyone involved."

The big man's broad, dark face had little of its usual joviality. The truth of Amahle's words weighed on him, perhaps making him doubt his role as their group's new commander.

"It's a tall order trying to lead my men in something like this. An all-or-nothing maneuver with so much at stake. Especially when I've been in command for such a short while.

"There's one important thing to keep in mind. We're moving directly against the Coven of Miracles this time. Striking a blow at the heart of the beast itself. Out in the hills, there won't be no risk to civilians this time around. Makes us all feel better knowing that much."

Eleanor studied him, noticing the mixture of fundamental decency and violent religious fervor. "Thank you, Ox. We're putting a great deal of trust in you."

He nodded. "Aye, I know. All your lives will be in our hands, towing the payload like that. I'll make sure your trust is well rewarded, mates. The Hellbreakers will come through. I give you my word, on my immortal soul."

Ty stared at the man. "I believe you."

For a moment, everyone was quiet. The only sounds came from the movie screen across the plateau where the actors were gearing up for a raid. One or two of the drive-in viewers shouted comments, but they were hard to make out.

Daria snapped her fingers. "I brought a little something. I thought it might be good to have on hand for emergencies, which means it escaped the fate of my house. Now would be the time to make use of it." Without explaining further, she returned to the

Autocutioner and dug around in the piles of stuff heaped into the rear compartment.

When she emerged, a bottle of vodka dangled from her hand. "I forgot glasses, however. Everyone who wishes, take a drink from the bottle and pass it on. To 'seal the deal,' as the Americans say, I believe. Whether we succeed or fail... Whatever happens once we put this plan into being, the fate of Atlantica will change forever."

Opening the bottle, she took a rather long swig herself before passing it to Ty, and around the circle it went. No one passed; everyone drank.

CHAPTER SIXTEEN

It was neither night nor morning. The darkness of pre-dawn had broken but hadn't yet given way to anything one could properly call *light* quite yet. There was only a lessening of the shadows, slight but perceptible, and a dim nimbus of light the color of faded ash on the horizon. The sun was about to begin its slow ascent.

The Executives had hidden their secret airfield well. It lay amid a particularly rugged stretch of terrain north of the city, in a lower-elevation zone of jagged and irregular small hills that made vehicular travel all but impossible. The exception was a discreet road bulldozed through the flatter portions. Its entrance off the highway was practically invisible unless one knew where to look.

It hadn't stopped nor fooled the Executioners, however. Or the Hellbreakers, who had never before gathered in their entirety for an operation in one place. That they had all moved so close to the facility without being noticed was a testament to their skill.

Since the Execs were relying upon secrecy and the threat of official reprisal to keep the place secure, it was surrounded only by a chain-link fence topped with a coil of low-quality barbed wire. Its garrison of security forces, meanwhile, was only a cursory force of about eight men.

The entirety of the Hellbreakers, combined with the Executioners, made a platoon of more than forty shooters. The Hellbreakers had a couple of explosives and a blowtorch, just to be safe.

Eleanor crouched within the APC. Riding in it wasn't the most pleasant experience. Although technically designed as a transport for a full squad of soldiers—nearly twice the number of the Executioners—it nonetheless seemed cramped and claustrophobic. It was too noisy for them to drive it up to the airfield before the attack began. She and Gage would stay behind while everyone else launched their surprise strike.

Ty had been driving. He shifted gears and brought the lumbering vehicle to a halt while Daria operated the radio, communicating with the Hellbreakers' advance scouts.

Nodding as they spoke into her headphones, she turned to Ty and the others. "Four men patrolling the perimeter, another four or five seem to be resting in the control building. Only one turret. As long as we aren't detected too soon, they're confident we can win this easily."

Ty grinned. "Good. Let's do it, then."

The others nodded their goodbyes to Gage and Eleanor and climbed out. Gage fired up one of the external cameras, which gave the two of them a halfway decent view of the southeast corner of the compound.

At first, there was nothing except motionless silence amid the pre-dawn gloom. Then a guard passed near the fence. Seconds after he was gone, she glimpsed dark, flitting shapes moving in, seeming to rise out of the shadows themselves.

"Ah," Gage observed with a satisfied note of appreciation in his voice. "I see how they're doing it. They're good at this. Under Gus, they seemed to favor direct assaults. But they do have ability and training at using stealth."

Eleanor watched as two silhouettes grabbed the guard and pulled him into the darkness. No shouts of alarm followed it. She wondered if they'd killed the man or merely incapacitated him. She'd seen plenty of violence in recent times, but something about the sneakiness and ruthlessness of the way the Hell-breakers had ambushed him made her faintly uncomfortable.

Then someone lit the blowtorch. Eleanor noted that they'd chosen that particular spot because a shed and the body of an airplane shielded it from the view of the turret and the control building.

Next, men streamed through the hole the torch operator had cut. Then the hammer stroke fell.

The air opened up as dozens of guns fired at once. Something exploded, and a giant ball of smoke and fire rose near the compound's center. It engulfed the turret while the structure crumbled at the base and fell over in pieces. A few guards rushed out of the central building only to find themselves surrounded.

Then it was over. Everything fell silent. The radio within the APC crackled.

"Okay, that was quick," Ty began. "They surrendered once they saw how completely outmatched they were. We're going to tie them up and toss them out in the woods. Move in. We need to get the choppers and get out fast. Over."

While Gage fired up the APC, Eleanor picked up the microphone. "Excellent news, Number One. We're on our way. Out."

The heavy vehicle roared and growled as the Nepali guided it through the hole in the fence. The opening wasn't big enough, but the bulk and power of the APC allowed it to rip through the rest with ease, uprooting a couple of poles and destroying a whole section of the barrier. It plowed across the ground, reaching the central area near the control building as the first pinkish light of true dawn appeared on the horizon.

As the APC rolled to a stop, Eleanor opened the hatch and popped out to examine things in more detail.

Half of the Hellbreakers were binding the prisoners. There were six of them, suggesting that two or three of the airfield's security detail had perished in the brief fight before the rest gave themselves up.

Ox's other men appeared to be planting explosives around the compound as well as selecting and securing the helicopters they would use. There were fifteen or sixteen to choose from, along with two planes.

Ty, Dante, Daria, and Amahle emerged from the control building. Ty took the scene in at a glance. "All right, all clear. Let's get nine of those choppers ready to fly." He gestured at the captive guards, "Take these guys and dump them on the road about a quarter-mile away. Then get back here post-haste. I want everyone airborne in twenty minutes."

A dozen Hellbreakers took away the prisoners, who only stared ashen-faced as their captors led them from the compound. They were shaken and wary but undoubtedly grateful they would be able to keep their lives. They wouldn't be in a position to do much of anything with their hands bound behind their backs, but they could still walk until someone rescued them.

Concurrently, those among the crew with flight experience started up the nine choppers. Five of them rose into the air and landed carefully around the APC. Then the Executioners hooked cables between the aircraft and the land craft.

Gage said, "Based on a brief test, the anti-gravity device seems to be working, but we should keep it at low power to avoid over-taxing it. So the helicopters must bear some of the weight themselves. This might slow them down, so it will be important for the other four to keep pace."

Ox barked, "Everybody got that?"

His men grunted their assent.

After conferring on the coordinates they'd be flying to and getting the men who'd dumped off the captives up to speed, the

Executioners piled into the APC. The Hellbreakers divided themselves among the choppers, three or four men in each one.

Dante murmured, "Now, the moment of truth. Do your thing, Gage."

The Gurkha hovered over the controls and fiddled with a couple of switches. The noise of the helicopters rose around them as the aircraft took to the sky, and another sound became impossible to ignore. They couldn't quite *hear* it, exactly. Rather, they felt it in their chests—the low, humming vibration of charged Atlanticore.

"Yes, it is working, and I have the power at only a low level. Let's see if—"

Everyone's stomachs lurched and sloshed as they struggled to keep their balance. The APC was rising. Too easily to be the sole work of the choppers, Eleanor could tell. The monitor hooked to the external camera showed the ground dropping away, the sky getting bigger, the airfield sinking into the distance.

As they left the facility behind, the bombs went off.

Another shockwave hit, and the Executioners all stumbled again. The helicopters they'd left behind, the planes, and the buildings all shattered to pieces amid clouds of smoky fire. The flames spread to consume the whole compound and render useless everything that still lay within it.

Ty laughed. "Ha-*ha!* Now that's what I call pulling the pin!"

CHAPTER SEVENTEEN

Eleanor squinted as she braced herself against the wall. She was pretty sure she heard something under the endless buzzing din of the choppers' propellers. Mercifully, it was mildly distracting her from the slight airsickness she was getting from their wobbly flight over Atlantica's hinterlands.

"Is that what I think it is?" She only half-expected anyone to answer her.

Daria perked up, intuiting that Eleanor was referring to a sound. She looked up, craned her head to the side, and nodded. "Yes, they're playing *Ride of the Valkyries*. I suppose it's a fitting choice even if I'm not fond of Wagner, for various reasons."

Ty noticed it too, and his typically grim and somber face split into a savage, wolf-like grin. "Ha! Good selection. I heard the pilots in Vietnam got a lot of mileage out of it whenever they did napalm runs."

Eleanor hadn't seen Tyler like this in quite some time. He seemed happy, but in a way that nearly scared her. They were finally taking the fight to the Coven and perhaps striking a blow from which they would never recover. That must have been it. The prospect was bringing his inner warrior out in ways that were almost less soldier-like and more akin to a bloodthirsty animal.

Their radio crackled, and Gage answered it. "This is E-Number Three. We read you. Over."

"Roger," an Australian-accented voice barked from the other end. "We have visual on the target just over the ridge. Comin' in from the inland side. ETA three minutes. With your permission, we'll attack immediately. If you need more time, tell us ASAP. Over."

Gage looked at Ty and Daria, who both nodded in affirmation.

"Yes, you may proceed. Continue with everything as planned. Good luck. Out." He hung up the mic, put both hands on his rifle, and exhaled slowly, his eyes focusing on some distant point as they grew brighter and more intense.

Eleanor looked down at the weapon in her grasp, a nine-millimeter Heckler & Koch MP5 submachine gun. It was a relatively new weapon and considered top-of-the-line. Some of Daria's connections had managed to procure one at the eleventh hour. As a pistol-caliber gun, it lacked the range and penetrative power of a rifle.

It was still enough to knock down or injure a man in light to medium armor, and she found it to be much easier to handle and control than the unwieldy, fire-breathing AR-10s that Ty, Gage, Amahle, and most of the Hellbreakers used. Daria still had her Uzi for much the same reasons, and Dante favored his pump shotgun.

Additionally, both the Hellbreakers and some of their smuggler acquaintances had provided everyone with at least two grenades or other small explosive devices, and most of them had pistols as sidearms. Going into the Coven's most secretive and valued sanctum, they couldn't afford to be anything less than armed to the teeth.

Of course, there were also the choppers themselves. And the

APC, with its mounted heavy machine gun and sheer kinetic bulk.

Eleanor leaned over and looked at the monitor hooked to the camera. The flight from the airfield to the secret facility hadn't taken too long, but it was still enough time that the light of early dawn had now transformed into full, glorious morning. Pink and gold sunshine bathed the hills and jungles and sparkled off the ocean waves in the distance behind them.

Up ahead, a broad, green, fern-choked incline marked the edge of their destination. They were nearly there. Then everything would come down to one final, massive endeavor—a well-planned, well-equipped attack that nevertheless carried with it the possibility of total failure. Not only for themselves but for the people who would end up in thrall to the Coven's elitist and autocratic methods should the attackers be captured or killed.

Zero Site was located primarily in the bowl-like valley formed by a low, sloping mountain that descended toward the coast on one side and a ring of higher, more jagged peaks across from it that looped in a semicircle. Four guard towers stood on the more accessible ridges, high enough that they might well have spotted the incoming first wave of choppers already.

From what the reports had said, along with Eleanor's vague memories of the initial construction plans, the valley contained staging grounds and a few outbuildings, forming a courtyard of sorts. The bulk of the facility—the true, beating heart of the operation—lay within the broad, coast-facing mountain. Whatever the Coven was hiding, they didn't feel comfortable keeping it aboveground where the light of the sun could show it.

Then the peace of the morning, the brief moment of wonder as they beheld the valley below them in the dappled sunlight, came to an abrupt and violent end. The first of Ox's fleet of choppers opened fire on the nearest guard tower with a rocket-propelled grenade launcher.

The projectile streaked out from the side of the lead helicopter, its course somewhat erratic. Despite the considerable distance across the valley, Eleanor still saw the grenade's smoke trail. It looked as though it was going to hit slightly off to the side of the tower proper, but the explosion might well still damage the foundations or start the whole thing on fire.

It struck a boulder on an incline to the side of the tower's base. The rock shattered and fire bloomed. The invisible shockwave kicked up earth and blasted apart the girders and blocks that formed the structure's lower reaches. Parts of the broken boulder and dirt from the hillside rolled down and crashed into the already-weakened foundation, and the tower tilted crazily to the side. A writhing human form toppled out of the perch and into the valley hundreds of feet below. Flames rose and curled around the rest of the structure.

"Well." Dante scratched his nose. "They're off to a pretty good start."

The next chopper of the four launched another RPG at a second tower. Unfortunately, a strong breeze had arisen, making it hard for the pilot to maintain a straight flight path, and the projectile went substantially off-course. It sailed past the tower and descended into the central depression where it blew up a random patch of ground, damaging one of the outbuildings and raising multiple small fires around the point of impact.

Ty shrugged. "At least they're still creating plenty of chaos. That's what we want. It would be better to take out all the towers before our fleet gets in. Speaking of which, our guys still have a couple of RPGs as well."

The rest of Ox's small squadron came in, now firing with rifles and machine guns, peppering the towers and other minor fortifications along the peaks and cliffs with regular gunfire.

One chopper swooped in close enough for someone to toss a hand grenade out the side. It bounced off an outcropping of rock and detonated next to a footpath leading up to the second tower, where an Executive Security goon rushed to join the fight. The explosion blew him apart along with the fencing rail on the path beside him. Most of the pieces tumbled into the valley.

Berger, piloting one of the choppers that towed the APC, radioed the Executioners. "It's Subcommander Berger. We'll be within their approximate range of fire within one minute. That should be the same time when the men on the ground attack from the interior side. Everyone get ready. This is where things get difficult. Our gunners will provide supporting fire as soon as we can, but there's no goddamn doubt that they'll see the APC at some point and figure out what we're doing. Balls to the wall. Out."

Eleanor watched through the camera, still rapt as Zero Site loomed closer. It was hard to tell for sure, but it looked like the ground force was launching their attack as well. The helicopters had dropped off twenty men a safe distance away, leaving two in each attack chopper, a pilot and a gunner. They would provide additional distractions and more carefully targeted attacks on the Coven's defenses.

Speaking of which, the facility was coming alive with activity. The Hellbreakers had done some damage before their enemies could tell what was happening, but the key period of shock and awe was rapidly ending. Security personnel streamed out of hidden doors, and Eleanor saw with mounting dread that some kind of large, automated gun turret mounted on a crane was rising from a hatch in one of the outbuildings' roofs.

The three remaining guard towers suddenly blazed with return fire, unloading on the choppers with machine guns. They largely missed, but one of the aircraft took some damage to its hull and rear propeller, causing it to wobble a bit in the air.

Dante was watching the monitor by Eleanor's side. "Uh-oh."

The crane holding the large, odd-looking weapon reached the top of its ascent. It was now able to aim over the edge of the mountainsides. Eleanor noticed something disturbing for the first time. Within the interior of the gun's chassis was a distinctive and radiant blue light. Atlanticore powered it.

Dante snatched the mic from the radio. "Tell our guys to get clear of that thing. It's some Coven-tech weapon. Bad news. Out."

"Roger," someone replied. Too late, however.

The crystal flashed, and a transparent ripple went through the air toward the faltering helicopter. Tyler and Amahle both gasped, the sound dry and hissing.

Eleanor *felt* the weapon before she heard or saw what it did. It affected the air in a faint but undeniable fashion, like ozone buildup during a lightning storm, and sent out a low but incredibly powerful subsonic vibration in an expanding wave.

Rocks along the ridge, nearby trees, and plants disintegrated into clouds of debris. The invisible projectile, or beam, or whatever it was, struck the chopper's rear half. The pilot couldn't evade quickly enough due to the damage from the machine guns.

The aircraft's entire back portion exploded into a mass of pieces and sparks. Blades detached from the main propeller and scythed in various directions. The front half smoked and frayed as the gunner screamed and toppled through the ragged hole to his doom. The pilot presumably held on, but it was hopeless. The chopper's front half crashed into the hillside and burst into flames before rolling down into the valley and coming to rest on a patch of dirt.

Eleanor squeezed her eyes shut. "*Madre de Dios*. How do we get past that thing?"

Ty's lips were stretched back across his face, his clenched teeth standing out as though he meant to pounce on their enemies and bite their throats out. "Blow it the fuck up," he snarled. He snatched the mic from Dante and shouted, "This is Number One. Concentrate all firepower on that central turret. We cannot afford to lose anyone else to that goddamn thing!"

Berger snapped, "Way ahead of you. Out."

Eleanor inhaled. There was nothing she could do yet. The

only thing was to trust their allies, the Hellbreakers, the men she'd insisted they befriend. So far, they'd been reliable.

However, the odds against them looked stiffer by the minute. The Coven's ground troops were taking up positions in fortified nests on the hillsides, and one of them launched a rocket at Ox's choppers, narrowly missing. All along the mountains, the machine guns boomed and chattered.

At last, the defenders realized that a second flight of helicopters was coming at them from the opposite direction. Men ran around within the valley. The giant Atlanticore disruptor swiveled on its crane, aiming now toward Berger's fleet—and by extension, the APC suspended below it.

Before it had finished moving, the cannon fired again.

"No!" Eleanor gasped.

This time the buzzing shockwave was much stronger, as though someone had sent a high-decibel sound directly through their flesh like an electric current. Above them, something exploded. The noise rattled the steel around them, and fiery light flashed the monitor, combined with raining debris.

Ty muttered, "Oh, *shit.*"

It felt as though the APC's bottom fell out from beneath their feet, like the initial drop in an elevator, but far worse. The beam had taken out at least one of the choppers towing them. They were sinking. The other helicopters couldn't support the weight.

Gage dashed to the controls, wildly gesturing at the radio. "Tell them I will increase the power of the anti-gravity device. They must hurry to get us within the compound."

Amahle retorted, "That won't matter if we get blasted out of the sky. Tell them to destroy that weapon!"

Dante sputtered and cursed under his breath, snatched up the mic again, and repeated both of his teammates' suggestions. Berger and the others didn't answer, but it seemed as though they began moving faster.

Then, as Gage increased the power and the awful feeling of

falling lessened, a rocket streaked down from one of the choppers above them. Its aim was true. It struck the Atlanticore cannon at the juncture of the gun and the crane that raised it into the sky.

The explosion detonated the crystal within. The monitor went pure white as the massive blast overwhelmed the camera's ability to process what it saw, and the crack was like a peal of thunder—higher, sharper, and somehow more violent than the boom of the rocket explosion preceding it.

When the light cleared, Eleanor saw that the cannon, crane, and the building that had housed them were no more, having been blown to particles. The blast had also wrought significant damage on the valley's inner hillsides, killing at least half a dozen Coven troops that she could see.

Ty pumped his fist. "Yes! Good work. Now get us the hell in there so we can finish the job."

They were almost to the crest of the coast-side mountain. Once they crossed it, there would be no turning back. They would be within the lion's den itself.

Both fleets of choppers exchanged gunfire with the remaining turrets. While the Hellbreakers' ground-based infantry couldn't break through the dug-in active defenses that survived the explosion, they at least kept them busy with constant, alternating bursts of rifle fire and the occasional hand grenade.

Eleanor grimaced. In addition to at least two choppers the disruptor cannon had downed, it looked as though the Hellbreakers' infantry had lost about four men. It was only a fraction of their force, but enough that victory would come at a major and painful cost. Freed from Gus's unstable influence, though, they were terrifyingly disciplined and held the line in the face of withering return fire.

The APC drifted over the peak of the broad seaside mountain. At once, the remaining pilots in the towing fleet descended, and once more Eleanor and the others felt sickening waves of nausea as they struggled to stay on their feet.

Berger radioed them. "We can't dip much farther without crashing. You'll have to drift the rest of the way down yourselves."

Gage was already increasing the power on the anti-gravity device. It was working. Their descent seemed slower and gentler. However, Eleanor noticed a faint electric burning smell that disturbed her.

The Nepali frantically waved as Dante radioed Berger back, giving them the green light to cut the APC loose.

Eleanor shut her eyes and prayed to God.

The gunners in the aircraft above them released the cables. Everyone lost balance and tried not to be sick as gravity seized them, only for Gage and the prototype Atlanticore device to fight back, cushioning their fall. They were still plummeting far too fast. The impact would snap their limbs, break their spines, crush their skulls against the steel walls around them.

"Hold on!" Gage cried, struggling against the controls while half-sprawled in the corner.

The crystal hummed louder in the last second or two of their descent as the device went into overdrive. It was as though they were sinking into an enormous blanket of cotton, and everyone found their footing again...

Only to lose it as the ground rose to meet them and slammed into the APC's treads.

Their guts churned horribly within their bodies, making it feel like they were still falling seconds after the vehicle had settled upon the ground. Everyone had fallen, stumbled, or crashed into some part of the compartment. In many cases, they'd also collided with each other. Their heads and limbs ached from the impact.

There was no time to feel pain, no time to be disoriented. Quick and overwhelming force was their only hope, the one advantage they could press now that they were beyond using the element of surprise. Outside, the defenders had taken a bead on the vehicle and were hammering it with machine-gun fire although their bullets couldn't penetrate the thick armor.

Eleanor forced her head to clear itself, exerted as much sheer will as she could muster, and dragged herself to her feet, raising her submachine gun and preparing to do whatever was necessary. They were rushing in blind, and there was no time to waste.

Ty pounced onto the ladder and climbed it, opening the top hatch and hurling himself onto the APC's mounted gun. Almost before he had time to assess the situation around him, he opened fire.

The sound was painful, practically deafening. Eleanor's ears throbbed and rang as the weapon roared to life. It would've been worse if it were inside the vehicle proper, but too much of the noise still filtered down through the hatch.

Daria waved for them all to follow her and she, too, climbed out. Gage stayed within. He would use the APC as a weapon until they opened the way into the main facility.

As Eleanor clambered out, Ty aimed the mounted gun at a fortified nest near the crotch of two ridges, where four Exec Security goons exchanged shots with the Hellbreakers' infantry. He pummeled them with heavy rounds, killing two of them outright and pinning the others down beneath the powerful barrage. It was enough time for one of the Hellbreakers to haul himself onto the ridge's crest and drop a grenade into the nest. The enemy troops within failed to get out before it detonated. The flash of fire and kinetic pulse liquidated them and collapsed part of the valley wall.

Daria pointed at Eleanor and Ty, indicating that she wanted the three of them to stick together. With their weaker submachine guns, the two women could concentrate on cursory suppressive fire. Ty would do the more surgical work with his rifle against the defenders in the valley courtyard who posed an immediate threat.

Meanwhile, Dante and Amahle jumped off and made for the main entrance into the mountainside sanctum, taking with them a bundle of dynamite and a small wad of plastic explosives.

The mounted gun fell silent as Ty spent the last of its ammo. Having taken out over half of the surviving Exec Security goons within the valley, it had served its purpose. He hopped down while Eleanor and Daria covered him with bursts of fire as Gage drove off.

Something boomed, and sprays of dirt kicked up near them, growing closer. One of the guard towers at the complex's far end had targeted them and tried to sweep them with a machine gun.

Ty swung his rifle up and squeezed off a few rounds, but there was no time to make such a precise shot at his present distance. He gestured, and he, Eleanor, and Daria all ran for cover, hiding behind a shed made of brick and concrete. It wouldn't hold up indefinitely, but it was far better than nothing.

Meanwhile, Gage drove the APC straight toward the tower.

Eleanor marveled during a lull in the endless shooting, "What is he doing?" She popped out her half-empty magazine to save for later and slapped in a fresh one. Behind her, gunshots slammed into the shed, causing brick dust and chunks of concrete to rain down around her.

Daria shrugged. "What he's supposed to. He's far better protected than we are, is he not?"

Ty scowled. "That hill is damn steep, though. I hope he knows what he's doing. He's the one who made that heap of junk work again so I guess if anyone would know, it's him."

The APC rumbled across the valley's central floor, which the Coven or Executive Security had turned into something like a cargo staging area or perhaps a parade ground. He was heading for the slope beneath the active guard tower. Above them, the helicopters continued to circle, taking pot shots at Security goons and sweeping the other two towers.

Noticing Gage's approach, the gunners within the tower stopped shooting at the shed and adjusted their aim, spraying the heavy vehicle with lead. The metal grew badly dented, sparks flew, and Eleanor watched in dismay as small pieces fell off the exterior hull. The APC's design could withstand small arms fire, but the turret guns were powerful enough to wear it down gradually. Too much sustained fire would finish Gage.

Suddenly, the enemy fire halted. Either the gun's barrel overheated and needed replacing, or the men operating it had to load a fresh belt. As the APC plowed up the slope, slowing but still moving inexorably forward, a man jumped out of the turret to roll down the hillside, then tried to flee to a fenced-off overhang along the cliffside path.

Ty muttered, "Sorry, pal." He raised his rifle and fired twice in semi-auto. The man toppled, rolled, and lay still.

Another burst of fire came at them from somewhere higher on the slope closest to them. Eleanor reflexively jumped back and crouched, snapping up her MP5. She and Daria sprayed nine-millimeter rounds toward the attackers, not sure if they were hitting anything but discouraging them if nothing else.

Eleanor checked on Gage's progress. The APC had picked up speed, moving in its highest gear despite the hillside's angle. It slammed into the guard tower as the remaining man finished readying his machine gun and opened fire again.

The structure's base collapsed. The entire thing tottered, and Gage reversed as fast as he could, swerving from side to side while the tower fell nearly on top of him. It finally shattered against the rocks a couple of yards to the vehicle's right. Gage rumbled back to the valley's center and parked the APC in the space between the shed and the main entrance to provide decent cover for the trio as they rushed to join Dante and Amahle.

The physician and the sniper had reached the main doors. As

they'd expected, the defenders had shut, locked, and sealed them after they'd deployed enough of the garrison to man the outer fortifications.

Dante placed the bundle of dynamite against the juncture of the two door parts. "What do you say we do this the simple way? Just have you shoot the dynamite from a nice safe distance. Pretty sure it will take care of this."

A burst of gunfire from below rang out. When it quieted, Amahle said, "You have great faith in my marksmanship, I see. Yes, that makes as much sense as anything else."

They ran sideways along the girded walkway ringing the middle of the valley wall until they were above where Ty, Daria, and Eleanor crouched. Then, while Dante covered her by blasting more or less at random with his shotgun, Amahle got to her knees and raised her rifle.

The dynamite was bright red, making it a little easier to see in the gloom below the overhanging cliff. The morning sun wasn't yet high enough to illuminate the particular cranny where the dug-in entrance lay. She exhaled, focused with a total singularity of purpose on the target, and squeezed the trigger.

A booming *crackle* became a thunder of utter devastation. The shockwave practically knocked the Executioners off their feet. Fire blossomed and twisted pieces of steel shot out across the open space below while parts of the cliff wall collapsed, showering dirt and rock across the ground. When the smoke cleared, they'd clearly breached the entrance, but the miniature landslides on either side had come dangerously close to blocking it off as soon as it had opened.

Dante loaded extra shells into his Ithaca 37. "Maybe we should've used a little less explosive."

Amahle twisted a finger in her ringing ear. "Oh, you don't say?" As she got back to her feet, the hatch of the APC opened and Gage at last climbed out. "The crystal is destroyed. This vehicle is barely drivable, but it served its purpose."

Ty looked around at all of them. "Enough bullshit. Everyone in. The Hellbreakers have the rest of them out here at a stalemate. We need to get in, get what we can, and get the hell out. Now."

With a last scan of the devastated valley for any immediate threats, the six of them dashed toward the entrance. No new guards were rushing out to fight them yet, but they all doubted that whatever the Coven had inside the mountain had been left unprotected.

As the oddly bright, silver-colored hallway beyond the blasted entrance and heaps of debris took shape in her field of vision, Eleanor had an unpleasant premonition that the worst was yet to come.

CHAPTER EIGHTEEN

The half-dozen Executioners fell into a battle order that would suit them best in close quarters combat. Ty and Dante were out in front, Eleanor and Daria in the middle, and Amahle and Gage brought up the rear. Beyond the ravaged entrance, the silver corridor stretched for about ten yards before it opened into a lobby or foyer of sorts.

In the back of her mind, Eleanor wondered what their objective was. At no point had they determined the precise nature of it. They only had a general plan to storm Zero Site, inflict as much damage as they could, and find something—anything—they could potentially use against the Coven.

Now wasn't the time to ask. Of greater concern was that they also had no idea the kind of opposition they might face.

They reached the end of the hall. Ty and Dante stormed out and spread to the sides, their gun muzzles covering the room beyond while Eleanor and Daria raised theirs to open fire on anyone or anything who attacked them. If need be, they could drop to their knees and allow Amahle and Gage to join in as well.

The chamber at the end of the hall appeared to be empty. There was a single small desk, likewise decorated in an indeterminate silver-colored substance, and on the rear wall was an insignia the size of a man—a hexagram on its side so two points faced up, two down, and one each to the sides.

Eleanor had seen it before, stamped on one or two envelopes containing official documents that the Executives had forbidden her from opening and reading. The sigil of the Coven of Miracles.

As the group moved to occupy the room completely, she snapped back to the present. "What is our objective? What, specifically, must we do?"

Ty grunted. "You tell us. You know more about their operation than we do. I suppose they kept you out of the loop concerning the juiciest stuff. In lieu of any other clear-cut goal, I say we sweep the place, kill anyone who fucks with us, and raid the file cabinets for evidence."

Daria wasted no time voicing her support. "That's the best option we have. If we can find incriminating materials that show how the Coven has been manipulating us all, and their schemes for taking over the island and ruling with an iron fist, we can present it at the upcoming international conference. Or, failing that, we can seize more of their technology to use it against them in the future. Which would also hurt them on a financial basis since Atlanticore devices don't come cheap."

Eleanor nodded. "Yes, so be it. Their pockets are deep, but even the Executives don't have unlimited funds, nor can they buy off the entire world if they seek to evade justice for their crimes."

Dante had advanced to the opposite wall. From the small central lobby, corridors branched off in two directions, at angles from the room and leading deeper into the mountain. The physician pointed at a placard in the corner.

"Well, well," he intoned. "Looky here. It was nice of them to put a map of the facility where visitors could see it. Symmetrical layout, hallways loop around into major rooms on both sides and bend back toward what looks like an elevator at the rear. There are three floors. This is the top one." He turned and looked at the others.

Ty chewed on his lower lip. "I don't like dividing the force, but we don't have time to sweep through six whole wings of this place as one group. If they have more guys waiting for us, they'll have that much more time to prepare, not to mention they could be flying in reinforcements behind us as we speak."

Gage adjusted his glasses. "Yes, under the circumstances, splitting up might be the wiser option. Two teams, one can clear each wing of each floor, then we meet at the elevator and descend to the next floor together."

"It's settled." Ty was never one to agonize much over his decisions. Whether acting alone or as their de facto leader, he made quick assessments, stuck to them, and plowed ahead, dealing with every problem that arose through a mixture of brute force, cunning, and willpower.

He pointed at Eleanor and Daria. "Come with me. We'll take the left side. Gage, Dante, and Amahle, you take the right. Move fast, but don't skip anything important. Yell if you need help. Let's go!"

Taking the lead, he stomped into the left-hand corridor with Eleanor falling in behind him and Daria bringing up the rear. Eleanor looked back over her shoulder and saw the other three dashing into the opposite hallway. Dante was out in front. A sudden sharp pang in her chest made it impossible to ignore—she was worried about him. She didn't like the thought of him being in danger where she couldn't see him and be there to help.

He was a good fighter, she told herself, able to hold his own despite his lack of formal martial training, not to mention a doctor. If injured, he could probably save his own life under circumstances that would spell a death sentence for most people.

She cleared her mind of distracting thoughts as they plunged ahead into the unknown.

The hallways that branched off to the sides were far longer

than the one leading into the underground complex from the valley. It was hard to see what lay at the end despite the surprisingly bright fluorescent light that shone from the discreet translucent panels overhead.

As they approached the terminal point, Eleanor saw that whatever lay in the room beyond it was glowing blue. The illumination was faint but noticeable.

The group slowed as they reached the corner. It appeared that the chamber beyond was a kind of second miniature lobby, with chairs around the edges and doors leading to small offices or perhaps bathrooms. The glow came from an imperceptible point off to the right. Ty raised his fist, and they halted.

He looked at Daria and Eleanor and mouthed, "On three." Then he extended one, two, and finally three fingers before bursting forth and pivoting to the right.

"Jesus Christ!" he shrieked, stumbled over his feet, and pitched sidelong into a chair.

Eleanor, right behind him, was suddenly overwhelmed with fear. She had *never* seen Ty react to something like that before, and a split second after the awful sound of his scream told her that something was terribly wrong, she saw exactly what had affected him.

Two men stood guarding the next stretch of hallway. Or at least, they'd been men originally. They wore the same armored vests as regular security personnel. There the resemblance ended. Their skin had turned the color of dirty snow and looked wet and sticky. All of their hair had fallen out, including their eyebrows. Their eyes had a definite bluish radiance to them.

The strangest trait of all, and the one that promised the greatest pain, was the cannon-like attachment that had replaced each one's left arm with an organic mishmash of flesh, steel, and crystal. The barrels held orbs of blue fire, the source of the strange glow they'd seen.

Eleanor's jaw fell open, and she reflexively dropped to her

knees. Daria made a short gasping sound and hurled herself beyond the threshold into the room, rolling and crouching.

The women's automatic movements saved their lives. Both of the mutated guards raised their arm-cannons and fired in unison. The high-pitched sounds of tortured air rang out as they unleashed blazing streams of painfully bright blue plasma that sizzled into the silvery walls with phosphorus-like crackling white flames.

As Eleanor's knees struck the floor, her submachine gun came up, and her finger depressed the trigger. The MP5 snarled as it spat out its leaden payload, the muzzle rise drawing the course of the bullets up. The first two or three struck one of the mutants' vests to no avail, but then another three landed in his throat and face. Thin, steaming blood more brown than red spilled from the wounds as the deformed man slumped back against the wall.

Daria came out of her roll with her Uzi up and blasting away. Nine-millimeter rounds cut across the second mutant's legs, collapsing his knees and sending him to the floor.

Ty sprang back into action, ashen-faced but the master of his fear. His wakizashi flashed from its scabbard, and he drove the blade through the mutant's head, finishing him off before he could do any further harm.

Eleanor looked back. The fire started by the plasma beams had burned out quickly enough but had still done a lot of damage to the walls. To have been hit with it herself would've ensured a messy, painful, but at least not overly prolonged death.

Daria stared at the loathsome corpses. She mumbled something under her breath, perhaps in Hebrew rather than Polish.

Ty sheathed his sword. "These are the people we're up against," he stated in a low voice. "*This* is what they're willing to do for power. Let's move on."

At the same time, in the other hallway, Dante took the lead as the trio approached a similar suite of small lobby spaces with attached offices and closets. A yellow and black line across the floor demarcated the threshold between the corridor and the room.

Amahle noticed it first. "Wait."

Dante scoffed. "What, an alarm? After all the explosions we caused, who cares?" He stepped over it, haste and confidence momentarily blinding him to the fact that Amahle's instincts were usually good when it came to sensing a trap.

As he put his foot down beyond it, a hatch about the size of a playing card opened in the floor. It discharged a tiny silver device like a baseball studded with four pebble-sized blue crystals. It shot up into the air and hovered there at about chest height for half a second.

Amahle's hand clamped down on Dante's shoulder. "Back!" she screamed while pulling.

In that brief and terrible instant, Dante felt that he was choking—on fear, but also on guilt for potentially getting his friends killed with his recklessness. There was no time to save himself. Instead, using his greater size and weight, he shoved backward, sending Amahle tumbling back into Gage so both of them fell into the hallway behind the yellow line.

Then Dante tumbled to the floor within the room as the device activated. Two curved panels extended from either side of the sphere, each with one crystal studded in its center. The buzzing vibration was instantly familiar, as was the hazy appearance of the air.

Gasping, he flung himself into the corner, expecting another disruptor beam to reduce him to a gelatinous puddle. Instead, the field of distortion was oddly restricted. Moving, but confined. It *orbited* the device.

He snapped his fingers. "Gage! It's a, a, fuck. Planetary ring! Expanding. See?"

It made sense now. The panels projected the disruptor field in a cycling motion, then the whole device rotated in place, sweeping the destructive ring around the room's periphery. It would kill or destroy anyone who got too close without damaging the chamber's structure.

Gage crawled to the edge of the yellow line and looked at the device, his eyes shining with intellectual curiosity. "Fascinating. But most inconvenient." He looked down at the little hatch where the deadly sphere had emerged. Within it were naked circuits. "How foolish."

He unscrewed the cap of his canteen and tossed some water into the hole. Immediately, it sparked and gave off smoke, crackling as it shorted out. The rotating disruptor fields faded, the device slowed, and it crashed, rendered useless.

Amahle crept forward with her mouth agape. "What on Earth have these people been doing in their spare time?"

Gage smiled. "Science. But they are quite bad at it. Here, let me help you up."

Dante had already got to his feet. He coughed. "Sorry. Next time I'll listen, Amahle."

"Good. I have no time to scold or argue. Let us move on, please."

Minutes later, the two groups converged in the rear room. Hurriedly debriefing one another, they agreed that they'd found nothing of interest save the Coven's bizarre defensive systems. Ahead of them was the elevator, leading down to the other two floors.

As Ty was about to press the button, they heard a *ding*. The elevator had already been summoned downward and was now on its way up. Eyes widening, Ty motioned for them to separate and fall back into the hallway mouths.

Everyone rushed backward, barely getting their guns ready in time for the doors to open. Within the elevator were five or six Exec Security men getting lectured by their commanding officer.

"...Ought to have been neutralized by—*No!*"

The Executioners started shooting. Surprised and caught in a crossfire, the goons all died in seconds, cut apart by the mass barrage. As their corpses slumped to the floor, Ty was first out in front to check for any stragglers. Eleanor had to admire how quickly he'd recovered from his embarrassing reaction to the mutant troopers not long ago.

They pulled the bodies free from the elevator and went down to the next floor. There they found a complex of rooms and halls much like those above, but in this case, it seemed to be primarily a barracks. It was all but empty.

A single guard had remained behind. The terrified man tried to shoot the Executioners as soon as he saw them but was shaking so badly that he missed with not one but two shots. That was all the time Ty needed to put a bullet between his eyes.

Once they cleared the second floor, each team sweeping a different wing again, they converged back at the elevator and descended to the final floor.

The doors parted. Ty and Dante leapt out with weapons free, their faces set in grim determination to destroy any obstacle that stood in their way. Behind them, Eleanor dropped to one knee, giving Gage the freedom to shoot over her head if he had to. Daria pressed herself to the side of the hallway, creating a space for Amahle.

Ahead of them was a short corridor that ended in a single shimmering door. The layout of the third and deepest floor was slightly different from that of the two above, it appeared. From what Eleanor could recall, Dante had said that all three were nearly identical. Perhaps he'd mistaken that.

The door burst open a second before Tyler could seize the handle. Standing on the threshold and aiming its glowing arm-cannon at them was another of the mutant soldiers, drooling on himself as his furious eyes glowed bright blue.

"Shit!" Dante burst out, firing his shotgun almost before he knew what he was doing. Amahle squeezed off a round from her rifle at the same time.

The buckshot took the augmented trooper in the chest, failing to penetrate his armor but still blasting him back a step while Amahle's rifle bullet struck him directly in one of his luminous eyes. Letting out a ragged howl that quickly faded to a soft groan, the mutated guard fell back, his arm-cannon spewing blue plasma at the upper walls and ceiling. The fires it ignited burned brightly for a few seconds. Drops of melted plastic and chunks of burned concrete fell, then the uncanny miniature blaze extinguished itself.

Ty's rifle was up, and he was first through the door. "Clear." He stepped over the corpse, aiming his gun at it briefly while checking to ensure the man was dead, then waited for the others. His discomfort at being anywhere close to the creature was still quite obvious.

They jumped through in their usual order. Beyond, the hallway split into two diagonal corridors once again. There was something different about the bottommost floor, though. It was subtle, but Eleanor couldn't help noticing it.

The ceilings seemed higher, and the lights brighter. It was as though the Coven had designed this final level to be used and inhabited more often and by people of greater importance within their ranks. Thus, they'd constructed it with more care and attention to aesthetic detail.

Helpfully enough, another map lay at the juncture point of the two halls.

Dante was once again the first to notice it. "Conference room, that way." He pointed left. "Sounds like the kind of place they'd keep documentation. Eleanor, you should be the one to go that way."

"Roger," Ty said. "Same groups as before. What's down the other hall?"

Dante snorted. "Lab. That ought to be interesting. In a bad way, I'm sure. We'll tell you guys all about it later over a banana split or something."

Ty was already gliding down the left corridor, rifle at low ready. "Sounds great. Good luck, Executioners. This is the home stretch. Remember that our fan club is moving in behind us."

Eleanor and Daria jogged along behind him.

The hallway they'd chosen had no features on its right side, but three doors to the left opened into what looked like spacious offices or lounge-type areas. Ty swept his eyes over the windows in the first before kicking in the door. He hopped in with Eleanor coming up behind him in a low crouch.

Empty, or so it appeared. Daria watched the hallway while they moved in.

Ty pointed at a file cabinet. "Check that." As Eleanor moved toward it, he made certain no one was hiding under the desks or behind the chairs. There was also another internal door that turned out to lead to a small one-person bathroom, similarly unoccupied.

Eleanor opened each drawer in the cabinet. All were empty. They contained folders but no documents. Frowning, she went to the two major desks and looked in them as well, finding little except materials invoices. There was, however, an itinerary for a meeting from a week ago. The names of the attendees were mostly masses of initials and abbreviations, disguising their identities, but it was better than nothing. She slipped it into her jacket.

Ty saw her doing so and assumed they'd finished in here. He left the room behind, rejoining Daria, and the two of them moved down to the next office while Eleanor trailed them and kept a wary eye on the hall toward the elevator. It sounded faintly like someone might be moving around on the floor above, but the thick layers of earth separating the facility's levels did a disturbingly good job of absorbing noise.

They checked the next two offices and found nothing. At the end of the hallway, the windows revealed what could only be the conference room Dante had mentioned. At least one person was within, trying to stay out of sight but not quite succeeding.

Ty raised his rifle to chest height. "On three. One, two...*three.*" He shouldered through the door, and they all burst in with him in the lead.

In the corner was a safe. It lay open. An older man in a black tuxedo with a white mustache stood nearby, and a middle-aged woman in a tan dress was pulling things out of it. Both of them turned their heads and saw the intruders at the same time.

The man exclaimed, "Shut it! *Shut it!*" He frantically gestured with a spotted hand.

The woman had an armload of folders, dossiers, and stacks of paper. She hurled them clumsily back into the compartment with one hand while seizing the safe door with the other.

"Stop!" Ty ordered her. When she ignored him, he shot her through the chest. She fell back, gasping and bleeding, and went stiff and motionless seconds later.

Eleanor's gut clenched up. She didn't know the woman personally but had seen her before at corporate functions and had one or two brief, reasonably pleasant interactions. She couldn't recall her name.

Ty held his rifle on the man, who was trembling and breathing in short, ragged gasps, his eyes rolling in shock and horror. "Don't move, friend," Ty threatened him. His face fell. "Shit, I think he's having a heart attack."

Daria rushed over to the man while pointing behind her. "Eleanor! Check that stuff. See what's so important that they tried to hide it."

She did. Rushing over, she found the documents in a couple of haphazard piles, but initial glances and a bit of thumbing through confirmed that it was probably what they were looking for.

Records of experiments. Invoices for shady business deals involving Atlanticore transfers, semi-legal weapons purchases, and what could only have been bribes and kickbacks. Outlines for political initiatives that circumvented local rules and customs.

"Yes," she announced. "I think this is what we need. With these documents, we can cast a tremendous amount of aspersion on the Junior Board of the Executives. This means we'll also get the Senior Board, and through them, the Coven itself."

Before she could ask how the man was doing, a faint humming sound impressed itself on her consciousness, followed by the sound she *least* wanted to hear—the *ding* of the elevator doors opening at the end of the hall.

Daria cursed in Polish, trying to keep the old Exec alive as he thrashed around on a tabletop while Ty threw himself toward the door. "Eleanor! Gather as much of that shit as you can. We're taking it out of here, and they are *not* getting it back."

With that vow on his lips, he broke into a bloodcurdling war cry and flung open the door, raising his rifle and blasting on full auto toward the staging hall before the elevator. A man screamed faintly at the other end, and a short burst of gunfire came back at them once Ty's magazine ran dry. He sidestepped back into the conference chamber instantly, dodging it as he ejected the mag and let it clatter to the floor.

Daria rose from the table and stepped back. "This man is finished. I can do nothing for him. Maybe Dante would've been able to save him."

"Whatever," Ty snarled as a couple of potshots came at them from the hall. "Help me kill these fucks."

Daria picked up her Uzi. "If you insist, Mr. Katakura." She slammed the gun's barrel into a hole in the wall blown by their foes and sprayed lead blindly toward the intruders.

Eleanor was trying to gather up the most pertinent of the

paperwork. She would only be able to carry so much, but there wasn't time to sift through it all in fine detail. She looked around for a suitcase or something of the sort, cursing herself for not having thought to bring a satchel or backpack.

On the floor near the dead woman was a purse. It wasn't as big as Eleanor would've preferred, but it would do. She snatched it up, opened it, and stuffed in documents, focusing on the ones that seemed to involve questionable business practices, violent power plays, or scientific research that violated the Nuremberg laws.

In other words, anything that would hit the Coven where it would hurt the most.

The gunfire kept crackling back and forth. In a lull between volleys, Ty asked, "You almost done? I want to take the fight to them."

"Yes." Eleanor could barely squeeze the top flap shut over the thick masses of paper within. "Let's go."

CHAPTER NINETEEN

Dante saw the guard first. By the time the man realized how close the enemy was and raised his rifle, the Ithaca had already gone off. The glass window of the first lab room shattered. His face came apart under the combined onslaught of buckshot and glass, and he died instantly, the rest of him flopping uselessly to the floor.

"Good shot," Amahle said. "You're using a shotgun at close range, yes, but it was still nicely done."

He gave his shoulders a short roll, acknowledging the half-hearted compliment, and kicked open the door.

Within, a scientist in a white coat cowered under a table. Various devices and implements were scattered around. The shot that had killed the guard had damaged some of them.

While Amahle took the scientist by the elbow and hauled him aside, Gage stepped into the room.

Dante backed out into the hall. "This looks like your department, Gage. Technological stuff rather than biological, I think. I'll keep watch out here."

The Nepali moved in, surveying the dizzying array of half-assembled devices and trying to keep his head from spinning.

"There is so much. There is no way I could study even a small fraction of these things." He looked at their captive. "Sir, what is all of this? What lies in the other laboratory?"

The man was trembling in abject terror, and it was difficult for him to form coherent words. Furthermore, he seemed to hail from Central Asia and spoke with a thick Turkic-influenced accent. Gage discerned a couple of essential points through the near-gibberish.

First, most of the tech scattered around the room was biological after all, in a fashion. It related to the Coven's ongoing research into Atlanticore machines that could be implanted into the body to achieve extraordinary healing powers, feats of physical strength, and the like.

Second, in the other lab was where the remaining researchers were conducting their most important experiment, involving "the boss." Whoever that was.

The three Executioners all exchanged glances. Dante was first to speak.

"As fascinating as all this crap is, I think we need to see what's in the other room before we worry about any of it. Sounds pretty major."

Amahle nodded. She hauled the scientist to his feet, forced him out the door, and ordered him to march toward the elevator. He did so with stiff mechanical steps, trying not to look behind him.

The South African turned her eyes to her partners. "I will stand watch here. You two check the other room."

Dante went out first while topping off his shotgun. Gage was at his elbow. The door to the second lab area, which they sensed was larger than the first, was solid steel. No windows looked out upon the hallway. Dante reached out and grabbed the handle. To his surprise, it wasn't locked and didn't seem to *have* a lock. The Coven was rather lax on security this deep into their home turf.

The instant he opened the door, two or three voices shouted in near-unison, "Don't shoot! Don't shoot, please!"

Both he and Gage had their weapons ready, but they made no move to open fire yet. Each hopped into the room, moving to one side or the other, scanning everything before them for any sign of threats.

Both men gasped, nearly crying out in shock despite themselves.

The lab as a whole somewhat resembled a vast operating theater, but the floor was entirely level. Its decor, atmosphere, *feng shui*, and so forth all put Dante instantly in mind of a place where people performed surgery, something he'd learned to pick up on throughout his education and career.

Off to his left, a woman scientist crouched on the floor with her hands on her head. To the right, there was another scientist, a man, who stood with arms outstretched and finger-splayed hands shaking in the air. Behind him was a third individual—a tall man in an old-fashioned black military uniform, like those worn by some present-day monarchs.

The pair noted all of these details, but the thing in the center of the chamber was what stupefied them with awe and horror.

Suspended chest-deep in a clear fluid within a transparent cylinder and with multiple wires and tubes sprouting out in all directions was Jori Singh. He wasn't dead—somehow they both instantly knew that the machine was either keeping him alive or had revived him—but he was still a fair ways off from what most people would consider "living."

The holes in his body had mostly healed despite the passage of mere days since his apparent death. His eyes were open and glassy, mostly white, and his mouth and chest moved ever so slightly in a sluggish parody of breathing. His arms were straight down by his sides as though bound there, but no restraints were visible aside from the cylindrical compartment's walls.

It was hard to be sure at first glance, but a faint blue glow emanated from various parts of his body. Dante's immediate suspicion was that they'd implanted crystals in his flesh for whatever bizarre purpose the Coven had once again tried to revive him.

Gage went over to the crouching woman and shoved her toward the two men, keeping all of the prisoners together. He held his rifle on them, but his eyes kept turning toward Singh.

Dante shook his head, dumbfounded. "Oh, no. *Hell* no. This fucking guy again? They killed him. The Coven took him out. Now they're trying to say that he's the *leader* of the whole operation? I don't get it."

The tall man in the uniform spoke up in a gloomy but dignified tone. "The Coven has no single leader. A younger faction decided that Singh had become a liability and tried to remove him. After he was gunned down, my faction overruled them. We retrieved his body and brought it here.

"He alone has been able to balance the competing interests, and he is by far the most knowledgeable of us all. He acted as an elder statesman, an advisor, more than anything. If this procedure works, he *will* be our leader, as perhaps he always should have been."

Dante looked at the man. "Well, that clears up a few things. Thanks for saying so without us having to beat you up and point guns in your face."

Then Singh blinked and sighed. The latter's sound was deep, resonant, and strangely echoing in the lab's confined space, with a powerful vibration to it like a milder version of the Coven's sonic disruptor guns. The skin on Dante's spine crawled up and down.

"*Yes,*" Jori Singh said. "Yes. The time *has* come, at last, to complete our work. If it requires me to take on a new and more direct role, so be it."

His voice continued to reverberate as though the machine preserving his life were amplifying it by artificial means. Yet his tone was only half-lucid, dreamy and detached. Dante couldn't tell if the glassy white eyes could see anything or if Singh had the slightest idea to whom he was speaking.

Gage beseeched the old man, "Singh! It is me, Dr. Gurung, do you remember? If you are now leading these people, you must convince them to stop what they're doing. Atlantica will become no more than a dictatorship, no matter how good you think your intentions are."

"*No,*" Singh responded, and despite the dreamy, drawn-out quality of his voice, there was something icy and final about the way he said it. "We have tried, time and again, to accomplish what must happen the easy way. What *must* happen. Now we are out of time. We cannot delay our goals any longer. Think of what our success will mean for the world. Atlantica will become the first place to witness the next phase in human evolution. That is worth more than the lives of—"

"Bullshit," Dante snapped back. "You always had your head in the clouds, as near as I can tell, but you're not talking *any* sense now. Whatever the hell they're doing to you, it's affecting your brain."

He turned to the two scientists and the other man, the Senior Board member, whoever he was. "You guys are creating a monster here. Putting this thing in charge of an organization like yours is only going to end badly for everyone."

The tall man's face contorted in a sneer of contempt. "What ended badly was giving you people—you peasants, you mercenaries—so much authority to begin with. Once Mr. Singh's transformation is complete, we will possess total power over the full potential of Atlanticore and be able to bring our entire species to the brink of transcendence. The tragedy of the human condition will be no more. We all will be as gods."

"*Yes,*" Singh agreed, and the almost childlike longing in his voice instilled a brief sense of awe...but also fear and loathing. Everything about the spectacle before them was fundamentally wrong. "I will be the first of the new gods. The rest of you may follow me as my children."

The blue glow was getting stronger. Gage moved closer to the tube and exclaimed something in his native language.

Dante admitted to himself that he was terrified. The Coven was meddling with forces that were largely beyond human comprehension, and they were doing so in ways far less controlled or competent than he would've guessed. "What is it, Gage?"

The Gurkha replied, "Singh doesn't have implanted crystals. He is *becoming* the crystal. It is overtaking his body like a disease. I think the procedure's design is to make him a living conduit for Atlanticore energy."

"Exactly," the man in the uniform drawled.

Dante gaped. "You idiot! Atlanticore is so unstable that even your people haven't figured out how to use it safely yet. You're turning a guy who already had a screw loose into a wannabe mad god *and* a living bomb at the same time. It never occurred to you that this might be a bad idea?"

The man moved closer to the tube and his new savior, scowling. The scientists stayed put.

Singh's voice rose again, echoing and crackling. "I can feel it. Everything I learned throughout a lifetime, all the knowledge that made me so well-valued by my esteemed colleagues. The duke is right. With this new and perfect body, I can make better use of my gifts than ever before. Look! See how much control I have over it all!"

His limbs twitched, and a slow writhing shudder went through his entire lanky frame. The clear liquid within the container bubbled and steamed. The blue glow grew brighter and stronger.

Gage backed away. "The crystal is spreading rapidly." Around them, the sense of the air electrifying grew alarmingly denser and more threatening. Something began to hum. The sound was everywhere but centered on the tube. "He is overcharging the system to force the transformation to take place faster. There is a chance he will simply, ah, explode."

The duke trembled with rage. "Absurd. The whole point of fusing crystal with living tissue is to reduce its instability. We proved this theoretically and mathematically over a month ago. We would've gone forward with the experiments had you not distracted us by destroying our centrifuge."

Dante stared at him. His confidence was shaky. The duke must have *known* that Gage was probably right but refused to admit it. The Coven was in far more dire straits than they'd let on. They were willing to risk everything on this final, madcap experiment, potentially destroying even themselves if it meant they could overcome the deficits that had accumulated during their megalomaniacal program.

The physician stated simply, "We have to get the hell out of here."

Behind them and down the hall, the elevator *dinged*. Amahle shouted, "Everyone get down!"

Dante and Gage, well accustomed to knowing when lead was about to start flying, dropped into deep crouches at once. As rifle fire barked down the hallway, the scientists and the duke hesitated, frozen in dumb confusion.

A couple of bullets punched through the wall. One found its way into the female scientist's neck, severing her throat and spine in one swift motion. She flopped to the ground in a rapidly spreading puddle of blood.

Another bullet struck a throbbing, vein-like tube that ran from something beyond the wall into Singh's resuscitation tube. Steam sprayed from it, and the bubbling within the cylinder grew more violent. Singh turned to look at Dante and Gage, his whitened eyes now gleaming like sapphires.

"It is inevitable. You cannot stop humanity's destiny. Here, I will show you. Let me lead the way!"

A crack appeared in the tube's upper glass, then from it jumped an arcing blue bolt of sheer power. It struck the duke square in the chest. His arrogant expression turned to alarm for a fraction of a second before he exploded. His blood and bodily water content turned to red steam, and the rest of him to carbon deposits. The dust and ash scattered all across the lab.

The remaining male scientist screamed, jumped up, and ran out the door. Amahle, who had been backing toward the second lab as she fired short bursts from her rifle, pivoted on instinct and slammed the butt of her gun into the man's face. The impact drove his nasal bone back into his brain, killing him instantly.

Amahle blinked. "Dammit. Why did he sneak up on me?"

Dante crawled forward as another blue bolt of Atlanticore-powered plasma streaked overhead, melting a hole in the far wall. "Amahle! We need to shoot our way out of here, *right now*. Singh is about to blow the whole place!"

"What? *Singh?*" She glanced back at them as though they had gone mad. "I thought he was dead. Again."

Gage sprang to his feet, firing past her into the corridor and dropping an overenthusiastic Security goon who tried to rush them. "No time to explain. We must gather the others and escape."

The three of them dashed out of the lab together, casting one final glance at Jori Singh. He now resembled a statue of Atlanticore, save his face, the one part of him that was still faintly human. The uncanny expression of ecstasy in his eyes haunted them all until the end of their days.

Ty's group had begun firing on the Security squad from the other direction, and the combined crossfire finished them off in short order. Only a handful of them must have made it through the base, the Hellbreakers having picked off the rest. Even with the Coven's goons neutralized, Singh posed a far greater threat. One which would only abate with distance. *Lots* of distance.

The two trios met at the junctures of the hallways. Dante

shouted, "We need to get out of here, fast. The place is going to blow!"

"Figures," Ty muttered. "Eleanor, you got all that stuff?"

She nodded. "Yes. It will be enough to finish them."

Not bothering to question what she meant by that, Dante shoved her into the elevator, getting everyone else over its threshold before he jumped in himself. The doors seemed to take an agonizingly long time to close. A blue glow was filling the whole of the bottom floor, stronger and brighter by the second.

The elevator began its ascent. The six Executioners stood unspeaking, hating the necessity of waiting. Daria had struck the button for the top floor, skipping the middle one. It would be a far faster and more direct way to escape but made the ride seem unbearably tedious.

Yet, so far, they'd all made it. They hadn't lost any of their friends in the battle to sweep the facility. Dante was a badly lapsed Catholic, but he gave thanks to the Almighty for that much if nothing else.

As the elevator began to slow near the first floor, lightning struck. A crackling sound, close in volume to a rifle, filled the enclosed space along with a blue-white flash. The elevator stopped where it was.

"No!" Dante exclaimed as a static electricity jolt shocked him. It wasn't from pain but the prospect of being trapped so close to the exit.

The doors opened, then shut again, and repeated the motion, short-circuited by the unleashed power of whatever Singh had become. Dante shoved his foot onto the threshold. Bizarrely, the doors stayed open as if their sensors were still working. The bottom of the floor lay at the level of their shoulders.

Amahle grumbled, "This again? Eleanor, you go first." She and Gage helped Ms. Cervantes climb up and out, then the others followed, with Dante insisting on being last. Once everyone else was out, Ty and Amahle pulled him up and through. Behind him, the doors closed, and the elevator sank back into the depths.

The humming, the subsonic vibration, was stronger now than it had been, despite the distance of two floors and hundreds of feet of earth between them and the Coven's erstwhile elder statesman.

Ty commanded, "Move, move!"

He went first, not out of self-preservation, but simply because he trusted himself to deal with any foes they might encounter. There were none. It seemed the Executioners had eliminated all of their immediate opposition. Behind Ty, the others sprinted down the entrance hallway and out the shattered entrance into the fresh air and natural light.

Shockingly, the battle between the Hellbreakers and the last of the Executive Security forces was still ongoing. By now the helicopters must have been getting low on fuel, but they still circled overhead, taking potshots at a couple of well-dug-in clusters of the Coven's men, who fired back in turn. The sporadic nature of the gunfire suggested that everyone was getting low on ammo. They were probably out of explosives, too.

Ty sprang out into the valley and emptied a full magazine of .308 rounds at the entrenched Security goons, sending them ducking for cover while also getting the attention of the chopper pilots. Eleanor waved them down, and two flew into the valley while Daria, Gage, and Amahle kept covering their escape with suppressive fire.

When the choppers landed, Ty shoved Eleanor, Dante, and Gage into the first one before he, Daria, and Amahle crowded into the second. The pilots took off, rising through air that seemed increasingly thick and oppressive with electrical activity.

For the first time, Eleanor noticed that the pilot of the chopper they'd climbed into was none other than Ox. "Good day," he greeted them. "Hope you found what you were lookin' for since I'd say it's about time to go."

"Yes," Eleanor responded. "We need to leave immediately."

Dante clarified, "They have an experiment down there involving a shit-ton of destabilized Atlanticore. This whole stretch of mountains is about to become a rubble pile, and it could happen any moment."

Ox shook his head. "Bloody hell. Well, we're off. Shoot at those bastards on the hillside, would you?"

Gage was the only one with a loaded rifle. He aimed and squeezed off a couple of bursts at their few remaining foes. It bought them enough time and space to get clear of the mountains. Soon they and the other surviving choppers were sailing into the sky over the jungle.

Eleanor's heart leapt into her throat. "Wait. The men of yours on the ground. We can't leave them behind."

Ox waved that off. "Other choppers already picked them up. All is well."

She exhaled. It wasn't over yet. She and Dante looked into each other's eyes, silently praying that they would get clear in time to spend more hours, more days, perhaps more years together.

Then, when the fleet was about a mile away, Jori Singh finally reached the fullness of his power at the same instant that his third iteration of life came to a dramatic end.

Everything went quiet as reality struggled to accommodate the explosion. The blast seemed to suck all light and sound into itself before the white flash spread across the mountains and valley, sending waves of earth tumbling in violent avalanches and clouds of dust and blue fire into the air. The sloping mountain above the main facility ceased to exist, collapsing altogether. The peaks of the others broke off and fell, either into the valley or out into the surrounding forest. Ridges flattened, and low points rose as they filled with burned debris.

The shockwave kicked up a temporary windstorm as well, and the helicopters all bucked alarmingly in the gale.

"Whoa! Turbulence," Ox remarked. "Think I got it under control, though."

Dante held Eleanor, who held onto the interior railing to stabilize herself. She wanted to throw up.

It was over. Of that, she was now quite sure. They'd made it. The purse filled with their precious collateral still hung by her side.

CHAPTER TWENTY

The street was dark despite the lamps. This was one of the poorer sections of the capital city and therefore had to make do with cheap sodium lights rather than the brilliant Atlanticore ones that adorned the more upscale parts of town.

Eleanor approached the phone booth, looking both ways. There was no point in trying to look inconspicuous or pretend that she *wasn't* checking for anyone watching her. If someone intended to harm her, then knowing about it and alerting her friends was more important than maintaining the ruse of nonchalance.

No one else was around. At least, no one else was readily visible. In high windows nearby, Amahle and Ty crouched with scoped rifles, scanning the pavement, the alleys, and the windows of other buildings. Amahle was on the top floor of the highest structure nearby. It gave her the best field of vision, not to mention guaranteed that anyone working for the Coven didn't take the best available sniper spot.

Ty was in a mid-level window, closer to the booth, so he could provide sniper support if necessary but could also rush out into the street quickly should something of a more close-quarters nature be needed.

Dante, Gage, Daria, and Berger, who'd insisted on accompanying them, lay hidden in pairs nearby. At the first sign of trouble, they would spring out and deal with the threat.

So far, the proverbial coast was clear. Eleanor opened the phone booth door and walked in. She deposited a couple of coins and dialed a number she'd memorized long ago. It wasn't a number she often used since it was officially reserved for emergencies and other matters of exceptional importance.

The dial went through its *clicking* motions. The tones came through the receiver, and the phone on the other end rang once. Immediately after the ringing faded, someone picked up.

"You do not need to speak," Eleanor said instantly. "I know who you are. I think you know who I am, as well. You only need to listen to what I have to say."

The sound of low, controlled breathing was audible, but otherwise, the person on the other end stayed silent.

"There is no point in trying to trace this call. I'm in a remote location with plenty of backup, and I imagine you have very few people left whom you could send after me, anyway. You would leave yourself defenseless while launching an attack that would likely fail. I do not think you're that stupid."

The faint breathing seemed to stop for about two seconds, then it resumed.

Eleanor sucked in oxygen through her nose, and in a louder voice, declared, "The Executives have failed, and the Coven of Miracles is finished. Allow me to repeat that—*finished*. You cannot recover from what we have done.

"You will not be the ones who seize the initiative at the coming international conference. If you try, you will only bring further disgrace upon yourselves. You have almost nothing to back up your claims. The best thing you can hope for now is a quiet exit and a life in which you cease your malevolent schemes and leave decent people to their destinies."

It was difficult to be sure, but she thought she heard another person breathing nearby. Farther from the phone, but heavier and louder so the two seemed to be about the same volume. One exhaled as the other inhaled, and their respirations became a constant, steady *thrum*.

"You have two days," Eleanor told them. "It is now ten o'clock in the evening. We will be generous and allow you until midnight, fifty hours from now, rather than a strict forty-eight. Flee Atlantica. Go away and never return. We offer you a chance, which is probably more than you deserve.

"Do not mistake our graciousness for weakness. 'Justice Before Mercy' is our motto, as you well know. We only make this offer to spare ourselves the annoyance and to decrease the risks to innocent bystanders as well as your dupes and patsies."

Something rustled, as though one of the people in the room was shifting around and checking something, or perhaps tugging on the sleeve of the other.

Eleanor decided it was time to wrap up. She didn't have much to say. The message was, after all, quite simple and direct.

"If you do not leave, the Executioners will come for you and take you on a little trip out to sea." She hung up.

The street was still empty and silent, save for a single car that rolled by without incident, ignoring her. Eleanor crossed the road, and Dante and Daria rose from the shadows to follow her. They regrouped with Gage and Berger and waited for Ty and Amahle.

Dante gave her a brief but tight hug. "So, how did it go?"

She flashed him a faint smile. "As well as can be expected. What they do now will be up to them, and we will react accordingly. The one thing I can say with absolute certainty is that they *listened*."

Daria nodded. "Then they're not so stupid as we'd feared. There might be hope for this island yet."

Time had passed. Following the flight of the Senior Board and their supporters—including all of what remained of the Coven—Atlantica had gone through another period of growing pains. Life became more peaceful in some regards and more chaotic in others. So it always was when there was a vacuum of power in a fledgling civilization.

The conference was approaching. Everyone knew that after said event, when the world acknowledged the island and decided at last what to do with it, Atlantican society would change forever.

Whether it changed for the better or worse was, of course, the Executioners' primary concern. In that regard, they represented the whole population.

The passage of so many months had wrought no particular alterations upon the drive-in movie theater that still lay on the natural terrace above the small boomtown of Northvale. The six Executioners gathered there, as they had many times before.

Ox and Berger weren't with them this time. With their mission accomplished, the Hellbreakers had formally disbanded. Many of them had left the island, electing to go back to America or Australia, albeit under assumed identities to avoid court-martial for their desertion from the Army. Fake IDs were fairly easy to get on Atlantica if one knew where to look. Those who remained had drifted into private security work or had found nonviolent civilian jobs wherever they could get them.

As for the Executioners, they still had their one remaining Autocutioner. With the Coven effectively defeated and their role in society increasingly ambiguous, they had largely taken to driving regular cars instead. Now their myriad vehicles formed a semicircle around their usual spot in the far corner of the drive-in's designated plateau.

Ty stood and looked at each of them in turn, assuming once more the role of unofficial leader. "All right. It's good to see you all again, under more peaceful circumstances. But we have a fight coming up; one which we may not be prepared to handle. The Third Atlantican Conference is in two weeks."

Nods went around the group. They all knew the day was coming. Whether they'd discussed it among themselves lately or devoted intentional, conscious thought, it had been lurking in the back of all their minds.

Behind Ty on the massive drive-in screen, a new American film called *Dirty Harry* was playing. Apparently, it wasn't even out in U.S. theaters yet, and the drive-in's owners had obtained an early bootleg copy. Clint Eastwood played a hardnosed San Francisco cop. Amahle seemed oddly enthralled by the movie, and her attention kept drifting toward the screen, which she watched with widened eyes and a faint but rather vicious smile.

Ty began, "First, we need to decide *who* should be the one to give the presentation to the various, uh, esteemed world leaders and so forth."

Dante glanced at the woman by his side. "Eleanor, of course."

Gage nodded. "Eleanor."

"Eleanor," Daria agreed.

Amahle looked briefly away from the movie. "Oh, Eleanor."

Ty cleared his throat. "I vote for Eleanor. She has the most experience in these sorts of matters."

Eleanor glowered at the space between Ty and Dante. "I vote for Dante," she quipped. "Since he's so charming and all. It would appear that you've all outvoted me. Yes, after working for the Executives for so long, I suppose I am the most qualified." She lowered her voice. "Unfortunately."

Ty allowed himself a smile. "Good, I'm glad we're in near-unanimous agreement on that. An even more important question remains. Namely, *what* do we present? What are the things we need to prioritize to get the point across to these people?"

Snapping her fingers, Daria added, "Indeed. We must think not only in terms of what has been relevant and important in the years since Atlantica became a working civilization, but also what is newly relevant since the Coven collapsed. And what will be important to us all in the months and years to come."

Each of them threw out their suggestion about what sorts of issues mattered most to them. Daria seemed most concerned with free commerce and how there might be a continuity of justice in society. Dante recommended they develop the island's medical infrastructure.

Gage mentioned technological development and alluded to the unfinished archaeological digs at sites where ancient ruins still lay. Amahle wanted to ensure that no government grew too overbearing. Eleanor said that all of the above were important but that getting them all to function in tandem with one another was the most difficult part.

Having heard their pieces, Tyler gave a slow head bow. "You all make good points. Let me make mine. We will be going before these people first and foremost as the notorious Atlantican Executioners, and they will want to hear about our specific role. *That* should be the focus of the presentation. I'd bet money that they particularly want to know whether or not we've declared a military dictatorship yet."

"Why?" Daria inquired with a sardonic cock of her right eyebrow. "Had you considered setting one up, Mr. Katakura? You would probably make an excellent evil dictator."

"No," he riposted. "No, I had not. Atlantica is still catching its breath after the long struggle between too much chaos and too much order. We emerged from the power plays and factionalism as perhaps the kings of the proverbial hill. But simply having us rule the island as some kind of feudal warrior aristocracy... No. It's not what I want, and it's not what Atlantica needs."

His parents had come from a land where some people still remembered a society of that nature. Many of his fellow Americans had risked life and limb to defeat it in far-flung islands across the Pacific. The memory was made even more painful by the shabby and disgraceful way the U.S. government had treated his family.

Eleanor thought over what Ty had said and added her two cents.

"Atlantica's population continues to grow. So does its infrastructure. This points toward us needing something closer to a regular police force. Our former employers tried to create one in the form of Executive Security, but in practice, it was little more than a thuggish private army that carried out their whims with little thought to the general benefit. How, then, do we keep such a force from becoming a threat to the very people and ideals we wish for it to protect?"

She had posed the question not rhetorically but as one she sought an answer to. While Daria, Gage, and Dante thought it over, the two most violent group members gave curt and unhesitant responses.

"I don't like the idea much," Ty grumbled. "Not sure you *can* prevent it from becoming a threat."

Amahle had once again focused on Officer Callahan's exploits, in this case, a scene in which he was shooting it out in a park with a psychopath in a red mask. "A police force in a place like Atlantica can be little else besides hired thugs, I should think. I do like him, though." She pointed at the screen, her face lighting up with juvenile enthusiasm.

Daria stroked her chin. "We cannot avoid something more standardized and official at this point. Yes, I say that as a career criminal. One thing people are often unaware of is that the underworld of smugglers and other such people does, in fact, have rules, codes, and standards of ethical conduct. If a police force is to be viable, it must operate under similar such standards."

Dante looked at her, then turned his face to the others with a kind of grim smile of resignation. "I agree. With Atlantica becoming a real country, the lack of proper law enforcement opens the door for the place to turn into an endless battleground between gangsters and warlords."

Ty frowned as he listened, but listen he did, without interrupting.

The doctor went on, "In a way, we've been like surgeons taking care of a significant health issue. Still, every time a person has a problem, no matter how minor, and they go in for surgery or other invasive methods, well... The constant use of the scalpel might keep them from death, but they'll never grow fully healthy because they're being sedated, cut open, and stitched back up all the time. The intrusions make it impossible to return to normality."

Gage mused, "So, we need to find a way to keep the Executioners' goal of justice first, but without being invasive."

Ty snorted. "Speak for yourself. Invasiveness is what got the job done for us."

Daria pointed out, "It will not be *us* much longer. Even if the conference ratifies our ideas, others will take our place."

Ty's demeanor had grown sulky. He sometimes got that way when a complication undermined his usual straightforward confidence. "I suppose so."

Gage had another idea. "What if the justice we seek is absolute, but only as long as it deals with public spaces?"

The others took a moment to think it over. Behind them, the sounds of Clint's .44 Magnum revolver filled the air.

Daria sought clarification. "So, your business in your own home is only your business, then? Do as you like?"

Eleanor was intrigued by the possibilities, both good and bad.

"Therefore you can snort cocaine while shooting holes in your couch with a rifle."

"Yes, and enjoy it, I am most sure," Gage said. "But the minute a stray shot leaves your property and harms someone else..."

Ty smirked a little. "Your ass is grass."

"Or perhaps just wet," Daria tossed out. "I think we should keep the old system of taking them out to sea."

Dante squinted at her. "For every infraction?"

She shrugged. "Maybe for the first offense, they're simply dropped into the water and can swim back or have someone pick them up. As for the second time..."

Once more, Ty finished the thought. "Then they can try swimming with a bullet in their head."

Amahle's eyes remained fixed on the movie screen, but they all could tell she was listening carefully. "Hmm, yes. I think Dirty Harry could get behind that. You know, I wish this film had come out sooner."

CHAPTER TWENTY-ONE

The Third Atlantican Conference was held in the ballroom of the Golden Fern Grand Hotel in the swankiest part of downtown, at seven o'clock at night. It was an event for which the host organizers had spared no expense, but there was a distinct lack of "party atmosphere" about the whole thing. Dignified and somber were the bywords of the evening.

The various business and political leaders of the world were there to discuss matters of great importance, and a curious sense of mutual agreement had permeated their ranks. They largely ignored Atlantica's freewheeling nature. No one seemed to have brought any drugs or prostitutes despite no laws against them, and the hotel served fine wine but not champagne.

Media coverage of the event also reflected its no-nonsense nature. Only respectable outlets had received invitations to observe and photograph. The more tabloid- or gossip-oriented publications would have to be content with half-baked paparazzi-style photographs of the various VIPs leaving the establishment later.

Eleanor had put on her best dress, a sleek black one that flattered her figure but in a tasteful way. It had a slit that ran up only to the knee and a relatively high neckline. She supplemented it with a necklace of pearls. Ironically, she'd received it as a gift from a Junior Board member years ago. Her wavy dark hair was done little differently than it always was, albeit with greater care.

Around her were her friends and partners, the other Executioners. Unlike her, they'd chosen to wear the dress uniforms of their order. It emphasized their status as a team and marked them out as a paramilitary unit—servants of the public, rather than would-be leaders or rulers. They didn't dress the way politicians would.

The Executioners were seated off in the corner. Whoever had handled all the seating arrangements had cleverly positioned them so they were visible at all times to virtually everyone in the ballroom but tactfully away from the main stage area.

The first hour passed uneventfully. Half of it seemed to consist of the various leaders and functionaries repeating the same canned pleasantries and ritualistically acknowledging how important they all were, and what a momentous occasion today was, et cetera. Eleanor had long experience with events of this nature, but she still found it all rather boring.

Yet, they would call upon her to represent not only her friends but the entire island soon. She was used to public speaking, too, but the nervousness that came with such a large and important occasion was impossible to dismiss. Her stomach gnawed and fluttered, her hands were sweaty, and her feet twitched beneath the hem of her dress.

Dante, who sat closest to her, noticed and put a hand on her wrist. "Hey. You look great, kid."

She fluttered her eyelashes at him, but the twist of her mouth was sardonic. "Kid? Why would you call me that?"

He sighed. "It's an American thing. Humphrey Bogart said it. It's supposed to be a compliment. Anyway, even though you look better than all the rest of us put together, remember this. You're still one of us. You deserve one of these uniforms every bit as much as we do. We just figured that all the gentlemen in the audience would respond better to the dress."

"The dress was my idea," she pointed out. "But thank you. I'm sure I will manage. The real question is, will they listen to what I have to say?"

She had a rough idea of what the political orientations of the world's major countries were and the personalities of their leaders. She knew where they drew the lines in the Cold War. Still, she had spent years in no place other than Atlantica. There was a risk that for all the event's pomp, the dignitaries regarded the place as too much of a backwater for anything its rude prototype law enforcement cabal might have to say to carry much weight.

Finally, it was her turn to speak.

"...now turn the floor over to Ms. Eleanor Cervantes, formerly an assistant to the Junior Board of the Atlantican Development Council, and since inducted into the Order of Executioners. Ms. Cervantes?"

The emcee looked at her, bowed, and gestured. She rose, returned the bow, and strode to the podium carrying the handful of cards on which she'd scribbled her main notes. Polite but reasonably enthusiastic applause filled the ballroom. Dante had probably been right; the dress was helping.

As she took her place behind the podium and adjusted the microphone to suit her relatively small frame, the weight of the world itself seemed to descend upon her shoulders.

She'd been called upon to present what the Executioners had accomplished and hopefully validate their existence. She would be responsible for offering a new path forward, based on what Atlantica's most up-to-date needs were. Her words could change the course of history. A right or wrong turn of phrase would tilt the whole course and balance of events for not only the fledgling island's civilization but, perhaps, the entire planet.

As she straightened the cards, she cast a final glance over her shoulder at her friends. They were proud of her. Their presence was reassuring, and Dante's warm smile most of all. She couldn't ask for better backup.

She was the last of the Executioners to join and in some ways was the "least" of them, having less experience with combat and survival than any. She came from a privileged background. However, they'd accepted her and given her the chance to handle this monumental task.

So, drawing in her breath, she allowed the emotions to mingle freely for a second or two before she dispelled them. It was as exciting as it was nerve-wracking, and gratitude also consumed her.

Then it all went away, and Eleanor had only to say the words.

"Esteemed leaders, friends, and interested parties—we of humble Atlantica cannot thank you enough for your presence. Our time to join the world community is now, and having toiled for so long in obscurity, we are profoundly honored to have you here."

The crowd seemed amenable so far. She saw the varying motivations of some of them. The often greedy calculations, but tempered by legitimate goodwill in some cases, or at least good *sense* in others.

Eleanor gave a summary of the island's history, its discovery during the Second World War, and the burying of said discovery within the U.S. government's classified files until the early 1960s when at last Atlantica was reopened for business and settlement. She even slipped in a joke about how the British had insisted on calling the place "Avalonia," just to be difficult, which got a few laughs from the leaders of Western Europe.

Next, she described the founding of the Executioners. For reasons of prudence and expediency, she glossed over the fact that the Executives—the same people who became their greatest enemies—were also their original benefactors. Rather than specifics, she referred vaguely to "ambitious investors" and "concerned citizens of means," which was technically true, anyway.

In the early years of their existence, the Executioners had stopped an almost incalculable number of crimes, and Eleanor elaborated upon several of the most dramatic examples.

"No formalized code of laws exists here," she explained. "Yet there are certain things which we universally acknowledge as crimes all the same; acts which offend the moral conscience of all humanity or threaten the basic fabric of society. Such infractions are the ones our order sought to pursue. And punish."

Eleanor described how Tyler, the first, and Daria, the second, had taken down an elite operation to smuggle Atlanticore while killing workers to cover up the crime. How Daria and Gage had similarly shut down a corrupt mining endeavor that was also killing people, and how Gage and Dante had then defeated a "foreign-sponsored" hit squad. She had little doubt that the Soviet delegates knew she was talking about an operation of theirs, but it was important to be polite.

She mentioned the operation against the "hunters' lodge" they'd also taken down and the rampage by rogue assassins in that mission's wake. Various maneuvers against gun runners, drug dealers, human traffickers. The removal from leadership of a vigilante religious fanatic whose personal army became as bad as the problems they purported to solve.

Finally, she spoke of the Executioners' overthrow of an exceptionally well-organized and well-connected group of conspirators who, blinded by megalomaniacal visions, had tried to take over the island altogether.

At no point did she name names. It was unnecessary and would create more problems than it could solve. Instead, she judiciously spoke of the ongoing struggle between tyrannical aspirations and the yearning for freedom.

"Various malefactors arranged in hostile factions against the self-determination of the Atlantican people had to be excised by us, so Atlantica could grow strong without their interference.

Now, the Executioners have served our purpose. A new means by which Atlantica can pursue justice has become necessary."

She glanced at Dante, mentally thanking him for the surgical metaphor—it had not been part of her notes. Instead, she'd thrown it in on a whim. Continuing the analogy, she repeated much of what he'd said two weeks ago almost word for word. She would have to trust him not to be too offended by her plagiarism.

"Once the organism is healthy, it can handle small maladies by itself, without the interference of the surgeon's knife."

The audience was attentive. She gave them a moment so that the point would sink in.

"The Executioners have been the knife but the time has come for Atlantica to heal and grow without us. We have assembled a comprehensive plan for the new Atlantica Justice System, to be constructed according to what we've dubbed the Callahan Model."

Eleanor glanced at Amahle, who smiled with deep satisfaction.

"Atlantica is supposed to be a place of unmatched opportunity, more than anything else. That surpasses its reputation as a rowdy and lawless frontier, as well as its status as the world's only source of Atlanticore crystal. Opportunity is what brought all of us here. Opportunity is what will define our future. It will permit us to continue what is well on its way to becoming a noble tradition without falling to machinations of those with ill intent. Past, present, and future."

She paused and bowed. "Thank you."

In the split second before the applause began, she only had to wonder how loud and genuine it would be and what sorts of questions people would ask later. She felt that she'd done her duty, and more than adequately.

It was up to the rest of the world to decide.

CHAPTER TWENTY-TWO

A month had passed since the conference. A certain ambivalence still prevailed in some corners of the world and some schools of thought. However, the approximate consensus was that the event had been a resounding success and that the rest of the Earth looked forward to opening its arms to their isle.

With that purpose served—with the door closing on the past and another door opening on the future—the time had arrived for the six to say goodbye.

On a whim, they'd selected a touristy beachside bar. It was a place none of them had ever been to before, recently constructed along Atlantica's burgeoning riviera. Eleanor found the idea of *having* a riviera odd and faintly amusing. She remembered, all too well, the days when the island's waterfronts had served no purpose other than to provide docking for supply ships and subsistence fishing for poor refugees.

There was a central building to prepare the drinks and snacks and seating for those who wanted it. Most patrons chose to drink out on the beach proper, in the open air, but with large umbrellas mounted on the tables since Atlantica was often rainy. Today it was partially sunny, faintly misty, but on the warm side. Pleasant enough.

Ty alone sat with his back to the ocean, facing the others and the rest of the island beyond it. His companions sat to his sides or across from him around the glass table. Golden sand lay spread around, and other patrons sipped their drinks at tables nearby, paying them no heed. Deep blue waves crashed upon the beach.

"Things are changing," Ty stated. "It sure didn't take long. It's for the best; that's what we wanted. From what I hear, the AJS will be up and running within two months, at least on a baseline level."

He referred, of course, to the Atlantica Justice System. The whole culture of the island would be transformed—hopefully for the better—by introducing a formalized police apparatus, albeit one tailored to the unique conditions that prevailed here.

Daria ran a finger around the edge of her glass. Since it was a fruity drink with rather weak alcohol content, she had less interest in simply guzzling it than if it had been straight vodka. There wasn't much point. "It will be a relief, in truth. Transferring the burden of power to this new regime. My shoulders are tired of the weight. I am past forty now. Soon I will be as old as Gage is. Or was."

Gage bobbed his head and smiled. "Yes, I understand what you intended to say, even if you didn't quite succeed. We all pass a point at which our struggles must become the struggles of the younger generation."

"Well, I am glad that they think they can implement the Callahan Method," Amahle commented. "And that they kept the name intact. It gives me some hope that the spirit of this place won't change too much. I have come to like it here."

Dante took a swig of his beer. He'd opted for the most basic beverage they had, perhaps out of solidarity with his old friends back in his working-class Italian neighborhood in New York. "The whole point is to balance things out, according to our experience, which I'd say makes for a pretty good representative sample of humanity in general. Kind of. Weighing the rights of the individual against the needs of the community."

Eleanor added, "And the cycles and processes of growth which underlie them both."

Ty spread his hands. "We've done what we can as far as the political stuff goes. Next up, it falls to the individuals who have to implement it on a day-by-day basis. Which reminds me." He paused to exhale and faintly looked like he expected to be mocked or hounded. "I'm staying on."

Eleanor blinked. "You mean..."

"As a consultant for the AJS," Ty clarified. "A trainer and advisor. There's going to be some growing pains. They could use the help and advice of someone who... Well... What the hell else am I good at?"

Amahle, who sat next to him as usual, put a hand over his. "There is no shame in that. I was thinking the same. Someone must teach them to move silently and how to shoot straight."

Gage chuckled and folded his hands behind his head. "It has been a most interesting experience, fighting alongside you people, but I am a scientist at heart. I was never able to complete the research that Dr. Limbu began. I wish to return to archaeology, which has long been my great passion."

"Good deal," Dante said. "I was afraid you were going to say engineering. You did enough of that for the Executioners. Me, I'm going back to stitching people up. God, I killed and maimed so many people these last few years, I think I *need* to make up for it."

Eleanor smiled at him. It was strangely good to hear him say that. She'd never fully recovered from her guilt at participating in so much violence, even if the circumstances had justified much of it. Recent developments had led her to pay more attention to his caring, nurturing side.

"You're a fine doctor, Dante. I will remain on the island as well, I think, and return to business. I have yet to make my fortune. My family is proud of me, or so they say, but I don't wish to return to Mexico until I don't need *their* fortune."

Daria had kept silent. She didn't offer her plans, thus forcing Tyler to pry.

"Daria," he intoned. "Speak. What are you doing next?"

She rolled her shoulders and stared at the waves. "I believe I will get away for a time. Take a vacation. I have more money than I need for the time being. Perhaps not as much as Eleanor seems to desire, but it's sufficient to purchase a boat and be at one with the sea for a while. Too much time on land is too much like imprisonment."

They lounged quietly for a couple of minutes, none of them desiring to say anything but comfortable in one another's presence all the same. They'd been through so much together.

Eleanor was curious about something else, though. "Has Atlantica fulfilled our hopes and dreams? Not only in terms of such things as money and base survival. But the...ideal of Atlantica and what it represents. And how we affected it ourselves."

She had mixed feelings. She wasn't shocked or disappointed to discover that the others all did, as well.

Daria mused, "Perhaps it was naïve of us to think we could find a place, anyplace, where the corrupting temptations of greed and power aren't trying to burrow in at all times. There are still far more fresh starts and second chances to be found here than in some other places, yes?"

Gage beamed. "I believe so. We have made a difference here and saved many innocent people."

"While putting down many *bad* people," Amahle clarified, with a certain grim satisfaction.

Ty nodded. "It's not perfect. But if I had to leave a legacy, that is the kind I would hope for."

The sun came fully out above them. The wind had finally

blown enough of the clouds away to simulate a clear summer's day on the mainland. The mood around the table lightened along with the day itself. They proposed toasts and joked about stupid things for the sake of hearing one another's voices and seeing each other laugh. It might be the last time they all gathered this way.

No one particularly noticed that Eleanor had refrained from alcohol, even though she'd had no compunctions about drinking in the past.

When the levity started to wear thin, Ty stood. "I'm going swimming."

Amahle, none too surprisingly, was first to stand beside him. "I'll join you."

The pair rushed out into the surf, suddenly seeming years younger and without any cares in the world.

The other four stood and moved away from the table at a more casual pace, taking their drinks with them, and walked along the sand. Beyond the area owned by the bar was a broad public beach with a sprinkling of bathers, but nowhere near as crowded as it would be on a hotter, sunnier day.

When they reached a quiet spot, partially secluded from the view of anyone farther inland, Eleanor stopped, and Dante stopped alongside her.

Daria and Gage kept walking. They turned their heads in acknowledgment before moving on, and Daria raised the glass in her hand, still half-full with a weak daiquiri. Gage casually sipped his martini, and it sounded like they were beginning a conversation about the properties of Atlanticore crystal.

Dr. Costa and Ms. Cervantes watched them go, standing in place and looking toward the horizon.

Dante put his hands in his pockets. "I wonder. How can we...transition from the lives we were living, for all that time? Switch over from all that to live the life we want to have now. Together, I mean. You and me."

She slipped an arm around his waist. "What do you mean?"

"Not only pursuing our passions and career interests and stuff but also being free from danger and stupid adventures." He sighed. "I worry that stuff might magnetically draw us to it. Which isn't... You know. Not good for people who are trying to create a life together."

He knew.

Eleanor took his hand by the wrist, extracting it from his pocket and moving it over to her stomach. It was still very early, but judging by the way he tensed with excitement, he felt the small bump, the unmistakable indication of what awaited them in the months to come. Something any medical doctor would recognize at once.

She moved closer, stretched up, and kissed his ear. "This is Atlantica, *mi amor*. Anything is possible."

AUTHOR NOTES MICHAEL ANDERLE

FEBRUARY 14, 2022

Thank you for not only reading this book but these author notes as well!

Okay, it's Valentine's Day, and I'm in Cabo San Lucas...

Now, I've been married for a while, so I should KNOW better. I purchased a (totally practical) item for Judith that she asked to receive for Valentine's day and figured I was good.

#Probably

(Editor's Note: #ManWhoLikesToLiveDangerously)

I'm typing this while waiting in a government office in Cabo San Lucas, Mexico. There are no shops around, so I can't sneak out and pick up anything for Valentine's Day.

Now, my wife isn't one to really worry because I got her what she asked for and we called it good.

However, I am fifty-something-something years old, and I remember from my twenties and thirties that taking a woman at her word about Valentine's Day was at best questionable and at worse a great way to ruin your day, likely your week, and in very poor situations, your month.

Are you guys out there shaking your head with me? I thought so.

So, it's 10:15 in the morning, and it's looking pretty good for me to be okay this Valentine's Day since I don't have anything else to give her.

Except, you know, my love and affection. But is that ever enough? We shall see.

At the moment, it appears to be enough.

Why am I in a government office in Mexico?

We are in the (and I'm trying to type this from the name on the wall) *SECRETARÍA DE GOBERNACIÓN INSTITUTO DE MIGRACION* office, sitting on some chairs that have been here…awhile.

Gray and semi-comfortable (thank God), and the temperature in here is a reasonable seventy degrees or so.

Like a Department of Transportation in just about every state in the US, it is slow, and you are not sure you will ever be seen. Who says people around the world are different? The governments sure seem to work the same way.

We have purchased a house down here and are working to acquire temporary residence permission so we can open a bank account here in Mexico. Why? When you deal with utility bills (and other items), you kinda need access to a Mexican bank account.

Thus, I'm sitting in a government office, thinking how much it is like any other government office I've been in during my life.

I guess I'll get to work. Since I can work with a laptop from just about anywhere, I might as well continue typing.

While I work on my next story idea, I hope you have a fantastic week or weekend. Talk to you in the next book!

Ad Aeternitatem,
Michael Anderle

OTHER ATLANTICA BOOKS

John Chambers Books

Her Mother's Pendant (Book 1)

The Mystery Deepens (Book 2)

One Last Choice (Book 3)

Valentina Winters

The Red Countess (Book 1)

One Night to Kill (Book 2)

One Death Too Few (Book 3)

Terra Kris

She is the Law (Book 1)

Law or Justice (Book 2)

Justice Served (Book 3)

Santana Sokolov

Law of the Jungle (Book 1)

Inner City Jungle (Book 2)

Rumble in the Jungle (Book 3)

BOOKS BY MICHAEL ANDERLE

Sign up for the LMBPN email list to be notified of new releases and special deals!

http://lmbpn.com/email

For a complete list of books by Michael Anderle, please visit:

www.lmbpn.com/ma-books/

CONNECT WITH THE AUTHOR

Connect with Michael Anderle

Website: http://lmbpn.com

Email List: http://lmbpn.com/email/

https://www.facebook.com/LMBPNPublishing

https://twitter.com/MichaelAnderle

https://www.instagram.com/lmbpn_publishing/

https://www.bookbub.com/authors/michael-anderle

www.ingramcontent.com/pod-product-compliance
Lightning Source LLC
Chambersburg PA
CBHW022127310726
48972CB00007B/2233